PRAISE FOR *ALL ARE WELCOME*

"There's also Liz Parker's *All Are Welcome*, a rom-com misadventure of a bride getting ready to marry the woman of her dreams and the familial secrets and drama that come with it."

—*Entertainment Tonight*

"Very fresh, real and hysterically funny . . . There aren't nearly enough lesbian romantic comedies meant to be read on the beach."

—ED by Ellen

"A tender, funny, wise debut novel in which a couple of women embark with their families to their destination wedding in Bermuda, only to watch in horror as their best-laid plans threaten to turn into disaster."

—*Oprah Daily*

"Parker writes with breezy, biting wit, perfectly skewering a demographic that keeps up appearances at all costs."

—*Booklist*

"A dramatic and darkly funny dose of WASP culture. Liz Parker takes on dysfunctional families, destination weddings, and the fact that sometimes the most difficult person to accept is yourself."

—Laura Hankin, author of *Happy & You Know It*

"In her buoyant, sharply observed, and painfully hilarious debut novel, *All Are Welcome*, Liz Parker tells the big story of a small lesbian wedding. Over a meticulously planned weekend at a sunstruck Bermuda beach club, the hard-packed, jovial WASP surfaces of two seemingly similar Connecticut families come loose to expose long-buried secrets, uncomfortable truths, and a monsoon of dysfunction. By the time the clouds part, Parker has illustrated with blistering wisdom how, for many of us, finding happiness—alone or with another—begins with first seeing who we've been in, and to, our families, and then deciding who it is we will be."

—Bill Clegg, author of *The End of the Day*

"In *All Are Welcome*, Liz Parker vividly describes a young couple on the brink of their future who must also face their past when their destination beach wedding goes somewhat awry. Over the course of a tumultuous, rum-punch-fueled weekend, secrets are revealed and love is tested. Parker's keen eye for detail and sense of humor had me both laughing and tearing up, and her sharp plot twists kept me guessing until the last page. With equal parts heart, drama, comedy, and emotion, *All Are Welcome* is a classic destination-wedding story turned on its head for a discerning modern reader."

—Julia Spiro, author of *Someone Else's Secret*

THE
FAMILY
COMPOUND

ALSO BY LIZ PARKER

All Are Welcome

THE
FAMILY
COMPOUND

A NOVEL

LIZ PARKER

Text copyright © 2022 by Elizabeth L. Parker
All rights reserved.

No part of this book may be reproduced, or stored in a retrieval system, or transmitted in any form or by any means, electronic, mechanical, photocopying, recording, or otherwise, without express written permission of the publisher.

Published by Lake Union Publishing, Seattle

www.apub.com

Amazon, the Amazon logo, and Lake Union Publishing are trademarks of Amazon.com, Inc., or its affiliates.

ISBN-13: 9781542036559
ISBN-10: 1542036550

Cover design by Philip Pascuzzo

Printed in the United States of America

To my brother, Mike, and our cousins on the hill:
Sage, Courtney, and Graham, and Story and Ellie

CHAPTER ONE

Their father died on a Tuesday, and on the next Saturday, after saying goodbye to his body at the graveyard near the church, the siblings drove home in a line of black cars, like ants marching up the road. The color of the cars didn't have anything to do with the funeral; Penny and Chris and Laurie just happened to drive black cars. Chris's was large, a Suburban he had no business owning in New York City, and Penny's was tiny, a MINI Cooper that was often almost driven off the road by all the trucks on the interstate. Laurie drove a BMW, a 4 Series, at once sporty and bored, not unlike Laurie herself.

He wasn't supposed to die this soon. He'd been seventy, fit, an enjoyer of long walks and fishing, wearer of custom button-down shirts and a well-worn loafer. He wasn't sick; he wasn't poorly rested. He had a balanced diet and drank only sparingly. But down he went, right there in the vegetable garden. Penny was visiting from Burlington for the weekend, as much a break from her nocturnal roommate as an opportunity to see her widowed father. She'd gone inside briefly to get them both some lemonade. She didn't even like lemonade. It was far too sweet.

She heard the spade hit the post holding up the birdhouse. "Wait, Dad! I'm coming!" she yelled from inside, thinking he'd tripped. She was jogging before she realized she was jogging, having dropped the full glasses on the porch when she saw him collapsed on the ground. Penny was screaming then, at once dialing 911 and throwing her body over his, checking in vain to see if he was breathing. She knew he wasn't. She knew he'd died before he hit the ground. He'd all but waved as she walked inside.

He was not supposed to die this soon. They'd buried their mother, breast cancer, quick, nearly invisible, only a year earlier. The cancer moved so quickly, she didn't have time to put up a fight. It seemed like by the time they'd booked her an appointment for a second opinion, she was gone. Their father was the last of his generation. His brothers and sisters had died like dominoes the few years before, leaving a roost of adult children still modestly confused that the world did not come with a meal plan. Penny was sure her family was cursed—not a soul lived past seventy, except for a single great-grandmother who was so evil and had been bedridden for so long, it was like God kept her alive as a punishment. Penny did not want to be like Nona.

Later that night, Penny called her sister from the phone in the living room, distracted by the relic of a landline while she told her what happened.

"I don't understand why you left him in the first place," Laurie said, her voice tight from crying.

"I didn't *leave* him," Penny enunciated. "I was getting us a drink. *I was taking care of him.*"

"Clearly not well enough," Laurie said, her voice now huffy.

Penny inhaled and exhaled very loudly, making sure to breathe right into the phone. "Laurie, are you accusing me of killing our father?"

Laurie didn't miss a beat.

"Of course not. All I'm saying is we can't be sure he would be gone if you hadn't left."

On the best days, Penny tolerated her sister. Laurie was older by five years, an eternity as children and an equal eternity as adults when one so proudly lorded her accomplishments over the other. If Laurie told

Penny one more time about the importance of starting a 401(k) while she was still young . . . Her imagination had run out of things to do.

Penny hung up the phone and looked at her brother. Chris, who had been in town for a spontaneous long weekend, was in their father's living room, his legs stretched over a patterned ottoman. He was nursing a beer, but when Penny looked down, she saw six empty bottles next to the armchair.

"You shouldn't drink those so fast," she said.

Chris shrugged and took a long sip. "Did Laurie really just accuse you of killing Dad?"

Penny nodded and folded her lips into each other.

Chris took another sip and held up the bottle. "Do you want one?"

"I'm not drinking. No." She said it as much for herself as for him. The seconds ticking by felt like hours, and the thoughts moved so quickly through her brain that she couldn't even try to keep up. Ever since a trip gone horribly wrong in 2015, leaving her without any friends to speak of, Penny had rapid cycled between drinking and not. Her mother had drunk too much, her father hardly at all, and Penny was somewhere in between. Her siblings never seemed to worry about it.

Chris raised his eyebrows. "Suit yourself."

Penny sat down on the couch opposite her brother. CNN was on, barely audible. She squinted to see the screen. "What do we do now?"

Chris looked at her like she'd just arrived. His eyes flared for a second, as if he might actually say something, and Penny braced for impact. But the second passed and his eyes went back to their normal size, and Chris shrugged. "Is that Thai place still open?"

Their father was dead. Their last parent. And Penny might have killed him. How could Chris be thinking about food at a time like this?

Penny looked at the beer bottles lined up by her brother. He'd turned up the TV. He was like a robot, and Penny wondered if she was supposed to go ahead and punch the Father-Just-Died-Unexpectedly program into his socket. What would the program look like, she thought, now up from her seat and walking through the room and into the main hallway connecting too many rooms and finally ending up in the bar off the main kitchen. She caught a glimpse of the vegetable garden in the early-evening moonlight and paused. The tomato plants now looked menacing, like they could engulf the entire hill. Penny couldn't fathom ever going back in there. Her ears rang with the din of her father's spade hitting rock. She shuddered and forced herself to look away.

The evening had fallen into night, and Penny thumbed around the wall until she found the light switch. Had she killed her father?

That wasn't how heart attacks worked, right? The paramedics hadn't seemed accusatory when they'd tried CPR. They hadn't asked why on earth she'd gone to get lemonade right before he collapsed. Penny took a bottle of wine out of the small fridge and turned it around in her hands. Chardonnay, California, a vineyard they'd been to as a family when her mother had first gotten into wine.

Her phone started vibrating as she finished pouring a glass. Laurie.

"Was the accusation too soft? Did you want to call again to really drive it home?" Penny said, not waiting for Laurie to say hello.

"How was Dad right before?" her sister asked.

"I told you. He was fine. Completely fine."

"No, I mean, how *was* he?" Laurie didn't mince words, and Penny couldn't figure out what she was trying to learn.

"Laurie, you're torturing me. I didn't kill our father."

"I know that," Laurie snapped. Penny recoiled, even five hundred miles away. She heard the sharp inhale of someone who had just started to cry.

"We were in the garden. Talking about what we should have for dinner."

Penny turned the light off in the bar and went into the man cave, falling into an oversize armchair. The same one her father had liked to read in.

Laurie sighed on the other end of the phone. Penny knew to wait.

"What were you going to have?"

"Are you serious?"

"I am," Laurie said. Penny heard a sniffle.

"We were debating pizza or grilling steak and making a salad from the garden," Penny said. The nearness of the memory broke the area surrounding her heart, like her body knew the organ needed more space to pump. Early pain expanded into the entire chest cavity.

"I shouldn't have suggested you killed him. I'll be there by nine," Laurie said. Penny heard the click of a lighter and her sister inhale.

"Those can kill you, you know."

"I love you, Pen. I'm sorry I'm not there already."

~

The next morning, Laurie arrived at nine on the dot. She hit the mailbox on her way into the driveway and Penny woke up to the crash just outside her window.

"Dammit," Laurie said, slamming the car door as she walked to the front of the vehicle. Penny stood by the curtain and debated opening the window and sticking her head outside. The car's left headlight was shattered.

Laurie alternated between leaning over to assess the damage and kicking the now-defunct mailbox. "I hate that mailbox."

"What's the commotion?" Chris sauntered outside, his hair a mess of bedhead, his sweatpants far too low on his hips. Penny rolled her eyes.

"Just the fucking mailbox Dad never got fixed," Laurie said, letting out an audible sigh and throwing her arms from over her head to by her sides.

Chris showed his support by giving the mailbox a light kick. Her brother and sister hugged easily, and Penny watched, suddenly not wanting to be seen. She leaned against the wall, not visible through the window, until she heard the front door open and close and two sets of feet pad into the house.

"Pen!" Laurie called from downstairs. "I'm here!"

Laurie always arrived like an event. Penny was sure she'd never entered a room quietly, positive she'd never left a room quietly either. Laurie was forty and on paper boasted adulthood. She was in-house counsel for a large makeup conglomerate. She had a 401(k) that promised more than a decade of easy living. She owned her apartment on 68th between Columbus and Central Park West. She drove a black BMW she parked at a garage in her building, and she'd once been dumped by a man for being too steady. This last part wasn't on paper, and Penny knew for a fact that Laurie was an emotional grenade waiting to get unpinned. But her sister on paper ate Penny on paper for breakfast.

"Hi, morning," Penny said as she walked down the stairs to the kitchen. "How was the drive? You must have been up at what, four?"

She kissed her sister on the cheek, but they didn't actually touch.

"Out the door at four on the dot," Laurie said, her head now six inches deep in the fridge. "Don't you guys have anything to eat?"

"Dad was planning to go to the market yesterday, you see," Chris said dryly, slouched over a barstool at the open kitchen counter.

"We should probably start telling people," Penny said, going so far as to pull out her cell phone.

Chris looked down at his empty cereal bowl. Laurie closed the refrigerator door too gently. Penny waited for one of them to say something.

Laurie finally spoke.

"We should. I know we should." Her voice broke. "It just makes it real."

Seeing Laurie cry made Penny cry and soon they were embracing properly, their chests hugged against each other and their hands stroking the other's back. Chris came around the bar and joined them, his body like a papa bear to their babies.

"How did this happen?" Laurie asked, the three of them not moving out of the hug. "He wasn't supposed to go yet."

"At least he gets to be with Mom," Penny said.

This only made Laurie cry harder. "Mom drove him crazy!" she wailed.

"That's what family is," Penny said. "Love them like crazy while they drive you crazy."

Chris broke the moment first by patting both women on the back and saying, "Well, okay, very good," like someone trying to impersonate an old banker type. He hadn't caught on to the "strong men can be vulnerable" trend yet.

"What next?" Penny asked.

"Well, who have you called?" Laurie asked, her hand reaching into her pants pocket and pulling out an iPhone. Chris and Penny looked at each other and then looked at her. "Let me rephrase: Have you called anyone?" she asked, her inflection higher this time.

Neither Penny nor Chris answered. Penny bit her lip and looked out the window, checking the neighboring driveway for cars. A station wagon and sedan were both parked.

Laurie followed her gaze. "Do you mean to tell me that Halsey and William are home, and they don't know their uncle died yesterday in our family's collective vegetable garden?"

"Technically, one car belongs to Halsey and one car is left over from Aunt Jean," Chris said, putting his hands up when he realized that wasn't the right technicality to mention.

"I'm sure William isn't around," Penny said. "Halsey and Miles are there, though you know Halsey. When she wants to see us, she shows up."

Laurie let out something between a whistle and a sigh and muttered about how she always needed to fix everything. When she opened the front door, clearly walking over to their cousins' house, neither Penny nor Chris moved to join her.

~

It turned out Laurie was incredibly adept at Dealing with Death. Penny watched for the most part from the overstuffed armchair in the living room, her mind on a loop that she would get up to help after the next episode of *Friends* was over. Chris was nearby and equally unhelpful, but he had more points because at least he knew to mock Penny's choice of show. "That show is literally for people with horrible senses of humor," he said, and Laurie laughed from the other room as she hung up one call and dialed another.

Three days passed like this, Penny on the armchair and Chris on the couch in the living room, Laurie behind them on a chair in the dining room calling everyone in the world who had known their father. Would they be more functional if they had kids? Penny thought. At least Chris would disappear throughout the day to take a work call or finish a spreadsheet. Penny could not bring herself to move, even if she wanted to move, and even if she hated herself for not moving. If not for her job at Harvest Market, the local grocer, she would have stayed completely isolated from the outside world.

"Thanks, Hals, I'll keep you posted," Penny heard Laurie say into the phone. She was positive it had taken Halsey three days to call her cousin back. And yet, not thirty seconds later, Halsey burst into the house with her six-year-old, Miles, at her side. Halsey had gotten divorced from her husband, Chad, a few months earlier, and no one ever talked about it.

"I'm so sorry, you three," Halsey said, her voice perfectly emotional, her hug perfectly tight. "We've got you now. Will is on his way too and we've got you. Family first, right?" she said, releasing Penny from a hug and looking her square in the eye. Halsey had always scared Penny a little bit. She was like an animal who couldn't decide between cuddling you and killing you.

Laurie got a hug next. "Sweet, sweet Laurie," Halsey said. Penny stifled a grin. Halsey, like her late mother, Jean, could lay it on a little thick. Chris stood off to the side, polite enough to know he couldn't get away without hugging her too. When it finally became his turn, Penny watched Laurie shake herself out a little. Hugs weren't supposed to crack ribs.

Halsey was the oldest, ripe and wise at forty-five, and she prided herself on being the oldest cousin. Penny, the youngest at thirty-five, always felt like she was catching up.

"If you three need anything, and I mean *anything*, we are just across the driveway."

"Thanks, Hals," Chris said for the group.

"Should we do dinner tonight? Over at our place? I'll organize!" Halsey said. The siblings looked quickly at each other. Halsey was notorious for excitedly making plans and then either pretending she hadn't or claiming it was an obligation she simply couldn't honor. Halsey didn't wait for an answer. "We're family. We're here. We are *here*." She said the last part as the door closed behind her and she jump-jogged back across the driveway. Miles tried to keep up.

The two houses were on a property that had been in their family for nearly seventy years. The front doors faced each other, with a two-hundred-foot-long driveway between them. Close enough to tell if someone was home, far enough away to not see into the windows.

~

The funeral was on Saturday at eleven a.m. at the church on Main Street. It was standing room only, but Penny barely recognized a soul. Chris gave a eulogy that suggested their father had never left them a day in his life. Laurie gave a reading that was an utterly indecipherable poem. Penny stayed seated, sweat spitting from her forehead and rolling like marbles down her face. She finally used the program to try and sop up some of the moisture but decided halfway through that her dress would work much better. When she realized what she was doing, her dress off her leg and on her chin, it felt like the entire church was staring.

CHAPTER TWO

In the dream, she was floating six inches above the bed, her body wrapped in towels that magically kept her warm and cooled her off at the same time. Someone was massaging her neck while someone else was rubbing her feet while even someone else was stretching and kneading her hands. This was the life, Halsey thought, her eyelids cool under lightly placed cucumber slices. She flexed her right foot up, stretching her arch, to tell the masseuse to knead harder. Someone dug into her feet at the right clip and Halsey went back to relaxing. Did this count as busy? She wondered.

Her toes were suddenly cold. Was the masseuse blowing cold air on her feet? Her husband, ex-husband, Chad, had slept with socks on—that was one of the things that had ruined them as a couple—but in this moment, sleeping in socks seemed like a good idea.

She squirmed her feet to make sure they were under the covers. The blowing continued. *Come on, Mr. Masseuse, don't lose me here.*

She now moved her whole foot, rotated it to the right like she was stretching out her ankle. No use. The cold air felt like the wind.

Every dream got weird. Even the ones that featured a handful of masseuses and made your comfort its top priority. Halsey sighed in her dream. She was awake enough to know it was a dream and asleep enough to keep it going.

The cold was now creeping up Halsey's calf. This wasn't fun. Or ignorable.

Halsey pushed up the energy through her body to her head and opened her eyes. *Hello, world, I'm back.* But the cold air . . . was still blowing?

"What the—" Halsey sat up and saw her six-year-old son at her feet. She had to will herself to breathe and not kick him in the face. "Miles, honey, why are you holding a fan on Mommy's feet?"

Miles looked up, unaware of just how creepy it was to hold a fan on his mother's feet and legs for no reason. "I wanted to wake you up, but I didn't want to disturb you," he said.

Halsey nodded. "Okay. But why didn't you gently touch my shoulder or rub my back or even whisper *Mommy*?" A learning specialist had told her that if you're going to reason with the child, you also need to provide options of what they could do or not do instead.

Miles didn't miss a beat. "You tend to jump."

"I *tend* to jump?"

Miles nodded assertively. "When you wake up. You go—" Here he went to the floor to impersonate Halsey startling at a touch so violently as to bounce off the ground, flail an arm toward the ceiling, and shout, "What! What happened!"

The kid had a point.

"Okay," she said, biting her lip and starting to sit up properly.

"I wanted to try something new," Miles said.

Halsey looked again at her son. He wore his Thomas the Tank Engine pajamas; even though he hadn't cared about Thomas the Tank Engine in years, he was loyal to the merchandise. His brown hair was perfectly mussed, and his eyes were like hazel plates on his face. He was, in a word, adorable.

But he'd also woken her up with a fan, and Halsey didn't quite know how to turn this into a teaching moment.

"How do you wake up your dad?" she asked, looking for a clue. Maybe Chad had already dealt with this. They weren't exactly mastering the coparenting these days.

Miles dramatically shrugged, exasperated by the question. "Dad is far worse, Mommy. He kicks. I would never go near his feet."

"So how do you wake him up?" Halsey sat against the bed frame. She was genuinely curious. Chad had always slept part-bear.

"It's best with loud noises," Miles said. Halsey laughed at the idea of Chad being woken up by various sounds.

"What kind of noises?" she asked, still laughing.

"The *Baby Shark* theme song," Miles said. Halsey laughed harder. It was beautiful payback: cheat on your wife with a colleague, who also happened to be her college classmate, blame your wife for not paying enough attention to your needs, then spend the rest of your life being awoken with the one song that drives parents off actual cliffs.

Miles sat at Halsey's feet expectantly, and she remembered that she hadn't yet asked why he'd woken her up in the first place.

"I'm sorry, buddy. You woke me up and I immediately hit you with all sorts of questions. What do you need?" she asked him.

"I just wanted a waffle," he said, getting up and walking toward the door.

"Where are you going, buddy?" Halsey called.

"*Paw Patrol*," Miles said without turning around.

"Do you still want a waffle?" She moved her legs to get out of bed.

"Of course I still want a waffle," Miles said in an obvious tone.

～

Halsey found William doing yoga in the backyard. His phone was sticking out of a selfie stick, which hung precariously from a nearby tree. He'd driven up from Hudson as soon as she'd told him that their uncle Frank had died. To William's credit, he was in the car before they'd even hung up. Now, even several days after their uncle's funeral, it was clear he felt no rush to leave. Time for William was not so much a tangible device to work with as it was a light wind that gusted over his life. For William, if it needed to be rushed, it was best abandoned.

"And that, my friends, is what we call a sun salutation," he said to the camera, which Halsey realized was rolling. She'd interrupted enough of his videos to know she'd better wait until he finished. When he leaned into a deep stretch with his back facing the camera and exhaled—"When we stretch, we're telling our bodies, *I love you. I value you. I'm there for you*"—she knew she needed to wait inside.

William was only eighteen months younger than Halsey, nearing his forty-fourth birthday with gusto and not a single responsibility. He was a yogi by training and an influencer for what Halsey could only assume was modest money and, apart from a young woman named Tina in the mid-2000s, had never been attached to anyone longer than a few months. And she only remembered Tina because he'd brought her to Halsey's wedding. He was a free spirit—Halsey knew this—but as she watched him go into a lunge and wave to the camera, she wished he could be the kind of free spirit who was at least artsy or had a wanderlust or was the type to run a tour-guide business. William rarely left Hudson, New York, a place he'd found a full decade before it became popular.

"My friends, today is the day we find our dreams. Today is the day we look to the earth and to the sky and say, *Yes, I am worth it*," William said, sitting cross-legged on the grass. "Namaste." He leaned dramatically forward, holding his nose to the ground for so long, Halsey thought he might lick the grass.

The bow ended and William sat and stood up in one fluid motion.

"Whew!" he said, finally acknowledging Halsey and moving to turn off his camera. "My followers are thirsty today." He shook his head for effect.

"Was it a live class?" Halsey asked.

William turned to look at her. "It doesn't need to be live for me to feel them."

He was serious, she realized, and closed her mouth from saying anything.

"So, we have that meeting today with the lawyer," Halsey said. "We all have to be present. He's either going to read the will or we have to go over the property."

"Guess the Compound is finally up for grabs," he said, gesturing around him.

Their family had owned two houses sitting on 150 acres since the 1950s, and when their uncle Frank passed away, the land officially transferred down to the next generation. Of course, they had three cousins and only two of them, meaning unless they got a cousin to their side, they'd always be outvoted.

"Time to hear the rules, at least," Halsey said, leaning against the house.

"What do you think will happen?" William asked. His yoga mat was now rolled up.

"I guess everything should get divided in half. You and I stay here, hopefully," Halsey said.

"It's weird, you know?" he said.

"What do you mean?"

William walked them back outside. The morning sun had dried the dew, and the late-summer fields looked almost golden, with only a few green blades poking through. "I never really imagined this"—he gestured to the valley—"would actually be ours. It's a lot, you know?"

"Don't tell me you'd let this place go?" Halsey asked, feeling her blood pressure start to rise. This was her son's home. This was the only place she knew.

"I didn't say that."

"But you didn't *not* say that," Halsey said.

William didn't answer.

CHAPTER THREE

The meeting was scheduled to start at eleven a.m. at the offices of Patrick Durkin Associates, a family law office that had been in practice for as long as the Nolans had owned the property in Vermont. Patrick had been Harry Nolan's oldest friend, and now his grandson Trevor was Chris Nolan's oldest friend. Which made a meeting like this utterly painless.

Laurie wanted to drive to the meeting herself. It had been almost two weeks straight with her siblings and Halsey and William just across the driveway. She needed a moment to get her thoughts together. She drove the long way to the Durkin offices, following a loop that traveled around the meat of residential Stowe, Vermont, passing the high school and accompanying fields, too many red barns to count, a stop sign that every year threatened to turn into a light. She flicked on her right blinker as she turned away from the white church that was not to be confused with the white church on Main Street, soon driving by a two-block stretch chock-full of bars, restaurants, and home-decor stores.

Would she stay up in Stowe until everything was sorted out? Could she stay? Work had been forgiving thus far—everyone knows to be nice to an orphan—but despite the company's "we are flexible" mantra, office hours were as vital now as they'd been before. She stopped at a crosswalk to allow a family of bikers to ride from one side of the bike path to the other. It certainly was a great excuse, she thought again, especially the bit about settling an estate, and she knew no one at work would think to question it. The Compound was legend in her New York City circle, her Williams circle too, for that matter, at once the place she brought every boy she was starting to get serious about and the setting for a series of increasingly unbelievable parties. The Compound was always going to be hers, or at least majority-owned by her and her siblings, she thought, now coasting into town proper and nearing the law office. She hadn't expected it to be theirs this soon, and she still wasn't sure how the land would be divided up among the five of them. But that was something for Trevor to figure out.

She pulled into the parking lot at 10:58 a.m., unsurprised by her punctuality. None of them ran late, not even Penny, who couldn't keep down a job but never lost track of time. Laurie assumed it was being raised predominantly by a German nanny, a buxom woman named Grietje who was at once mother bear and drill sergeant and who lived by the code that to be on time was to be late.

The Compound would probably fall on her and Chris to manage. Chris especially fancied himself the de facto leader, even if he was pompous and drove everyone crazy with his pompousness. He, along with Laurie, was the only one who held a "career" job. Halsey and William had never taken to working, and Penny did her best to get through the day. Laurie wasn't the oldest—Halsey had nearly five whole years on her and three on Chris—but she was the most put together, the most organized, and it was only right that the land's fate be up to her. The others would have a vote, of course they would. But she and Chris should carry the weight.

Chris knocking on the window broke her out of her trance.

"Come on, we're going to be late," he said, using a key-chain ring to tap the glass. The clock now said 11:02 a.m. She smoothed down her hair and opened the door. Chris stood back so she could get out.

"Hey, Laur," he said, giving her a side hug. She felt him shimmy and could see it made his pants slide a few inches down his thighs. The cuffs hit right above his ankles, offering key attention to his new Gucci sneakers.

"Those new?" she asked, staring at his feet.

"Nah, I've had these for years," he said. She knew he was lying. He'd bought them the day after their father had died, a nod to what was to come in this very meeting.

They walked together into the office building, one that looked much more like a Colonial home than it did a law practice. The entryway even boasted an antique wooden table for keys and mail, and Chris almost dropped his down.

"Guys!" Trevor said, greeting them in the foyer. "Hey, glad you could make it."

Laurie and Chris each hugged Trevor, Laurie's including an air kiss on the cheek.

"Where are the others?" she asked, but Trevor was already leading them inside to the conference room, where they saw their younger sister and two cousins sitting at the table.

No one got up to greet them, and Chris and Laurie maneuvered the chairs so all five Nolans were sitting on the same side of the table with Trevor facing them. Trevor's longtime assistant, Harriet, sat at the far head, fingers already poised over a laptop to take notes.

Chris nodded to both Halsey and William, who looked put together in a highly choreographed way. Halsey had gained a lot of weight since having Miles. Meanwhile, William was as thin as Laurie had ever seen him, his cheekbones now jutting out like elbows on his face. They were a yin and yang, and neither looked particularly healthy.

"This meeting is to provide an official reading of the last will and testament for a Mr. Frank Lawrence Nolan," Trevor began, reading from a script in front of him. All five Nolans leaned forward.

"The land, heretofore known as the Family Compound, comprises a trust established by Harold Lawrence Nolan in 1956 and, upon the death of the last child of Harold Lawrence Nolan, is to be shared equally by the descendants of Frank Lawrence Nolan and Jean Nolan Ridge and their descendants Christopher MacArthur Nolan, Laura Elizabeth Nolan, Penelope Lawrence Nolan, Halsey Ridge Thomas, and William Nolan Ridge. To that end, no material decision pertaining to the Family Compound may be acted on without the universal agreement from the owners. Should an owner wish to terminate their ownership of the Family Compound, the remaining owners shall offer the terminating owner a onetime sum of one hundred dollars, that sum not to be adjusted for inflation or change in the property's appraised value. Should additional owners wish to terminate their ownership of the Family Compound, the remaining owners shall offer the terminating owners a onetime sum of one hundred dollars, and so on and so forth, until there is a single owner of the Family Compound. Should additional individuals wish to become partial owners of the Family Compound, all existing owners must vote on the additional individual. Ownership through marriage is not valid until all existing owners agree."

Laurie now understood why Halsey's ex-husband, Chad, had never been considered part of the family.

No one sitting at the table said anything as Trevor evened out the pages in front of him and lightly tapped them before setting them down in front of him.

"Any questions?" he asked, his voice slightly hoarse from the lengthy reading.

Laurie felt droplets of sweat rolling down the length of her spine. This was going to be complicated. This was a group of people who could barely agree on what to make for dinner. They had always relied on their parents to keep them together. But as just five people out in the world? What did they have, except a little shared blood?

"So the Family Compound is divided evenly, then?" William was the first to speak.

"The Family Compound is *shared* evenly," Trevor clarified. "There isn't a division of the land here. You are all equal owners of the property."

"But what if one of us wants to build?" Laurie asked. She was sitting up straight, a practice she'd assumed since law school. When she was at her desk in private, she sat more like a humpback whale.

"Any decision must come with agreement from every party," Trevor said. He was speaking carefully and avoiding Chris's eyes. They were friends from way back, and Laurie could only imagine the fury simmering in Chris that he hadn't gotten any sort of heads-up. She knew her brother had walked into this meeting assuming he would somehow have more position than the rest of them. Men.

"Well, it's certainly lucky we are so close," Halsey said emphatically, even going so far as to hit her hand lightly on the table. Penny and William both nodded along, though Laurie remained still, her eyes locked on Trevor.

"We are so close," Penny said, her voice like a junior imitation of Halsey's. Laurie rolled her eyes without meaning to. Her sister had never paid rent, at least not without their parents' help, forget knowing the first thing about running something like their family's property.

Chris felt obligated to speak. "We are close," he agreed, "so I'm sure we can come to an agreement on everything that needs to be done with the property." He used his work voice for effect.

"Exactly," said Halsey, leaning forward to look him in the eye. "We are perfectly poised for this. Perfectly."

Trevor looked palpably relieved.

"This is a great start!" he said. The cousins all looked quite pleased with themselves. "I suppose we should get right to business."

Chris cocked his head in Trevor's direction, finally catching his eye for the first time all morning. "What business exactly?" he asked.

"Maintenance, really," Trevor said. "We need to officially transition any utility accounts to ensure there isn't an interruption in service."

"Can't all that come out of the estate?" Chris asked.

Trevor shook his head subtly from side to side, causing Laurie to perch on the edge of her seat. "Not exactly."

"Not exactly?" Chris asked.

"No. In this case, the extent of your father's estate was, well, this property. To keep it up and running will demand a fresh insurgence of equity that will need to come from the new owners." Trevor spoke like he was racing to include the words before he ran out of breath.

Laurie watched Chris look down at his feet. Suddenly his new Gucci sneakers looked ridiculous. As did her new watch and Penny's bag.

"He was out of money?" Laurie asked.

Trevor grimaced slightly. "His estate is not one with many primary assets."

Halsey looked confused, and Chris muttered, "Nothing liquid. Nothing easily transferrable to beneficiaries."

Thanks, Halsey mouthed to him.

"Going back to maintenance," Laurie said, trying to get a handle. "What do you mean?"

"It's the utilities, really," Trevor said.

Chris exhaled. Utilities were nothing to worry about. No more than a few thousand a cycle, slightly more during the winter months.

"Fine. I assume as shared owners we will need to open an account in which everyone contributes an equal amount, and all bills pertaining to the property are drawn from said account," Chris said. He was the leader here. He sat up straighter and puffed out his chest to prove it. Never mind that his sneakered foot was tapping on the floor under the table so loud, it sounded like the bass track of an album.

"Not so fast," William said.

Chris turned his head to see his cousin. He raised his eyebrows for William to continue.

"We aren't all equal earners. Why should we all be putting in the same amount?"

Penny nodded to William, and Chris was unsurprised by this. Penny had jobs that hadn't turned into a career. She had a passion for food. She might have been a camp counselor once, and she might have been a dog walker once—

"William is right," Laurie said, breaking Chris's trance. "It actually isn't fair to base contributions on income. If everything is shared five ways, we can't have some of us contributing more than the others, or else we'll never make an objective decision."

She looked directly at her brother. If looks could kill, she'd be underground. And of course he would be alarmed: they were by far the high earners of the group, each bringing in more than a million dollars a year at this point, and he would be damned if he had to float this entire enterprise for 20 percent. He furrowed his brow at her. *Take it back. Take it back right now.*

Halsey opened her mouth to speak—

"We need to base contributions on what we've been given, which then gets us on equal footing. While the property is shared equally, the five of us come from two families. So that's two estates split five ways, equal thirds for the Nolans, equal halves for the Ridges. If we consider this a family property, and thus pull from family funds, then we are in effect equal owners." Laurie looked again at her brother. *See?*

"Except there is nothing," Halsey said matter-of-factly. Laurie cringed.

"There isn't nothing; there just isn't a significant amount," Trevor said.

"Trevor, would you mind, then, elaborating on what we do and do not have?" Chris said, clearly frustrated.

"There is enough to cover the basic costs of utilities and taxes for the next calendar year. But to be clear, and I am not an accountant, I am your attorney, that means if anything goes wrong or awry, you five"—Trevor made eye contact with each person for full effect—"will need to contribute the difference. Or you will lose the land, as simple as that."

Chris groaned.

"This goes back to my point, then," Laurie said. "We have a year, and the five of us, regardless of earning, put in the same amount, given that we are all determined to make sure that nothing goes wrong."

"Exactly what Laurie said," Chris said quickly.

Even Trevor nodded.

"That makes sense to me," Penny said.

Halsey and William stayed quiet but looked at each other like they were trying to have a conversation without any words.

They probably had nothing left, Laurie thought. It'd been at least five, maybe six, years since her aunt had passed away. Neither of them worked; Halsey's ex-husband had always preferred to treat life like a series of breaks, and William fancied himself a yoga influencer. The hard part about old money was that without new money, it all went away. Besides this property, which made them look awfully impressive, their reserves demanded a very shallow hole.

Halsey addressed the group. "We can agree to this so long as contributions are approved in advance."

"Are you talking monthly, quarterly, or annual approvals?" Laurie asked. She was truly no-bullshit, even with family.

Halsey and William exchanged looks again.

"Annual," William said.

"That means you have one opportunity each fiscal year to negotiate the monthly contribution," Laurie said.

"Monthly," William said.

Laurie turned back to Trevor. "Can you draw up these documents?"

"Of course," Trevor said. Harriet was typing furiously, like this was more activity than she was used to.

The meeting ended shortly after, with the five cousins loitering in the parking lot after, each half saying what they thought. They agreed to go to the Shed for dinner that night, an impromptu toast to their new chapter, and all got into their five separate cars. Environmentalists they were not.

It wasn't until Laurie was driving away that she realized even with family funds covering the houses for a year, and even with all five of them legally pretending that they got along, no one had said yet whether keeping this land was the right idea. This had been their grandfather's dream and their parents' lives. Only Halsey lived up here full-time. Did this mean she needed to move to Vermont? Did they all? Could they all? The person who would have known what to do was her father, and Laurie realized at the same moment that he was never coming back and that tears were rolling down her face.

CHAPTER FOUR

Halsey could feel the sun on her back. Her shoulders were toasted, she knew this; she could feel the crackles in her skin when she moved her arms too fast. But the area around the pond was brimming with frogs—she'd never seen so many at one time before. And she had her grandfather and uncle on bended knee helping her catch them.

Her mother, Jean, was near the cluster of pine trees they'd recently planted, stealing as much shade as she could while she tried to convince a fussy William that he actually did like cheese. Halsey's aunt was feeding Chris, two years younger than William.

"If you tilt his head this way and shift up here," Halsey heard her mom explain to her aunt, "he'll get the milk a little easier."

Halsey heard her little cousin start to fuss less. William reached over to help himself to the goldfish and started smacking on them.

"Hals," her uncle Frank said, "check it out." Halsey turned around and saw her uncle's hand outstretched, a frog perched in the middle.

"I got one!" her grandfather said, cupping his hands together and showing Halsey the goods.

She peered into his hands and helped him place the frog in the bucket stationed between the rock they liked to jump off and a small stream they'd built to flow into the pond. The bucket was a chorus of ribbits.

"We'll name this one Pepper," Halsey said, gently stroking its head. The frog tried to jump up the sides.

She put her feet in the water to cool down. The sun was cresting behind the hill, and Halsey watched the sky start to paint itself pink. She held up her finger like it was a paintbrush, moving it across the sky, like a cloud trail planes leave behind.

"It's beautiful, isn't it?" her grandfather said. He sat on the pond's bank a few feet from her.

"It really is," she said, surprised at just how beautiful it was. She'd known she lived in a beautiful place, but she hadn't ever felt it before. It was like her lungs were breathing in this land, making her part of it somehow.

"This is my favorite place on Earth," he said.

"Can we stay here forever?" Halsey asked.

"I hope so," her grandfather said. "That's certainly what I'm trying to do here. To create a place where you'd want to stay."

"Like with family," Halsey said, considering something. "Family is something you want to stay with." And it was: she looked over at the pine trees where her parents were with William. Her family. Where she wanted to stay.

Uncle Frank waved and said they should head up the hill to eat dinner. "We've got hamburgers and hot dogs at our house," he said.

Halsey stepped out of the pond and waited for her grandfather to stand up. They walked slowly up the hill, his breathing labored. At one point, he took a break to rest his hands on his hips. Twilight had taken over; the pink had turned to a deep blue.

"I really do hope you stay here forever," her grandfather said.

"We will, Grandpa. I promise."

They finished the walk, reaching her parents' porch. Her grandfather sat down and asked Halsey to bring him some water. As she walked inside, she stopped and watched him looking out, like he was waiting for the hills to tell him something. A secret maybe.

CHAPTER FIVE

Laurie spent the entire drive from Stowe to Manhattan debating whether she should turn around and stay at her parents' house. "At *my house*," she said aloud, turning on her blinker and cruising into the right lane. She'd been on the Merritt Parkway for the past two hours; her two-bedroom apartment in New York City was three merges and an exit off the West Side Highway. "At my house," she said again, still getting used to how it sounded. Perhaps the lack of traffic was a sign she had made the right decision.

The cousins had been up in Stowe for weeks now, combing through their father's will again and again, looking for loopholes in the language that would allow them to split the land into five equal portions. They'd even take splitting the property into halves, at least protecting their acreage, because while Penny was a wild card, three deciders was still easier than five deciders. But neither Trevor nor the lawyers she and Chris kept within shouting distance could see any path forward beyond what their grandfather had clearly stipulated. The land was theirs, plural.

"Luckily, we get along," Penny said. They were sitting in the garden just below the house, each nursing a glass of wine. Laurie nodded but didn't say anything. Her mind drifted to Halsey and William and how they were a bit like mud: easy to get stuck in. Halsey especially could ensnare Laurie in seconds, turning her words around to show how Laurie had misspoken. Laurie sometimes thought she hated Halsey, or she hated how Halsey made her feel, but she didn't dare say it: Halsey had the rest of them wrapped around her finger.

"You need to start working," Laurie said without meaning to.

Penny looked at her like she'd been hit, going so far as to drop her glass of wine in the grass. "Excuse me?"

Laurie sighed and closed her eyes. Why had she opened her mouth? Why?

"I have a job. At Harvest Market. Where I go *every day*," Penny said, her chin warbly.

"I didn't mean anything by it," Laurie said.

"Sure you didn't," Penny said, now crying. Her sister could fall into tears so quickly.

"Would it be *wrong* to want more?" Laurie asked. What was so awful about wanting a career?

"I work!" Penny's eyes flared into saucers. "I've worked for years!"

"May I ask what you do?" It was a genuine question.

Even Chris, who had been pretending to be utterly engrossed in whatever he was reading, put his iPad down.

Penny stood up and put her hands on her hips before she answered. Laurie recognized this as a power pose and begged her lips to stay in a straight line. She knew Penny well enough to know that if she so much as smirked, that wine would be thrown at her head.

"I work at Harvest Market. I specialize in produce, and I know everything grown in the state of Vermont. I am figuring out how best to turn those loves into something larger. I know I'm not a lawyer or in private equity like you, but I still do something that matters. Do *you* know the latest laws around produce regulation in this state?" Penny said this bravely. "Plus I garden, but"—she turned briefly to the now-abandoned vegetable garden—"I can't go back in there. Not yet."

Laurie and Chris waited for her to continue. Several seconds passed, and Penny did not elaborate. She was still in her power position.

"Of course, Pen, and those are wonderful interests," Laurie said, adopting the nicest tone she could muster. "And of course you work." Penny relaxed her stance. Laurie looked at Chris only to find him looking at her already. Which meant he was as lost as she was.

"Do you make any money, Pen?" Chris asked, grimacing as he spoke.

Penny's eyes flared again. "I have always had a job. Just because I'm not a fancy lawyer or a fancy equities trader does not mean I don't earn a paycheck."

Laurie raised her arms in surrender. She and her sister had always argued about money, and Laurie realized she needed to tread more carefully. She had come out of the womb arguing. Chris had spent his childhood playing with his cash register. Their parents had done everything they could to ensure both Laurie and Chris were fast-tracked into big jobs. They hadn't done that with Penny. Laurie had a feeling that their rift over money was this: Laurie was jealous their parents had never let her just be a child exploring her dreams. Penny was jealous their parents never pushed her to dream bigger.

Chris's shoulders were squared for a fight, and Laurie shot him a look that said, *Guns down.* His shoulders fell, and he leaned back with his iPad in such a fluid movement, it almost seemed choreographed.

"We're sorry, Penny," Laurie said, meaning it.

They didn't need Penny to succeed; they needed her to stay afloat. She was fragile, to put it mildly, often falling into or slowly climbing out of a breakdown. It had been easier when she was younger: she had friends, went to school. But for the past few years, she had been almost completely isolated from anyone she ever used to know, and neither Laurie nor Chris had any idea why. The last thing they needed was to lose Penny now, not when so much was hanging by a thread.

Before Laurie left her siblings, she and Chris huddled near the base-ment door. They were due at their cousins' house in less than an hour.

"So long as we stay united, we'll figure this out," Laurie said.

Chris nodded like he was showing that he was listening. "We stay united. What about Penny?"

"She's one of us. We watch her, just like Mom and Dad did."

~

Laurie's New York City luxury was that her apartment building had a parking garage. She reached her building on 68th and almost Central Park West just before dinner and spent the entire time unloading her stuff onto a luggage cart, waiting for the elevator as it creaked up to the tenth floor, unlocking her door, and unloading her stuff off the luggage cart, debating whether she should order sushi or moo shu.

"Hey, stranger," a male voice said, causing Laurie to look up. It was Paul, a junior associate from work. They'd been in an absolutely secret affair for nearly a year, and six months in, they'd been assigned to their first case together.

"What are you doing here?" Laurie said. She couldn't stop from smiling.

"You've been gone for weeks," Paul said, stepping toward her and reaching out to take the duffel bag from her arms. "I missed you."

He leaned in for a kiss, and she accepted.

"I missed you too," she said, taking the hand that wasn't holding her bag. "I'm sorry I've been so MIA."

"I'm glad you're here now," he said.

Paul was far too young, and she was crossing every HR line she could, but he was gorgeous and funny, and she lost all better judgment around him.

"Want to come in?" she asked him. He was already following her inside.

As soon as the door closed, they couldn't keep their hands off each other, and Laurie couldn't believe she'd allowed nearly a month to go by without seeing him. Not that Paul was for public consumption: not even her best friends knew they were seeing each other. He stopped kissing her for a moment and put a strand of her hair behind her ear.

"What happens in Vermont?" he asked, smiling coyly. She rolled her eyes and took his face in her hands.

"Not nearly enough of this," she said.

As she ushered him inside her bedroom, she made her thousandth vow (all previously broken) to tell HR the truth and do whatever she needed to do to make this young man her boyfriend.

～

Halsey called a few days later while Laurie was at work.

"There's a Halsey for you?" her assistant, Haley, said. She was standing at Laurie's office door with her eyebrows furrowed. "I'm sorry, but she didn't give her last name."

Laurie rolled her eyes. "It's my cousin. She's never had a job, so she's never called an office, so she doesn't know that when you do call an office, you introduce yourself first and last name."

Haley nodded a little like she was learning something.

Laurie turned on her headset. "Hey, Hals," she said.

"Laurie, thank God it's you." Halsey sounded either excited or out of breath or both.

"What can I—"

"It's the house. The houses! We share property now." Halsey's voice went into an awkward falsetto.

"And?"

"It seems the pump in the well has gone dry. Extra use on the hill or something like that. We need a new pump."

"And you're saying what, that we need to split it?"

"I knew you'd understand, Laur."

"Do we need to split it?" Laurie said again.

"We do." Laurie could hear Halsey nodding through the phone.

"Have you gotten an estimate?"

"It'll be twenty thousand. Ten thousand a family."

Laurie leaned back in her chair and swiveled around to look at the window. Her office overlooked most of downtown Manhattan, high enough that the people were ants and the noise was mostly a hum.

Paul walked by her office without looking up but held a thumbs-up out of his back pocket, their secret signal. They navigated the illicit office romance by pretending to be strangers. A young partner could absolutely not get caught with a junior associate, no matter how real the relationship.

Ten thousand was a nuisance. Between their existing family pots, each side allotted $10,000 a month for everything. This meant she and Chris would have to dip into their own money, and given where she knew the Ridges were financially, they would probably have to do this for both sides.

"That's a little more than we can Venmo." Laurie tended to be sarcastic when she was uncomfortable.

Halsey laughed too loudly. "Laurie! You've always been so funny!"

Laurie stayed quiet a beat for Halsey to stop laughing. They weren't that kind of cousins.

"Okay, so you'll organize getting the pump fixed, or do I need to come back?"

"We can take care of it, sure," Halsey said, but Laurie could tell she wasn't finished talking.

"And . . . ?"

"I think we need you up here. While we get everything sorted. We both know William and Penny can only do so much. And Chris, well, Chris goes on long walks and drinks a lot of beer. Plus, you know he drove back to the city yesterday. And William is itching to get back to

Hudson; he'll leave any day. So it's really just me up here, and Miles is unstoppable right now . . ."

Chris hadn't told her he was coming back to the city. She even checked her texts from him yesterday—nothing after a photo of Camel's Hump and the caption, Not a bad hill we've got.

"Chris is really just getting his stuff together before coming back," Laurie said, hoping the lie would suffice.

"Sure. Whatever. Can you come?"

Laurie shook her head into the phone and raised her hands to the sky. Her assistant thought she was motioning for help, and they had an awkward, wordless exchange that resulted in Laurie gesticulating wildly with her arms in an attempt to get her assistant out of her office. How did Halsey do this to people? She was so good at getting what she wanted. Laurie often thought that if Halsey had gotten a degree in finance instead of meeting Chad, she would have been the most successful one of all of them.

"I need to move some things around, but yeah, I'll come back."

"Thanks, Laur! You're the best!" Halsey disconnected before Laurie could even say when she'd return. But of course, that was because she was supposed to come back that night. She texted Paul from a burner phone.

I have to go back to Vermont. How about a cocktail before I go?

She closed the phone and threw it in her desk drawer, debating how best to tell her partners that she needed to leave again.

CHAPTER SIX

Halsey heard the front door open above her and noticed Chad was dropping off Miles nearly three hours early. She pouted in the privacy of the basement, knowing her *90 Day Fiancé* binge was coming to an end.

"Whatever happened to no screens when it's sunny outside?" Miles asked from behind her, his question like a bomb to her silence. She turned around and expected to see rubble from the fallout.

"Hi, sweetie," she said, getting up from the overstuffed armchair and turning off the TV in one movement.

"Do you watch TV when you are alone?" Miles asked, looking between her and the television screen. Halsey wasn't ready to try and explain the draw of horrendous reality TV.

"I was helping out a friend; she needed me to check something on the screen. I wasn't really watching," she said, kicking herself for getting caught. She should have just walked upstairs as soon as she heard the door. Something must have happened anyway, she knew this—Chad never dropped him off early. Now Miles was probably going to run upstairs, find his father, and announce proudly that Mommy had been watching television all day alone.

Miles looked between her and the television screen and her again. He furrowed his eyebrows and cocked his head and opened his mouth to say something. Halsey braced herself with lies.

But then he closed his mouth. His face relaxed.

"Okay, Mommy." *Okay, Mommy?* "Can I have a grilled cheese?" *A grilled cheese?* Halsey stared at her son. This was the same boy who'd woken her up by blowing a fan on her feet because he felt like she was unpredictable in the morning. This boy did not accept a single answer to a single question. He needed no fewer than two answers per question. If it was raining, he needed to know why it was raining and for how long it would rain.

"Yes," Halsey said, not daring to look a gift horse in the mouth. "Let's go make you a grilled cheese."

They walked up the stairs, passing a wall brimming with framed family photos, and Halsey caught a glimpse of one from just after Miles was born. How had she looked better with a newborn than she did now?

Chad was standing at the top of the stairs, blocking their route to the kitchen. Halsey felt her heart climb into her throat.

"Well, hey there," she said, keeping her voice light.

Chad barely noticed her, his attention solely on Miles.

"Miles." Chad was using his angry-dad voice.

"Dad," Miles said back. He was pretending not to notice the angry-dad voice.

"What's up?" Halsey asked, trying to read her ex-husband. He was tense. Tense enough to clench his buttocks. His shoulders square. What on earth could their son have done?

"Miles, would you like to tell your mother what you just did in my shoes?"

Miles looked down. His hands took turns massaging each other.

"Miles, buddy?" Halsey tried. She looked again at Chad, still trying to get his eye.

He was focused squarely on his son. "Miles, I'll ask again. Would you like to tell your mother what you just did in my shoes?"

Miles let out an imperceptible murmur.

"What's that?" Halsey asked.

"They were sneakers," Miles said again, louder.

Finally, Chad looked at Halsey and mouthed, *He peed in my shoes!* His eyes were wide open, and his hands were in a field-goal position up by his shoulders.

Halsey closed her eyes and swallowed.

"Miles? Miles, look at me," she said.

Miles looked up for a second and then looked back down. He was now kneeling and tracing the carpet with his fingers.

"Do you want to talk about why you might have peed in your father's shoes?"

"I *told* you, they were sneakers."

Chad let out an exasperated sigh and turned around in a little circle, as if pacing in place.

"Okay, do you want to talk about why you might have peed in your father's *sneakers*?"

"Does it matter?" Chad wailed, now speaking to the ceiling.

"It does!" Halsey said sharply. "Eye on the prize, Chad. Dr. Spector told us if we don't get to the root of every behavior, it'll never get better."

"Dr. Spector never had his sneakers peed in for no good reason," Chad muttered, now walking in languid steps toward the doors leading out to the covered porch.

"We don't know that!" Halsey said too loudly.

She kneeled to where Miles now sat, still tracing the carpet with his fingers.

"Baby, it's okay that you peed in your dad's sneakers," she said, remembering Dr. Spector's words: "witness, validate, understand." She hadn't witnessed the act, but she could validate it. "Was it because you had to go really bad? Were they in the bathroom, maybe? And you got confused?" Sneakers could look like miniature toilets. Especially Chad's. White on the outside and a questionable mildew color on the inside.

Miles shook his head.

"Were you mad at Daddy?"

When Halsey thought about it, peeing in someone's shoe was an effective way to express anger.

Miles shook his head.

Why had she and Chad wanted more children? When they did things like pee in sneakers for no discernible reason?

"Hey, Chad?" Halsey called out. It was no use. He was now pacing on the porch but had closed the door, meaning he would hear her only if she shouted, and if Dr. Spector said anything, it was to never shout around the child after unwanted behavior. "I will pee in your sneakers too, I swear to God," she said under her breath. Chad had an uncanny ability to leave uncomfortable situations. Not the good kind, the kind where you're sixteen and too young to be around sex and drugs. No, the kind where a confrontation was necessary and, in the case of a six-year-old, where two against one was the only route to survival. Of course he'd left their marriage.

Miles murmured something.

"What, baby? Can you say it again for Mommy?"

"I was practicing."

"You were practicing?"

"I was practicing my aim."

Halsey looked up to where Chad, leaver of uncomfortable spaces, was still pacing. Their son, eager to master the art of peeing standing up, had been practicing. In his father's shoes, because on a technical level, they were instruments with an opening in the middle. They were arguably cloth's version of a toilet bowl. It made no sense, and it made perfect sense. Miles was looking at Halsey with a mix of hope and distraction. He was ready for this exchange to end. Chad showed no signs of slowing down. He should have been here, sitting with them, teaching their son about things like aim. It wasn't fair, that he left the hard talks to her.

"Well, listen," Halsey said, pulling Miles into her lap. He nuzzled her shoulder. "Well, listen," she said again. "I think we can agree that shoes aren't great places to pee. For one, there's no way to flush!" She raised her voice a little to let Miles know she was joking.

"You can't flush a shoe!" Miles said, letting out a small laugh.

"You cannot flush a shoe," Halsey agreed. "But I'll tell you what." She could think of one single way to get back at Chad.

"What?"

"If you want, we can keep this a secret from your dad." She thought of all the conversations Chad refused to have. She thought about how he'd tried to blame her, a woman at home with their son, for his affair with a colleague whom Halsey knew from college. Did Chad deserve to know that his son was peeing in his shoes for a truly understandable reason? Nope.

"But you said we don't keep secrets," Miles said. Halsey laughed and sighed in the same breath. Her attempt at delayed revenge was thwarted. Steel-trap Miles would never have let a secret fly. She should have known better.

"You're right. We don't keep secrets. I shouldn't have said that," she said.

Chad opened the porch door and stepped back inside. He took the necessary steps to where Halsey and Miles were sitting.

"So?" he asked, looking between mother and son.

"So?" Halsey asked back, smiling without opening her lips.

"Did we get to the bottom of it?"

Miles interrupted to ask if he could go play with his iPad and ran off before either parent could actually consent. Chad looked at Halsey expectantly.

"It's handled," Halsey said, getting up from her cross-legged position and audibly moaning as her knees cracked.

"What do you mean, it's handled?" Chad said. He'd made his way into the kitchen area of their open-floor-plan living area and helped himself to a beer. Halsey almost reminded him that he no longer laid claim over the contents of the fridge.

"What I said. It's handled. We talked. He explained himself. I don't think he'll do it again, but I also can't be sure." Halsey said this as breezily as she could muster.

"Don't you think that's a little soft?"

Halsey wanted a beer too.

"What about it?"

"He peed in my shoes, Halsey. How do you even get something like that out?"

"You put them in the washing machine like a big boy. I told you, it's handled. Don't worry about it."

She found a bottle of Heady Topper and used a bottle opener. The liquid was cold and brimming with bubbles in her mouth. She would drink one beer and a bottle of wine, and Chad could say anything he'd like because she would not listen to a word. He would be at his house with his new girlfriend anyway. She could drink in peace.

Chad sat down on the sofa and turned on the television.

"Chad, I mean this with kindness, but what are you doing? It's nearly six; Miles needs to eat. Are we pretending we still eat together?" Halsey checked the fridge again, this time for food instead of beer, and found leftover macaroni and cheese. And salad. "You can stay, but I can't accommodate the no-gluten stuff. It's pasta or nothing."

"I just don't feel comfortable knowing that our son sometimes pees in shoes," Chad said from the sofa. Halsey looked at him, his eyes behind glasses that were too small for his face. His haircut that was either three weeks past army training camp or three weeks before Wall Street executive. She knew she could easily put him out of his misery. Their son was simply figuring out his place in the world, an exercise accomplished by testing everything and everyone around him.

"Chin up, Chad," Halsey said, opening the bag of lettuce and pouring it in the salad bowl.

Chad got up from the sofa, put his empty bottle on the counter. "I gotta get going. I could bring some food home. For dinner," he said.

"By all means, please, have this macaroni and cheese I'm heating up," Halsey said. She didn't sound as sarcastic as she'd intended, and Chad gave her a confused look.

"I'm not sure that's—"

"I'm kidding, Chad. You cannot have my leftover macaroni and cheese. Namely because Miles and I need to eat it, but also because food is not part of our current coparenting arrangement. We find our own food—that's how this works."

Chad tried to laugh but failed. Halsey turned away from him so she could roll her eyes.

"Well, bye," Chad said, coming in close enough to try and kiss Halsey on the cheek. She took a step back, causing him to miss and slightly trip forward.

Miles rode in on his hoverboard.

"Bye, Daddy," he said, riding right up to Chad and giving him a hug. Halsey swooned at the sight. Chad drove her up the wall, but her heart melted every time she saw father and son together. Chad did his best to hug back without letting the wheels roll over his feet.

"Bye, champ. See you this week," he said, exiting through the front door.

"Hey, Miles," Halsey said, tossing the salad while she spoke. Miles looked her way. "I won't tell your dad why you were peeing in his shoes, but you know you should not do that, right?"

Miles pursed his lips and rode the hoverboard once around the dining room table.

"Miles?" she said again.

He stopped. Looked out the window. Looked at her.

"The openings are too small anyway," he said and rode the hoverboard down the hall.

CHAPTER SEVEN

Penny's room in the house was called the Birds Nest, because it was nestled between two significantly larger rooms and got direct sunlight for only an hour or so a day. A little longer in the summer and a little shorter in the winter. Penny was supposed to have gotten a proper Birdhouse, as named by her mother, but a deal gone bad at the last minute replaced the House with a Nest. As such, Penny was given free rein to design her room, and so her walls were washed with a light blue and covered with hand-painted murals. The rest of the house was a classic ski chalet, all dark wood and light stone and tumbled couches. On a good day, Penny's room felt like a vacation. On a bad day, it just felt weird.

Today, it felt weird. Penny had outgrown this room, she thought, pushing the covers off her and getting out of bed. It was just after eight a.m., which meant when she pulled up the blinds, two rays of sunlight would shine through the trees on the east side of the house. She traced the rays with her finger. So little sunlight in an otherwise sun-drenched house meant Penny treated this hour like an event. Her family assumed she slept late.

Penny had been alone at the house for a week now. Chris and Laurie were both back in New York City, though not together. They lived on opposite sides of the city, and it wasn't unusual for them to have absolutely no contact for weeks at a time. A week alone meant she'd easily retreated into her single-girl behaviors, the dominant of which were an old pair of sweatpants, eating peanut butter out of the jar, and lining up her weekly ration of alcohol. If not for work, she would not leave the house, and she would not interact with anyone else. She preferred it this way: people, the very presence of them, made her so anxious, it felt like her insides turned into marbles, rolling around this way and that with every breath she took.

For the past year, her ration had been one freshly made cocktail per night, either a gin and tonic or a margarita; one bottle of cold white wine, either Chardonnay or Sauvignon Blanc; one bottle of beer, either an IPA or a stout but always a microbrew. This allowed her to get drunk enough to easily pass the nighttime hours, but not so drunk that she got unbearably lonely or bored. She didn't want to wake up in the sauna or down by the pond without any recollection of how she got there, which was what had happened before she instituted the ration. When she was alone, she liked to line up each day's share on the kitchen counter and spend most of the day thinking about the bottles. By noon, it was an all-out countdown to six, when her shift would end and she'd roll in the door fifteen minutes later.

The house around her was immaculate. When she wasn't at work, she moved around like a train on a track, never extending beyond her route: bedroom, bathroom, hallway, kitchen, and repeat. She found the easiest way to keep the house clean was to move as little as possible. If she never changed, clothes didn't get dirty. If she only watched streaming television from her laptop in bed, the living room didn't need tidying.

She dressed in pants with a button and a shirt that showed the world she had a bust. It was uncomfortable. The pants fit but only technically. She put on a pair of shoes that were not slippers. She traded her fuzzy wool socks for low white ones. Her feet felt itchy against the new fabric, and as she looked at her legs for the first time, she realized she was now part bear. Did she mind this? She stroked her right calf. It reminded her of her high school boyfriend's calf.

"We're doing this. We're going out," Penny said to herself in the mirror. She did this every morning: a will and a pep talk to keep going.

She moved toward the door, the one that led from the mudroom to the porch to the driveway but stopped just before reaching the doorknob. Her outfit was all wrong, she decided, not even bothering to look down. She walked back upstairs, back down the hallway, stopping at the Birds Nest, first door on the left. Three attempts later, she was dressed. It was more or less the outfit she'd started with.

Her black MINI Cooper sat right outside the house, but there was another car in the shed a ways down the driveway. An old 4Runner that had no business running. It was a relic from when she had two parents and an aunt and an uncle and two siblings and two cousins and the families would gather for holidays that stretched across weeks in a flurry of activity. It was the car she commandeered in college, driving through the mountains to Dartmouth. It was the car she once drove over the lawn and through the weeds down to the property's swimming pond.

She tried the ignition and it worked.

"Good girl!" she cried, tapping the dashboard.

The drive down the hill was easy enough. Their property was at the end of a long dirt road that meandered up a hill, and Penny always wondered what people thought when they accidentally drove all the way up and had to turn around. The property itself was unassuming, two mailboxes in front of a simple wooden fence. But the fence, if the driver paid attention, trailed nearly half a mile.

Ten minutes and two stop signs later, she pulled into Harvest Market. It was Thursday, which meant it was shelf-stocking day. She melted easily into the rhythm of replenishment: grab a box from the back, record it, stock the shelves, and repeat. Today was mostly grains: rice, barley, pasta. An entire wall, all lined with various sizes and shapes of boxes. Penny subtly lined them up by color. Eight hours passed with hardly a glance up, and Penny felt as safe here as anywhere.

When six o'clock hit and her supervisor, Jake, sent her off for the day, Penny remembered she needed to replenish her booze. But going to only the liquor store meant she was some sad lady who drank too much. If she added a stop, then she was a lady running errands. It was completely different.

Penny got into the car and visualized the street around her, thinking about potential places to stop. She would go to the sports store in town, buy something that suggested outdoor activity, and then go to the liquor store on her way home. That way, the cashier at the liquor store would believe she'd just returned from a hike, merely picking up beverages on her way to a dinner party tonight. It was perfect. Penny turned left into the parking lot for Twin Tips, a sporting-goods store that had been around at least as long as Penny had been alive. She loved this place, even if she was more of a house cat than a coyote.

A male voice interrupted Penny comparing an insulated fleece and a ski parka: "Are you looking for anything in particular?" She looked up and saw that the face attached to the voice was attractive. Abercrombie & Fitch attractive, when that had meant something.

"I'm, um . . ." Penny gestured between the two jackets. She didn't know what to say next.

The man took a step toward her. "Is it between these two, then?" he asked.

It wasn't, because Penny had no intention of wearing either, but she couldn't look away from this guy.

"I guess so? I don't know—I need something warm."

"Something warm? Something warm for when you're . . . doing something active outside?" This guy was really trying. He even furrowed his brow a little.

"Yes! I mean, yes. Yes. I'm, um, preparing for a trip of sorts. An outdoor trip." What was she saying?

"That sounds fun," he said. Did he look interested?

"I'm going to hike up Mount Washington. Maybe even make it an overnight."

The guy's eyes flared. He was impressed. He took another step closer. "That's rad."

His saying "rad" made Penny deflate a little. She didn't interact with many people who said "rad."

"You need a bunch of stuff, don't you? A jacket, yes, but probably a tent? Cooking equipment? How are you for boots?"

Penny tried to remember how much room she had left on her credit cards.

"I do, that's true, but I . . ." She trailed off. It didn't feel like flirting to say she was broke yet technically a land baron.

"Say no more." The guy put up his hands. "I hear you. I too need to prepare for trips in stages."

Penny nodded with a touch too much enthusiasm. "Exactly!" She was *so* bad at flirting.

"Maybe we start with the jacket today, and then I can tell you when things go on sale?" He'd taken the parka off the hanger and was holding it up against her. "You want this one, by the way; it's warmer and better against the wind. It's water resistant too. That fleece is for a bonfire."

Penny realized she was nodding along.

"I'm Andrew," he said, holding the parka in one hand and sticking out his other. Penny took it in hers. It was strong and a little dry and a little clammy.

"Penny."

"Like the lane?"

"Like the coin."

Andrew laughed and led them toward the cash register at the front of the store.

"If you want to give me your number, I can tell you when stuff goes on sale." Andrew said this without even trying to hide the hope in his voice.

Penny gave him her number.

"When's the big trip anyway?"

"That's a good question," Penny said. Would she actually have to do this trip? Overnight?

"Well, maybe you'd want some company?" Andrew said. Penny must have looked horrified because he quickly followed up with, "Two tents, of course!"

"So a BYOT sort of thing?" Penny asked, her voice light.

"Bring your own . . ." Andrew trailed off.

"Tent," Penny finished.

"Of course, of course." Andrew thumbed in a code to the register. "The jacket is one sixty."

Penny handed over her credit card.

"Well, Penny like the coin, it was a pleasure doing business with you," Andrew said, handing her the shopping bag.

Penny finished her errands, replenishing her rations and even stopping to buy food, real, actual, nutritious food she could prepare as a meal to eat. She didn't know the last time she'd cared to cook something for herself, and as she crested the hill right before their property started, she thought about walking through their woods with Andrew. He was cute, "Abercrombie & Fitch as interpreted by a lifelong Phish fan" cute, and Penny realized with a little horror that she hadn't found someone—girl or boy—cute since well before her father died. She turned left at the road's dead end onto the Compound's driveway, pushing on the gas to get the 4Runner one final stretch of hill.

She didn't expect to see Chris's Suburban and Laurie's BMW already parked outside the house, with every light on inside. The first emotion to hit her was excitement, which was unexpected. Penny had gotten really good at being alone. It was easier that way, with far less chance of disappointing whoever she was with. Maybe she missed them, her brother and sister, as ornery and righteous as they were. Or maybe she just missed how they confirmed that she came from somewhere: the three of them looked so similar, it was like they were heightened versions of brother and sister. Penny felt like an alien so much of the time that seeing herself in another person was sometimes the only thing tethering her to Earth.

CHAPTER EIGHT

Laurie heard Penny's car putter up their driveway and went outside to meet her. The house had been shocking when Laurie had arrived, not because it was a mess but because not a thread was out of place. Laurie had lived alone for long enough to know that even one person left a wake in their living. The house looked positively empty, and Laurie knew her sister well enough to know that an intense cleaning regimen was not in her DNA. Nor was a budget for a cleaning service. Which meant Penny never left her bed. Even the cushions on the couch were still puffed correctly.

"We shouldn't have left," Laurie had said to Chris as soon as he walked in the door.

"What do you mean?" he asked.

Penny was clearly not okay on her own.

"She's cooped up in her room! Go open the door and I'll bet you a hundred dollars it smells like old cheese," she said.

Chris went upstairs as directed, and Laurie heard him open a door. Then she heard a door close and another open and then close, which meant he'd smelled whatever there was to smell and decided he would rather hide upstairs than talk to his sister. The dried-out well pump felt like a distant memory.

"Chris!" Laurie yelled up the stairs.

No response.

"Did it smell like cheese or not?" she yelled again.

A door opened.

"Not super cheesy," Chris called out.

The door closed.

Laurie walked up the stairs and into Chris's room.

"Do you think everything is okay?" His room was a little disorderly, now that Laurie looked around. He didn't answer. "I just want her to be okay, you know?" she said, softer.

Chris nodded and winced a little.

"Can you help me be less harsh? With Penny?" Laurie hated that she had to ask this. She felt like little knives were pricking behind her eyes.

"Just remind her how much you love her. I will too. I bet she's okay." Chris said the last part with a hopeful smile.

~

"Hey there!" Laurie said after walking downstairs and outside, immediately wishing she hadn't sounded so fake and upbeat. Why did she sound like an inflating balloon?

"Hi," Penny said, getting out of the car slowly, like an animal considering an imminent threat.

"I'm back. We're back. We came back," Laurie said.

"I can see that," Penny said.

"Running some errands?" Laurie asked, trying and failing to subtly see what was in the car.

"Groceries. And a new parka," Penny said, still too suspicious to fully get out of the car and close the door.

"Need help carrying stuff in?" Laurie took a step forward, and Penny looked like she was seriously contemplating getting back into the car and driving away.

"What's this about, Laur?" Penny asked. She'd shifted her weight to be fully out of the vehicle and closed the driver's door and stood in what appeared to be another power position. Legs shoulder-width apart, hands on her hips. Penny had clearly watched the TED Talk. If Laurie had been at work and Penny were a junior associate, Laurie would have laughed. Instead, Laurie hunched into herself and crossed her arms over her chest.

She didn't want to raise her adult sister. She wanted her sister to be an adult.

"Halsey called about something going wrong with the well," Laurie said, debating what to say next. Penny remained in her position. "She didn't ask me to come back, but she also didn't say I didn't need to come back, so here I am. Chris too. But then when I got here and didn't see your car and walked inside . . . I thought the worst, Pen. There were ten messages on the machine from Halsey. I assume you were ignoring your phone, but she called the house ten times before she finally called me at work. Where were you?" Laurie bit the inside of her cheek so she wouldn't cry.

Penny didn't say anything for several seconds, her eyes darting among Laurie, the groceries, and the house, like she was considering whether she could possibly bring her things inside instead of answering. Laurie inhaled and realized she'd been holding her breath.

"I've been around, but I've been busy. I didn't hear Halsey's messages," Penny finally said. Her hands were still on her hips. She looked like the statue of the girl in front of the bull on Wall Street.

"Busy with what?" Laurie couldn't help herself.

"What does it matter?" Penny said. Her arms shot up in the air like she was catching something out of the sky. "Whatever I say, you're still going to think I'm just a fuckup. So you know what? I'll keep being busy."

With that, she got back in the car, turned the ignition, and drove back down the driveway, leaving Laurie standing outside their front door.

Laurie shook her head and turned around.

"Chris!" she called, walking up the stairs to his room. She could hear him on the phone; low but emphatic rumblings pushed their way through the door. "Chris!" she said again, knocking twice before trying the knob.

"I'll call you back," Chris said as Laurie pushed her way into the room. "Knock much?" he said. He was sitting on the edge of his bed, facing the window that overlooked Camel's Hump.

"I literally just knocked," Laurie said, defiant. The same anxiety she felt with Penny transitioned immediately into aggression with Chris. It had always been that way.

"What's up?" Chris asked.

"Penny just drove away in a fit of rage," Laurie said, sitting in the armchair next to the bed.

"What else is new?"

"Aren't you worried? We have to come together now, you know? It's just us left." Laurie gestured for effect.

Chris shrugged. "This is what Penny does. She leaves, and she comes back."

"Even now? When it's just us?" Laurie asked.

"What else are we supposed to do?" he asked.

Laurie let out a deep breath and leaned back.

"What did Mom and Dad do?" Chris asked after a few moments.

Laurie felt herself welling up. None of them knew how to talk about their parents, not yet. For them, grief was right under the scab they covered carefully with a bandage. "I don't know," she said, swallowing hard to try and hold back the tears. "They just knew how to handle her, I guess."

Chris stood up and went to the window, which he opened to let in the late-summer breeze. Laurie could smell the fire burning from Halsey and William's house.

"Until we get this property settled, we need Penny with us," Chris said.

"Are you really bringing in the Compound right now?" Laurie couldn't believe her brother was being so crass.

Chris didn't turn around as he continued to speak. "She's the tie-breaker here. She's the swing state. There aren't any loopholes, but there are votes, and if Penny decides that maybe her cousins are nicer, or more supportive, or even, I don't know, smarter, well, then you and I are suddenly all alone."

"Do we even know what we want out of this?" Laurie asked.

"What do you mean?" Chris responded, cocking his head.

"Do we want this place? Or do we want to sell it? We haven't said it out loud yet," Laurie said.

"I don't see how it makes sense to keep this place intact. Not with five co-owners who have basically nothing in common besides shared blood and a few key memories."

"That's a little harsh, don't you think?" As her brother spoke, Laurie realized she disagreed with him. Intensely so.

"Okay, yes, fine. We share more than that. I'm just a little nervous about the five of us actually coming together. I don't know William and Halsey anymore. Not as adults. Dad was so good at smoothing everything over."

Her brother was right, Laurie thought, crossing one leg over the other. Their parents had always taken care of everything. But here they were, utterly out to sea. Her phone buzzed in her jacket pocket and she wished desperately it was Paul checking in. She hadn't expected him to lodge himself into her life like this.

"I wish I knew where she went," Laurie said. She needed to fix whatever this was.

"She'll be back. And we'll be here. And you'll apologize and we'll have a family meeting and come up with some ground rules for the house. Maybe you and I stick around for a little while, just as we get the property underway."

Laurie nodded and stood up. "You want some wine?" she asked.

"I'll meet you down there," Chris said, pulling his phone out of his pocket.

"Who were you on with earlier?" Laurie asked, gesturing to the phone.

Chris furrowed his brow and shook his head. "It doesn't concern you."

"I'm your sister?" Laurie asked, hoping her tone would keep the question light.

"And? It's not like we're close," Chris said without looking up.

"We could be, though. We used to be," Laurie said. "See you down-stairs." She walked out of his room. He was right, and it hurt to hear, and there was no one else who could make her feel so lonely.

CHAPTER NINE

Halsey tried calling William again. When it went to voice mail, she finally left a message. "Look," she started, "I realize I've now called you fourteen times. But you don't call me back, and frankly, you need to." She could feel herself getting more worked up. "You know we are having an issue with the well. Literally everyone is here except for you, and they have three of them and we only have two, and I need you to send money for the house account. It is not fair, William." She made sure to emphasize his name, like a disappointed parent. "And you need to do this." She needed something to hold over him. A few seconds passed with dead air on the message. "Or I'm telling all your followers that you can't actually do crow and that's why you never include it in your classes." She hit "End" and felt satisfied.

It was Tuesday, just before eleven, and Halsey was on her way to play tennis. She played twice a week, year-round. On Tuesdays, Miles was either at school or at camp, and Halsey had played with this particular foursome for the past three years—since Miles started school or camp. These women had gotten her through late-toddlerhood, predivorce, divorce, and post-divorce. They all lived in Stowe, and Halsey often considered them her lifeline to a semblance of a social life.

She pulled into the parking lot as one of her foursome-mates, Margot, got out of her car. Halsey gave her a little honk and pulled into the space next door.

"Howdy," Margot said with a little wave. She wore freshly pressed whites that fit well enough to look couture.

Halsey got out of her car and grabbed her tennis bag. Her own whites were slightly wrinkled, but she hoped they looked wrinkled from sitting in the car for too long. She did this sometimes: she'd wear a shirt with a stain or wrinkled pants or a too-scuffed shoe and pretend it had all just happened. She wanted to believe this worked, but she also couldn't be sure it did.

"Are the other girls out there already?" Halsey asked. She hated feeling late.

Margot shrugged. "We'll find out in a sec. How's Miles?"

"A dreamboat with pizzazz," Halsey said, smirking. Miles was a fan favorite among her friends. They especially loved the "practicing his aim in the ex-husband's shoes" storyline. "How's Mirabelle? Kristin?"

"Mirabelle believes it's her duty to protect her little sister from ever learning the truth about Santa Claus, which is very sweet during the holidays and less so during the rest of the year. Yesterday, we were walking down Main Street and I don't even know how she heard it, but someone said his name, and she screamed at the top of her lungs, 'Santa Claus is *real*.'"

"Spirited kids are the best kids," Halsey said, and Margot laughed while she nodded.

"I just wish she hadn't screamed into an old man's face. Kristin didn't even notice," Margot said.

"I had my cousins over for dinner a few nights ago, and Miles put out ex-lax, pretending it was just regular chocolate," Halsey said. "Not that he even understands what ex-lax is, just that it's not something he's supposed to eat." Chris had gone so far as to try and pick up a piece, and Halsey still didn't know how she managed to intercept it. Miles had been in the corner giggling, fully aware of the prank.

The other two women, Pamela and Melissa, were hitting balls when they reached the court. Halsey and Margot fell into place beside them, the four of them playing a round robin to warm up.

Pamela and Melissa were old friends from the ski team. Of all the cousins, Halsey had spent the most time in Stowe as a kid, attending camps and playing sports like a regular local. She was a natural skier, and her parents had been thrilled at the prospect of her ski racing instead of playing ice hockey, and they would load her and William into the car and make the trek three hours north every Friday night. The Nolans were more vacationers than weekenders and thus never made local friends like Halsey did.

Halsey played tennis easily, but Melissa was the one to beat. After a doubles set, each took turns playing a singles round, and the final came down to Melissa and Margot. Pamela and Halsey sat on a bench next to the court, watching as the women lobbed balls across the net, their game a bit like a dance.

"Have you met Jeremy's mom yet?" Pamela asked. Her daughter, India, was the same age as Miles.

"Have I?" Halsey asked. The town of Stowe was small enough that she was surprised to imagine anyone new.

"She's recently divorced too, and just moved back after a bunch of years in Boston. The ex also moved; I guess they figured everyone deserved a fresh start, and it wasn't fair to break up the family even more," Pamela explained.

"And Jeremy is in Miles and India's class?" Halsey asked.

"He will be this fall. He's a sweet kid. A little shy for India's taste, but Miles gets along with everyone," Pamela said.

"I wonder if he did any of the camps this summer," Halsey thought out loud.

"Who knows, but I met his mom, Heather, the other day at the Swimming Hole, and she's sweet. And looking for friends. We should invite her to cocktails sometime," Pamela said.

"Maybe I'll put something together for next week," Halsey said, just as Margot wailed a forehand cross court and won the game. It was unclear who of the four was most surprised at the upset.

The ladies gathered their belongings and started walking toward their respective cars. "Hals, if you want to put something together, I'll make sure Heather comes," Pamela said. Margot chimed in that she also had met and liked this Heather.

When Halsey got back to her car, she checked her phone and saw William had finally called her back. With his voice mail came the reminder that her entire life was suddenly on uneven footing. If she couldn't get her family to agree, she needed to find somewhere new to live. She wasn't ready to be an orphan. Or divorced. Or houseless.

"For the record," William's message started, "I absolutely know how to do crow. However, as you know, I have compromised elbows, and frankly, it's a detrimental pose for me personally, and it's entirely possible to have a vibrant and meaningful yoga practice without it." Halsey laughed out loud at his justification. "I can come back to the property," he continued, "but only for a few nights. We'll deal with the well and whatever else and hopefully make some sort of decision."

Halsey dialed her brother back.

"Hey, sis," he said.

"It's you!" she said, trying too hard to sound light.

"You got my message?"

"I sure did. Why can you only come back for a few nights?" Halsey asked.

"I've got a lot going on," William said plainly.

"What, in the world of influencing? I thought the best part about being an influencer is you can do it from anywhere," Halsey said.

"It's not that simple," William said. "I've got roots here."

"Roots? You put out yoga videos. How rooted can you possibly be?" Halsey said and immediately regretted it. William was not someone who welcomed even jovial criticism. She could hear him bristle in his breath.

"I have people here," he said.

"Did you meet someone?" Halsey asked. Maybe that was it. William fell in love hard and quick once every couple of years. It lasted between one season and three but never four, and the woman was never spoken of again.

William didn't say anything.

"Bro? Is that it? You're in love?" Halsey asked, her voice softer now.

"Maybe. It's early. We've known each other a long time. But yeah, she's here, and I want to stick around."

Halsey wasn't used to her brother being so forthcoming. She was touched.

"Why don't you just bring her, then? There's plenty of room here," she said.

"That would be incredibly complicated for many reasons," William said quickly and firmly.

Halsey knew better than to push this moment. The fact that she was actually on the phone with her brother was a small miracle.

"Got it, bro. No worries. Just get here when you can. And please, please don't vote to sell," Halsey said.

"Love you, sis," William said and hung up without waiting for her to respond.

She had forty-five minutes before Miles needed to get picked up from camp, which meant she could swing by Daedalus. If she was going to be a single mother and lose her home, then today she was going to treat herself to lunch, and next week she would host a cocktail party and welcome new girl Heather to town while she still had a home to host in.

CHAPTER TEN

Their grandfather was determined to ski in his eighties. "Are you sure, Dad?" Frank asked, looking nervously between his sister, Jean, and his wife, Bea.

"Don't be ridiculous—I've been skiing for seventy years, and I'm not stopping now," he said.

Laurie was in the new room of the old house, when it was still called the Red Shed and before her mother had finally put her foot down and said that unless a new house was built, she was never coming back. While her parents and grandfather had been arguing about the skiing, Laurie'd been getting ready for the day. She was ten. This meant she could ski alone, but only if another—older—family member was at the mountain.

"Hey, Grandpa," she said, walking into the mudroom. The adults turned around and looked at her. An old ladder that went up to the attic cut the room in half. Old one-piece ski suits hung from a rod against one wall, with a dozen pairs of skis, all ranging in size and quality, hung on the other wall.

"Yes, champ?" Grandpa said.

"I'll go skiing with you," she said. "I did Goat last weekend, and Dad says I can do Star if I keep leaning forward."

Laurie's grandfather broke into a smile and turned to his son. "That settles it. Laurie and I are going skiing."

This led to a chorus of murmurs, which eventually bore the consensus that everyone would go skiing—Frank, Bea, Harry, Halsey, Chris, and Laurie. Jean would stay in the lodge with William, who didn't care about skiing, and Penny, who was still a year away from ski school, a program aptly named Pooh's Corner.

~

It was a bluebird day: crisp, clear air, scattered clouds, the snowpack deep and firm. The group filled the eight-person gondola, and Grandpa declared while they were halfway up Mount Mansfield that he needed only a run, maybe two, to satisfy his goal. Laurie leaned into her grandfather. Even at ten, she could feel that he glued the family together. She didn't want to think about what would happen when he wasn't around anymore.

"Do you want to lead the way, Dad, or do you want to ski down to us?" Laurie's dad asked. By now, he was on board with Operation Ski In Your Eighties, and a smile was plastered on his face. He was proud.

"I think I'll ski down to you," Grandpa said, nodding as he spoke. "That way no one talks in my backswing."

The family skied down, leaving Grandpa behind. Laurie watched Halsey and Chris, their movements like a silk ribbon being guided down the hill. Halsey especially was a beautiful skier, her form at once relaxed and precise. Laurie copied her movements: she slid in behind her, pole planting when she pole planted, trying to tuck her body into each turn and accelerate into the next one. Chris barreled past both of them a few turns in, his ability to build speed almost God-given.

They stopped at the bottom of a large pitch, and Uncle Frank waved Grandpa down. Grandpa waved back and then leaned forward, letting his skis do the work. He was a natural skier without the speed of his younger family members, instead gliding more like a sail with the wind. His red coat billowed in the wind, and his old ski hat with a pom-pom bounced up and down. Laurie could see his smile and determination all the way from where she stood watching.

Grandpa reached the bottom and let out a hoot.

"And *that* is skiing in your eighties!" he said, beaming.

Laurie and Halsey and Chris kept skiing that day, even after the adults headed home. At first, they took advantage of being alone and raced, seeing who could go the longest without making a single turn. But after a while, they fell into a rhythm, their turns getting longer and slower, their runs feeling like a dance on the snow.

CHAPTER ELEVEN

The five cousins filed into the law offices of Trevor Durkin the following Monday. Chris had asked Trevor to organize the meeting after he came up with what he believed to be a bulletproof plan for moving forward. The key was accountability. He and Laurie made money. William, Halsey, and Penny did not. He was unwilling to float their lifestyles, even if it was built on a property where Chris had experienced the best times of his life. Chris explained all this to Laurie as if it were humane and obvious, and while she wanted to protect him from the outcry this plan would no doubt elicit, she also wanted him to experience it firsthand. Chris had hardened when his fiancée, Alison, left him three months into their engagement. It was like she'd taken with her Chris's ability to consider the gray—now he was all black and white, and neither Laurie nor Penny knew how to soften him.

The two sets of siblings had yet to spend any time together on the hill, despite all five now being back. Chris had gone over a few times to watch Disney+ with Miles, but Laurie wasn't great with kids. Penny showed no interest in crossing the driveway, but she also showed no interest in leaving her bedroom, and Laurie was pretty sure it had nothing to do with her cousins and everything to do with the thing that happened that no one talked about. Halsey had her life here, Laurie knew, but when she threw a cocktail party in their shared backyard without inviting any of the Nolans, it was impossible not to take it as a slight.

"Who cares?" Chris had said from his designated armchair, his eyes on the Patriots game.

Laurie stood at a point in the living room where she could watch the party without being seen. "I don't care. I just think it's rude," she said, wishing Penny were around because she would agree with her.

"If you don't care, why are you spying on the party?" Chris said. "Here," he added, reaching behind him to a mini fridge in the bar, "have a beer. It'll be good for you."

It looked like a fun party. That was the worst part. She wouldn't care if everyone were just milling about the lawn looking for something to do. It was the opposite. Great music was playing, conversations were lively, the food and drinks looked tasteful. Laurie could judge Halsey for many things—she was conniving, she was judgmental, she relied way too much on money she hadn't made—but she could never claim that Halsey did not know how to entertain.

Laurie sat at the conference table facing Halsey and William. Halsey was wearing sunglasses inside like she was Jackie O.

"Hey, cousins," William said. Penny and Chris both said "hey" back. Laurie gave a little wave.

"Why are we here again?" Halsey said to the room.

William cut in first. "For a plan moving forward, sis. You know that." He was leaned back and sipping from an espresso cup. William was that rare combination of poorly shaven and carefully dressed. If he weren't an influencer for yogis everywhere, he could have just as easily gotten obsessively involved in nonalcoholic craft beer and fit right in.

"That's right," Trevor said, cutting in. "Chris wanted us to gather today to talk about how the group might best protect the Shaw Hill property."

"I speak for all of us when I say Chris is not the only one concerned with what happens to the property?" Penny said with a slight inflection in her voice. The very assertion caused everyone to turn their heads and look right at her. Penny was not the sort to assert herself—ever.

"Of course," Trevor said quickly. "Chris was just the one who happened to reach out to schedule the meeting."

"Because you've been friends since you were ten," Penny confirmed. Trevor looked uncomfortable.

"Shut up, Pen. Obviously everyone cares. Can we please move on?" Chris said without trying to mask the irritation in his voice. "Trevor, please continue."

"Right. So, as I was saying, we need to implement a plan for protecting the property," Trevor said.

"Protect?" Penny said, her eyes widening. "What do you mean, protect?"

"Protect in the sense of getting everyone on the same page. The property needs a schedule of payments, a strategy for land appreciation, and a longer-term plan for if and when the deed holders decide to sell." Trevor spoke with an officialness in his voice Chris imagined he used more freely with other clients.

"Don't we already do that? The well pump just broke and that was handled easily," Halsey said, nodding along with herself.

"The issue is accountability," Chris said, sitting up straighter. "Let's take the well pump, for example. It was a twenty-thousand-dollar issue. We have that now, but to stretch the metaphor, who of us is actually putting new water into the well? At a certain point, the well itself will run dry."

The room was silent. Chris carried on.

"If Laurie and I earn most of the income for the family, it leaves us too exposed. We can't do anything as individuals, but it's individual income that's going to actually keep this land in the family." He felt himself getting increasingly heated. "If the three of you aren't going to change your lifestyles"—he looked between Penny, William, and

Halsey—"then we need to seriously consider moving on from this property."

Chris leaned back in his chair. The room erupted in a series of gasps and murmurs.

"I work, you know," Halsey said.

"You're a sometimes freelancer at a marketing firm. I would hardly call that a career," Chris said not unkindly.

"I came up with the slogan for Mrs. Butter's Buttery Biscuits!" Halsey said, now indignant.

"You did, and we're all very proud of the sixty-thousand-dollar bonus you got for it. How could we not be? You wouldn't stop talking about it. But that was ten years ago, and you haven't had a Mrs. Butter's Buttery Biscuits since," Chris said. Laurie watched the air deflate out of Halsey.

Halsey leaned forward to say more, but Chris interrupted the effort.

"Not so fast," she said to Chris, thwarting his attempt to jump in. "This property has been in our family for fifty years. Just because you and Laurie sacrificed any semblance of personal lives for professional ones does not mean that the rest of us have to give this up. Come up with another plan. I don't accept."

"Why don't you come up with another plan?" Chris said.

"I don't need to. I'm fine with the current arrangement of all of us splitting the property expenses and getting on with things. I want to live here. I want Miles to go to school here. I'm not selling." Halsey spoke with finality.

"No one said anything about selling," Trevor chimed in.

"Did Chris not just say that we needed to seriously consider moving on from this property?" Halsey shot back.

"He did," Trevor agreed. "What do the rest of you think?" He gestured to William and Penny and Laurie.

"I'm with Chris on this one," Laurie said. "We need to be strategic."

"Of course she is," Halsey said under her breath but loud enough for everyone to hear.

"I'm with Halsey. I don't think we need to consider selling just yet," William said. Halsey mouthed a *thank-you* in her brother's direction.

It all came down to Penny. The group looked at her, and Laurie tried to get a read on her little sister. She should understand where she and Chris were coming from. It simply wasn't fair that they float the others, not when neither of their cousins had ever actually worked. Old money went only so far. They weren't Rockefellers.

Penny looked down at the table and swallowed a few times. The air felt like the inside of a balloon.

"I don't want to sell this place. Not yet," she said softly, still not looking up.

"Penny—" Chris tried to interject.

"Yes!" Halsey said, pumping her fist in the air. "Take that, you money-grubbers! Three against two. The land stays."

"What does that even mean?" Chris said to Penny, ignoring Halsey's ridiculous celebrating.

Laurie stared at her sister, whose eyes were downcast and whose entire body was a little slumped over. She looked at her cousin, who appeared as someone who had just won a battle. What was the battle, though? Weren't they all stuck in time here, waiting to feel all grown up?

"I can draw up papers that better anticipate a budget of monthly contributions," Trevor said, hitting a small stack of papers against the table to line them up.

CHAPTER TWELVE

It had been Miles's idea for a playdate with Jeremy. The boys had met in gymnastics class, which at six years old really meant rolling around on gym mats. One of the girls had mastered a cartwheel, but she was alone in this accomplishment, and Halsey was fairly positive the girl's mother was making her practice around the clock. Miles had come halfway through a somersault before deciding the movement wasn't for him. But he had come away with a new friend, and Halsey was as pleased that Miles had a friend as she was that he lived down the street.

Halsey and Heather decided to do a playdate / lunch date on the Wednesday after Halloween.

"It'll be way too cold for us to sit outside, but we can sit on the covered porch and drink mulled wine while the boys play on the swing set," Heather said as they finalized logistics in the parking lot. Halsey wasn't used to making plans with people that required no additional logistics. A Wednesday playdate around lunchtime at a house down the hill from hers. It was radically simple. If Heather played tennis, Halsey decided she would invite her to join the group on Tuesdays.

The two mothers and two sons separated into their respective vehicles.

"Excited to see you next week!" Heather said, keeping eye contact and smiling.

"You too," Halsey said back, her stomach doing an undefined somersault of its own.

When they'd said the day, neither had really registered that it was the literal day after Halloween.

Halsey had texted: Apologies in advance if Miles has not yet recovered from what can only be described as an epic sugar crash. It's the one day of the year when all my parenting goes out the window and honestly, it's a day that lasts at least two before he's back to normal.

Heather had wasted no time in responding: Jeremy snuck out of bed last night to locate his candy basket, which I had expertly hidden above the fridge. He was elbow deep in chocolate at eleven p.m. There is a very good chance the boy you see today is not my son but a chocolate-crazed shell of a human.

The morning passed quickly, punctuated by a text from Chris that they needed to treat the pond for next year's swimming.

Do we do that every year? Halsey texted.

Every year you swim in a clear pond it's because our parents treated it, Chris replied. He was so smug, even over text.

Does that not come out of our property account? Halsey typed. She wasn't exactly rolling in cash. Not when Chad conveniently spent months at a time out of work and consequently let the child support payments slip on by.

It does and it doesn't. A little bit more this year because we had that weed outbreak. You and William both need to add another $1,000.

Halsey screamed into a pillow and mentally guessed at how she was going to find this money. Explaining cash flow to well-employed people was like explaining snow to someone who lives in the desert. Comprehension by idea only. She knew she needed to work again. Chad had been the earner, and their early marriage witnessed Halsey almost exclusively focused on getting pregnant. Then she got pregnant and had Miles. Now she had no idea where to start—all her contacts were in Boston, in the years she'd lived there between college and Miles being born. Every time she opened her email to send a note to someone who could help, she froze. What could she possibly offer them?

To Halsey's chagrin, Miles had not forgotten about Jeremy or the playdate. He hadn't glommed on to a friend before, and she was excited to watch this little-boy friendship blossom. At 11:25, Miles stood by the front door.

"Mommy!" he shouted. Halsey was in her bedroom tying her sneakers. She stood in front of the mirror to make sure the skinny jeans and the bare ankle and the low Keds looked as cute in real life as they had in her head. She switched her blue crew-neck T-shirt for a white V-neck. She moved her hair from a half-up pony to a low pony. She added her Ray-Bans to make sure they looked cute and—

"Mommy!" Miles shouted more urgently, breaking Halsey's outfit critique.

"Yes! I'm in here," she said loudly enough without shouting herself, and she could hear Miles's footsteps coming toward the room.

"You said eleven thirty and it is now eleven twenty-eight and you said we never rush because that is dangerous and there is no reason to try and shave off a minute, but if we don't rush, we'll be late, and you also said it's rude to be late." Miles was speaking quickly and with a precocious amount of condescension.

Halsey couldn't disagree with him. Everything he said was true. She folded the sunglasses and put them in the V of her collar and turned around. "Okay, buddy, you're right. Let's go!"

"I can't take you anywhere," Miles said, shaking his head and throwing his hands up in the air.

Halsey stared at her son. Children were parrots.

~

Despite always chastising Chad for his driving, Halsey drove fast down the hill, trying to save a little time. Still, they were only a few minutes late when she turned their wagon into Heather and Jeremy's driveway. Halsey realized she hadn't even asked if Jeremy had a dad. Or another mom. Either way. Two parents.

"Hey, Miles, does Jeremy have one parent or two?" she asked now.

Miles cocked his head to the side and seemed to think about it. "Two mommies and a daddy," he said with certainty.

"Two mommies who live together or a mommy and then a mommy and a daddy?" she asked, knowing as she spoke that she was asking too much.

Miles squinted and bit his lip. "Um," he started, wincing from all the thinking going on. "I don't know."

"That's okay, buddy," Halsey said. For a brief and intense and utterly unfamiliar moment, she wished it was not two mommies and a daddy, and the moment was so intense and so unfamiliar, she had to actually shake her head and blink as if to shoo it out of her body. Why on earth would she care about Jeremy's parents' makeup?

~

Heather and Jeremy were outside on the front porch as they drove up. Heather was in spandex and a workout top and Halsey was suddenly mortified she'd put on an actual outfit. It looked like she was trying too hard, the worst possible thing to do when trying to impress someone else. She couldn't even pretend these were her house-chore jeans or something. They were new and formfitting.

"Hey, you two!" Heather said while Jeremy waved next to her.

Miles was out of the car before she'd fully put it in park. Halsey caught Heather's eye and shook her head. *Kids!* her expression said.

Heather shrugged and smiled in return. The boys were around the corner of the house within seconds, their hands clasped as Jeremy led his friend to the playground.

"You follow me," Heather said, leading Halsey through the front door and into what could only be described as farmhouse-flip chic. Like Joanna Gaines but with a touch of Restoration Hardware.

"I love your house," Halsey said, taking in the cedar and white accents.

"Oh, thanks," Heather said. They were in an open-concept kitchen now, with accordion doors that opened into the backyard, where the boys now played. "I call this my divorce prize."

Divorce. So a mommy and then a daddy and a new mommy, Halsey thought.

"When the affair leads to a stepmom for your son, guilt gets the original mom a new house on her dream street," Heather said, reading Halsey's mind. Halsey nodded along as she tried to figure out what to say. Her friends weren't usually so open.

"That had to suck," she said. Was that the best she could come up with?

Heather let out a little laugh. "It did suck."

"Where's Jeremy's dad now?" Halsey asked.

"Charlotte. He's a pediatrician in Burlington, and Francine, that would be the affair-turned-stepmom, prefers the lake over the mountains." Heather gestured toward Mount Mansfield, visible to the right of the house. "I prefer the mountains."

"Isn't there a monster in that lake anyway?" Halsey said, helping herself to a stool by the counter. Heather had laid out a cheese plate and two wineglasses.

"There's a total monster," Heather said, her voice low for effect. She poured them each a glass full of rosé and Halsey felt like she didn't want the time to pass. She wanted to sit here in this kitchen forever.

"What was before Stowe?" Halsey asked. She knew the answer from Pamela—outside Boston—but if she didn't ask and then one day let it slip, Heather would know she was the talk of the town.

"Cambridge. When Jeremy's dad was still my husband, though not totally before Francine entered the picture? We'll never know, will we? I wanted a change. He wanted a change. We agreed that the change should involve us being in driving distance, so shared custody was not impossible. We took two separate cars north to 89 and figured it would be okay if one of us lived off exit ten and the other lived off exit twelve," Heather said. She shared this so easily, brimming with perspective and humor, and Halsey wanted to ask where she'd gotten the instruction manual for comfortable divorces.

Halsey had no idea how to ask a question like that, so she stayed silent for at least a minute too long. "So," Heather said, breaking the silence and rescuing Halsey from her divorce-tortured island, "you know the brushstrokes of my story. What's yours?" She spread some brie on a piece of perfectly toasted baguette.

"My story?"

"You can tell someone else's if you prefer, but I'd like a story either way." Heather was funny.

"We live up the hill, which you know. On that property at the end of the road my grandfather bought forever ago. It was my husband, Chad, and Miles and me for a long time; then Chad moved out and became my ex-husband, so it's then been just Miles and me, but then my uncle died recently, which means now my cousins and I have to figure out what to do with the land, so we're all sort of here at the moment." Halsey let out a breath. "That was probably more than you needed, I'm guessing?" She said this last part quickly.

Heather considered her. "That's a lot of people on the hill," she said, as if perfectly understanding Halsey without being told anything.

"And we have to figure out what to do," Halsey said.

"Well, I hope whatever you decide to do keeps you here," Heather said easily. "It's fun to have a new friend on the street." Halsey nodded and then got nervous she was nodding too emphatically, which caused her to abruptly stop nodding, which felt sudden, so she nodded again and realized her neck probably looked like a car stalled going up a hill.

"What do you do?" Halsey asked.

"An incredibly uninteresting job in insurance that also pays well and gives me the flexibility to hang with that one"—Heather used her thumb to point out toward Jeremy—"when he's not with his dad."

"Have you always had the same job?"

"I used to be an editor in New York. I mean, we are talking a lifetime ago, when I was happily broke and before Jeremy's dad came into the picture. The insurance company is like my divorce job. Ironic, right? That I go for insurance only after my life falls apart?"

Halsey laughed at Heather's laugh, but she was also blown away by Heather's openness and self-deprecation. Halsey could barely admit she was divorced.

"How about you? What do you do when you aren't momming or fretting about the land?" Heather asked before Halsey could come up with another question.

Halsey thought for a second. She'd had that job in marketing, so usually she said she was a marketer. But was that true, really? Her jobs never lasted long and were always a little bit of this and a little bit of that, and she was embarrassed by this, but she also didn't know what else to do. Her parents hadn't raised her with that industrious approach to life.

"I've always wanted to write a book," Halsey said, immediately regretting it. Write a book? Since when? She'd barely graduated from college.

"Why don't you write one?"

Halsey considered this. "It's awfully easy to talk to you," she said.

Heather smiled. "I get that a lot. Probably because I'm an open book."

"So I could just write you?" Halsey put her hand up to her mouth. She couldn't believe she'd just said that. Was she flirting?

Heather laughed and shook her head.

"Write your own story." She kept Halsey's gaze.

Their hands grazed by accident when each woman reached for a grape.

Halsey had to get out of here. This was too much, too unexpected. Halsey was not someone who flirted with women.

Heather noticed the energy shift and put up her hands. "I think what we need is to refill our wine and go find the boys outside."

Halsey could hear them screaming with glee. She looked out and saw them on the swings, little legs pumping up and down with abandon.

"That's perfect," she said, holding out her glass.

~

Halsey and Miles walked home as the sun started to set over the hill where Trapp Family Lodge was.

"Why are we walking, Mommy?" Miles said.

"Because sometimes when we have too much fun, it's a good idea to walk it off," Halsey answered, deciding this was the right blend of truth and omission. Miles scowled, clearly processing this.

Before he could say anything, Halsey spoke again. "The mommies had some mommy juice while you were playing, and you know my rule—"

"Mommy juice is for home!" Miles shouted out, doubled over with pride at the knowledge.

She could never say he didn't listen.

They marched up the rest of Shaw Hill, Halsey promising Miles pizza if they made it back without Miles needing another "sit rest."

What he called the desire to sit in the middle of the street and "wait for the energy tank to fill back up." She looked down at her phone and saw Heather had texted.

Hope the walk back was nice. Thanks for coming this afternoon, it made my day.

Halsey bit her lip as she typed a response.

Made my day too. Next time, you two come up here and I can provide the wine.

Her phone dinged a few seconds later.

Given that I have your car and your car keys, how about tomorrow?

Halsey felt something near her belly button, like a single butterfly exploring its surroundings as she typed that that sounded great.

CHAPTER THIRTEEN

Laurie caved and texted Paul. It was midday on Wednesday, and her eyes were glazing over from a brief. Work had felt disjointed since her father died, and no matter how present Laurie was over email and calls and Zooms, she still knew it wasn't the same as being in the office. The house was quiet: Chris was in Burlington for some work thing and Penny was at Harvest Market. Laurie's head was spinning the way it did when she had too many hours in a row of silence. Hell for Laurie was a library.

Howdy, stranger.

She stared at her phone, waiting for the three dots to appear. When they didn't, and after Laurie had endured the five stages of mortification from the lack of the three dots—give it a minute, turn the phone over on the table, check his Instagram, check the phone's signal, reread old texts to curb the spiraling—she called her office.

"Laurie Nolan's office," said a voice she didn't recognize.

"Who is this?" Laurie asked, willing her tone to sound friendly.

"Annette Baker," said the voice.

"Well, hi, Annette, this is Laurie Nolan," Laurie said.

"Hello," Annette said simply. Laurie caught herself squinting in the mirror. This was not how she was used to being received when she called her own office line.

"Are you my new assistant?" Laurie asked.

"Oh, no, I'm sorry!" Annette said quickly. "I'm just filling in. Haley left last week, you see, and HR is having us alternate who covers the phones."

Haley had been Laurie's assistant for two years. That she would leave unannounced shook Laurie to the core—was she that asleep at the wheel that she hadn't noticed? Laurie couldn't possibly admit to this person that she didn't know her assistant had left, and yet, there was no way to pretend otherwise.

"Thanks for filling in," Laurie said. "Can you transfer me to Paul Richards?" The request came out by accident, but by the time she said "transfer," it was too late.

"Of course, one second," Annette said.

Laurie exhaled. She and Paul had never acknowledged each other at work. It was part of their pact, driven mostly by Paul. Laurie had been suggesting they bring their relationship aboveboard for the past eight months, once even scheduling a meeting with HR, but Paul was as firmly against going public as he was persistent in pursuing her.

"Paul Richards's office," a voice answered after a single ring.

"It's Laurie Nolan for Paul."

Laurie thought she heard a barely perceptible though undeniably sharp intake of air on the other end of the receiver. She looked at her phone again. Her text remained unanswered.

"I'm sorry, Paul is away from his desk at the moment."

"No worries," Laurie said, trying to keep it light. "Any idea when he'll be back?"

The same sharp intake of air. The same two seconds of tense silence. "I'm afraid not."

"Could I—" Laurie started.

76

"I'll have him return your call once he's back in the office."

The line went dead before Laurie could say anything further. Whoever answered Paul's phone had somehow known to not entertain Laurie; it was as if the person had read from a script. Laurie's legs suddenly felt weak, the way anxiety can fool your body into thinking it's been doing manual labor for the past ten hours. Her muscles ached, and her heart was racing.

There is always a moment right before something goes wrong when you know something *has* gone wrong. It's often a silent exchange, a subtle energy shift that takes a moment from before to after. Laurie could feel herself in the middle of that moment: she was no longer the driver of her life but a subject within it. Whatever was happening was happening around her and despite her, and the feeling left her hollow. She couldn't pinpoint what was going on, only that something was and that the life she knew was somehow in jeopardy.

She looked at her phone again. Still nothing from Paul.

Laurie typed one more missive.

Called the office, even though I know I'm not supposed to. Hope everything is okay. It'd be great to talk to you soon.

CHAPTER FOURTEEN

If Penny were the type to gamble, she would bet 50:1 that her siblings had divided the day into four chunks of six hours, so someone was always monitoring her. At first it had felt like a coincidence. She'd come downstairs around midnight for some ice water, and Chris had been sitting at the bar in the kitchen reading something on his iPad.

"What are you doing up?" she'd asked. They were an "early to bed / early to rise" type family, typically in bed by eleven and awake around seven.

"Just catching up on some reading," Chris answered easily, even going so far as to smile.

Penny nodded, accepting the answer, and filled up her glass. "Well, good night," she said on her way back upstairs.

The next morning, it was early, maybe six, when Penny woke up to her stomach grumbling. Her stomach often woke up first, and she had recently caved to feeding herself despite believing wholeheartedly that breakfast was the worst way to keep a diet. This time, Laurie was sitting at the bar, typing away on her laptop.

"What are you doing up?" Penny asked.

Laurie kept typing as she spoke. "Early day at the office. I have Zooms starting at eight and need to be ahead of it." This felt accurate enough, Penny thought, taking two slices of gluten-free bread and putting them in the toaster.

"How is work?" she asked, now finding the almond butter and a sugar-free jam in the cupboard.

"It's taxing, I guess," Laurie said, looking up from her laptop. "The first few years when you're a partner, there is a ton of pressure to keep up. And it's this weird survival mentality, even though as a partner, it means technically you should be pretty secure in your job."

"They're lucky to have you," Penny said. She spread two minuscule and even layers of almond butter and jam on the toast.

"Thanks, Pen. I hope so," Laurie said.

Penny walked back upstairs with her breakfast.

It was a full thirty-six hours later, just before dinnertime, when Penny finally connected the dots. This time it was Laurie again at the bar, and Penny couldn't remember the last time she'd been in the kitchen, or even the house, alone. It had been two weeks at least. Every time she left, someone would be there to ask where she was going. It had happened again today, as Penny was on her way out.

"Where to, little sis?" Chris asked with too much enthusiasm. Again, he was sitting at the bar in the kitchen. It was just after nine in the morning.

"You do realize I have a job, right?" Penny asked while she filled a thermos with coffee.

"Of course, of course I know that," Chris said quickly. "But I didn't think you worked on Thursdays. Don't you get Thursdays and Sundays off?"

Penny took a second. She was impressed. How long had Chris kept track of her schedule?

"Fine, I'm just running some errands!" she answered, matching her brother's intonation.

"What errands?" Chris asked, getting up from the stool and walking over to where she was standing. Penny opened the back door to walk out.

"I don't know, just around?" she answered, closing the door before he could either follow her or follow up with another question.

~

Ten minutes later, Penny pulled into the parking lot of Twin Tips. Andrew was standing outside, putzing around the sale rack. He noticed her as she walked up the steps toward the store.

"You're back," he said, smiling.

"I'm back," she said.

"Still planning that Mount Washington summit?" he asked, opening the door and leading Penny inside. He remembered.

"I am," she said, "but I may have missed the window?" Outside it was dusting with snow, the ground hardened since before Halloween a few weeks previous.

"Nah, just means you need hardcore equipment."

Penny bit her lip.

"Or make it a day hike?" Andrew ventured, clearly wanting to undo the lip bite.

"What would I need for a day hike?" Penny asked.

Andrew considered, or pretended to consider, the question. "Well, it's a 'good news / bad news' sort of thing," he said. He started walking toward the women's apparel section and Penny followed.

"Which is?"

"The good news is that you really don't need anything much at all," Andrew said, stopping in front of a rack of Patagonia windbreakers. "You need a good warm layer and a parka. I'm assuming you've got hiking boots and a water bottle; those are pretty basic."

"Okay, a warm layer and a parka. The parka I think I bought the last time I was here," Penny said.

"Indeed, you did," Andrew said.

"What's the bad news?"

"You don't need to buy anything."

"Ah, so you aren't getting much out of this deal," Penny said. She'd never flirted with an outdoor kid before. Usually, her flirting consisted of the guy asking to buy her a shot and then asking if she was opposed to doing that shot off his body.

"I am not getting much out of this deal," Andrew agreed. He had drifted over to a section with ladies' boots. Penny debated what to say next.

"We could do the hike . . . together?"

Andrew met her eye. "I'm listening."

"I mean, I won't pay you to hike with me. But you can hike with me. To some, that's a coveted invitation." She felt witty and articulate. She liked this kind of flirting.

"You're inviting me on a hike?" Andrew said. It was like he was trying not to smile but couldn't help it.

"I am inviting you on a hike," Penny said, nodding along as she said it. She could be someone who invited a guy on a hike. She could be someone who hiked. This was a whole new Penny.

They had made their way back to the front of the store. A few other shoppers milled about, and when one man asked Andrew when this year's skis would go on sale, he yelled for someone named Michael to take over. Penny realized she had imagined Andrew worked here all alone. But of course, as she spanned a 360-degree look around, it was a huge store, with multiple levels. Obviously, this was not a one-person job.

"Well, when's the hike?" Andrew asked.

"Sunday?" Penny answered, turning to leave.

"Awesome. I'm off on Sundays. See you then, Penny Lane," Andrew said. "Let's meet at the trailhead at nine, after the sun warms us up a bit but early enough that we aren't chasing the daylight on our way back."

~

Penny was at the trailhead at 8:45, equally surprised that her punctuality extended to the early-morning hours and that she was arriving in a presentable state. Even Laurie and Chris hadn't hidden their surprise as she suited up in her warmest athletic gear and filled a water bottle at the kitchen sink.

"You're going hiking?" Laurie asked, loud enough for Chris to hear, so he too came into the kitchen to investigate.

"I am going hiking," Penny said. She felt so earnest, suiting up to go hiking with a boy.

"I'll be damned," Chris said, and Laurie swatted him.

"Don't say that," she hissed.

Penny pretended not to hear. "Just text me if you need anything," she said. "We're hiking Camel's Hump."

"I don't think I've done that since we were kids," Laurie said. "When Mom and Dad and Uncle Harry and Aunt Jean would load us up and we'd get sandwiches at the bottom of the hill."

"Remember when William had to go number two when we were almost to the top? And Dad took him behind a bush? Then he spent the rest of the day saying, 'A man's gotta do what a man's gotta do'?" Penny said, laughing as she fully remembered that day.

"Maybe we should be people who hike?" Chris suggested, though his posture also suggested he didn't totally mean it. No matter, both Laurie and Penny nodded emphatically.

"We should absolutely be people who hike," Laurie said. Even when she floated hypotheticals, she still sounded like she was in the middle of a high-stakes business meeting.

A few minutes later, Penny's siblings stood on the back porch staring as she drove down the driveway.

Andrew showed up at 8:55 in a Subaru Outback, exactly the car Penny expected him to drive. She heard Phish through the closed windows and wished she hadn't. This was not the type of guy she had any experience with. But then again, she was probably not the type of girl he had any experience with either.

"It's a great day for a hike!" Andrew said as he got out of his car. He was tall, well built, and just floppy enough to keep him relatable. Penny's stomach did a somersault. He was so not the guy she expected to be here with. Then again, she was hiking of her own volition. Obviously, something catastrophic had happened in the universe.

"I guess it is," Penny said. They both walked toward the trailhead, neither knowing how to embrace the other. Finally, Andrew leaned forward and gave Penny's shoulder an awkward pat.

"You good for the Monroe Trail?" Andrew asked. Penny furrowed her brow.

"Aren't we hiking Camel's Hump?"

Andrew thumbed toward the large map by the trailhead. "It's called the Monroe Trail. Camel's Hump is up top."

"Is now when you find out I don't hike a lot?" Penny asked, desperately trying to keep her voice light.

"No offense, but I didn't actually need to find out that you don't hike a lot," Andrew said. They started walking up the trail. Even with morning frost and a dusting of snow, a hardy brush stayed green. Penny felt like she was looking right at resilience.

"That obvious?"

"You walked into my store and said you were hoping to hike Mount Washington."

"So?"

"Mount Washington is in New Hampshire."

Penny squeezed her lips together and then smacked. Andrew turned around and smiled and then laughed. "Don't worry. I still think you're cute." He turned back around.

The morning was crisp, the perfect level of cold where Penny was happy for the extra heat between her back and her backpack. The air was breathable, incredibly so, and Penny thought about the last time she'd really considered her breathing. Was that what outdoor kids did? Take walks and breathe well?

They walked in an easy silence, Andrew pointing out a brush every now and then and Penny nodding and *uh-huh*-ing along. It felt as natural as it did unnatural, and Penny was happy this Monroe Trail, the trail that would take them to Camel's Hump and back, was over seven miles long.

"So how long are you in Stowe?" Andrew asked after a while.

Penny debated how to answer. "I sort of live here?"

This stopped Andrew in his tracks. "You live here? How did I not know that?"

Penny shrugged. "I'm not sure?"

"Who do you hang out with?" Andrew asked.

"I don't really hang out with anyone," Penny said.

"Like you mean, people from town?"

"Or people?" Penny said, not knowing quite how to describe her social situation. "I don't have a lot of friends these days." She tried to get her breath under control. The truth was, she had no friends these days. She hadn't had friends since she messed everything up at a bachelorette party in Las Vegas. It had been six years earlier and she couldn't fathom facing a single person who knew the story. Even Chris and Laurie had no idea what had really happened, just that Penny went away for the weekend with friends and came home without them.

"Well, socializing is overrated," Andrew said kindly.

Penny turned her head to catch Andrew's eye and smiled.

"Do you work in town?" he asked.

"Harvest Market. I'm a cashier and produce sorter," she said a little proudly.

"I don't know how I'd miss you," Andrew said, mostly to himself. Penny caught him even shaking his head a little bit. It made her warm from the inside. The idea that someone would berate themselves for not noticing her.

"It's a relatively new post, if that makes you feel better. Less than a year. Plus a short break when my dad died," Penny said.

"I'm really sorry about your dad," Andrew said.

Penny stretched her lips into a small smile and didn't say anything.

"Well, where do you live?" Andrew asked.

"I guess I live on Shaw Hill Road," Penny said. They started hiking again.

"You guess?"

"I live on Shaw Hill Road. It's complicated. My parents have a house. Had a house. They died. At separate times. My dad just. In August. And they left the house to my siblings and me. But there is another house next door that belongs to my cousins, and then there's also some land, and we're figuring out what to do."

"That sounds complicated."

"It is," Penny said, relieved to finally be talking about this. For the past few months, it had felt like she only talked to her family, and no one really knew what they wanted to do.

"How much land?" Andrew asked after a little silence.

"One hundred and fifty acres."

"*Whoa,*" Andrew said, not hiding his surprise. "That's a ton of land."

Penny sighed. "I know it's a ton of land. That's why we don't know what to do."

"I don't even know what I would do with that land. Definitely not work at an apparel shop."

"How long have you been at Twin Tips?" Penny asked, suddenly ravenous to talk about something else.

"Forever," Andrew said. "My parents own it. I'm basically their long-term volunteer until they retire or sell the store to me or disappear or some combination of all those things."

Andrew led the way around a corner in the trail that jutted up, and Penny realized they were nearing the top.

"That's pretty cool, though, that one day the store will be yours," she said. There was a simplicity to that: take over what was left to you, make it your own in time.

"Check out that hawk," Andrew said, stopping them in their tracks and pointing to the right.

"Good eye," Penny said, following his point. The hawk came to rest on a tree branch one hundred feet from them. By now, the sun had warmed up the earth as much as it would for the day, and Penny felt hot enough to unzip her parka. When had her legs worked so much in a single stretch?

They crested up to the summit, Camel's Hump really a small seal drilled into a boulder. Penny traced the seal with her thumb, feeling the ridges and the cold. Andrew reached into his pocket and pulled out a Clif Bar. Split it in two. Handed her a half. They each ate and looked around. Was this a date? Should they be standing closer? Penny considered Andrew. They were a good six feet apart, but they were also flirting.

"This is my favorite hike in Vermont," Andrew said, still looking out. They were surrounded by mountains that dipped into valleys that reached into mountains again. It wasn't anything like out west, where the sky almost felt like a dome, it was so big. Here it was more like sitting on the edge of something, the beginning of a magic carpet ride or enough hope that you would continue to travel. That today wasn't as far as you'd ever get.

Conversation ambled alongside their hiking as they worked their way back to the parking lot. The wind picked up slightly around noon, and Penny zipped her parka as high as it would go, sticking her chin down to try and cover some of her face. At one point, she even hiked with her hands in her pockets. Andrew seemed unfazed, continuing to look around and make quips about the wildlife and even at one point saying the day reminded him of a song.

When their cars came back into view, Penny felt equal parts relief and disappointment. She didn't want this day to end. It was as close to normal as she'd been in months. Andrew dipped down to hug her.

Penny meant to say that she'd had a lovely time, but instead she said, "I think my siblings are spying on me."

Andrew cocked his head and wrinkled up his forehead. "Come again?"

"I mean, I had a great time. I have no idea why I said that."

"Well, for your sake, I hope it isn't true. For my sake, can I see you again?" Andrew smiled as he said this last part.

Penny nodded.

"How about dinner?"

Penny nodded again. She was too afraid to say anything.

"Have you been to Plate?" Andrew asked.

Penny shook her head. Andrew nodded his, contemplating.

"No pressure, but if I commit to dinner, I'm definitely going to want you to talk. Cool?" he said, smirking.

Penny nodded and smiled through the side of her mouth. She turned around and unlocked her car and got in and rolled down her window before she backed out.

"I'll talk," she said. Andrew took a step toward the car, causing her to keep her foot on the brake. He leaned over the driver's side window.

"That's good," he said, kissing her lightly on the lips.

She kissed back.

CHAPTER FIFTEEN

Laurie had been in Stowe for two months, but at any given moment, it felt like two years or two days. This morning, she was upstairs at the desk, an old oak thing her parents had bought at a consignment shop in the nineties. Her father had positioned it in the center of the loft, offering the person seated at the desk unparalleled views of Camel's Hump.

Her father had always said looking out cleared his focus, but every time Laurie looked up from her computer, all she saw was out and all she thought was that she was failing.

It took her three full rings to realize it was her phone that was ringing. First, she needed to recognize the ringtone—it hadn't gone off in recent memory—and then she needed to recognize the caller: one of the managing partners at her firm.

"Tom, hi," Laurie answered.

"Hey, Laur, Laurie. How's it going?" Tom sounded stilted. Or distracted. Sometimes they were indistinguishable tones. Tom had been the one who'd ushered her from associate to the partnership.

"I can't believe I'm still here, to be honest," Laurie said.

"What's it been now?" Tom asked.

"It's been two months," Laurie said, cringing while she spoke. Who on earth took two months out of the office when a parent died? She was mortified. "I'm planning to come back—"

Tom cut her off. "Don't worry about timing right now. I think you need to focus on getting everything in order up there. It sounds like it's a beast of a problem."

Laurie remembered when a colleague, Cassandra, had gone on maternity leave. Toward the end of her three months at home, the partners had started calling her, one by one, checking in, though really making sure she was coming back. At first, she'd freaked out, suddenly nervous that she'd blown her entire career by having a kid. And then one of the other female partners, a woman a few years her senior, had clarified: Cassandra was needed. She was wanted. Her partners just wanted to make sure she needed and wanted them back.

But Tom, right now, was telling Laurie she didn't need to worry about coming back. Laurie swallowed a lump in her throat and sat up straight in her chair.

"Are you saying you don't need me back, Tom?" she asked.

Please say you need me back. Please say you need me back. Please, please, please—

"I'm not saying that at all. Of course not," he said.

Laurie didn't know what to say. Tom took her silence and continued.

"Have you worked much with one of the associates, Paul?" he asked. She could tell he was trying to keep his voice even.

"I haven't worked much with Paul, no," Laurie said. It was the truth. They had virtually no business together, by Laurie's design.

"Well, you keep doing what you need up there," Tom said, trying to wrap up the call.

"Why do you ask about Paul?" Laurie asked. It was too random to be innocuous. She felt her hands shaking.

"I didn't," Tom said plainly.

"You didn't?"

"I didn't," he said again.

"Okay, well, I guess I'll see you in a few weeks?" Laurie said, hoping with all her being that Tom would simply agree and they could hang up.

Instead, he inhaled sharply.

"Listen, I have to be honest. There is something being investigated here that I think would behoove you to stay where you are. Just for now. Just for a few weeks. Until everything blows over," Tom said. "You didn't hear this from me. But we've been through a lot together."

"Something is being investigated in regard to Paul?"

"The kid's got a story. But listen. It's all up in the air and I shouldn't have said anything anyway. You keep going as normal, and we'll touch base in a few weeks, okay?" Tom said, forcing a high note at the end.

They hung up and Laurie sat back in her chair, her insides something between a blender and a waterfall. It wouldn't be long before stuff started coming out.

An investigation was very bad. An investigation also explained why Paul had stopped responding to her toward the end of September. Her mind flashed back to that day they'd traded calls, and she called him from her work phone. She never should have been so stupid, she thought, clicking out of her work email and into her personal one. Trevor had emailed, and suddenly the investigation went to another side of her brain. No one could know what was going on, especially not her family, especially not when her livelihood affected the property itself. No way was Halsey going to turn this against her.

"Chris," she said, loud enough for him to hear from his bedroom.

"What?" he yelled back.

Laurie got up and found him sitting at a small desk in the corner of his room.

"I got an email from Trevor saying you haven't called him back about pricing out the new operating costs for next year," Laurie said.

"I've been busy." Chris kept his eyes glued on his computer screen.

"Well, don't we have to get back to him?" Laurie asked.

Chris turned around and sighed emphatically.

"Laurie," he said—she rolled her eyes internally; it was never good when he said her name. "Do you understand how complicated this situation is? That we have inherited a property that for all intents and purposes could set us up for life, whether we stay or we go, but only if everything goes exactly to plan?" He spoke with almost impressive patronization.

"Chris," she said in an equal tone, "I do understand. That is why I'm here, in Stowe, Vermont, six hours from my home and my office and my life, without any indication that I will have a home and an office and a life should I not return within the next few days. I'm standing here in the threshold of your doorway, resisting the urge to count the number of mallard duck figurines in this room alone, and asking if you might be responding to Trevor soon."

This made Chris turn his head to look at her. He clenched his jaw and narrowed his eyes.

"Do you think you are the only person who has put their life on hold to deal with this? Do you realize I also have a home and an office and a life somewhere else? It's not that simple. I can't just tell Trevor the operating cost. I don't *know* the operating cost, and I don't imagine Halsey or William or Penny or you, dear sister, know the operating cost either."

Laurie stood up straighter and opened her mouth to speak, but Chris kept going.

"What are you even doing here? At least I'm meeting with accounts and trying to figure this all out. You're just, what, 'working from home,' trying to be normal? I wouldn't say you're exactly moving the needle here, sis."

Laurie felt the air evaporate out of her chest. This was not the first time Chris had lashed out at her, but it was the first time since their father had died. Laurie wanted to be angry, she wanted so badly to be angry, but all that came was defeat. The combination of the phone call with Tom and this fight with Chris was almost too much to take. She looked down at the ground and tapped her foot to a silent beat.

"When did you get so hard?" she asked, almost afraid of his answer. The only thing worse than poking an angry bear was asking if that angry bear might be hungry.

"What?"

She asked anyway.

"I'm here to help, you know. I know it's just us with most of the adult stuff. And I know you're trying to be fair. But you also have to let me in sometimes," she said.

"Whatever," Chris said, turning back around.

Laurie took a step into the room so she could see his screen. There was an email up.

"Who is that from?" she asked.

Chris's shoulders fell almost imperceptibly. "Alison."

Alison had left him just before their engagement party two years earlier. Back when they still had two parents. It had been horrible and surprising, and no one had heard from her since. Not that they wanted to.

"Is she finally writing to apologize?"

Chris shook his head. "Apparently, I have a box of her things up here. She wants it because she's moving out to San Francisco."

"What a bitch," Laurie said, walking up close enough to touch her brother's shoulder. He shrugged it off.

"She's coming up here."

"From New York?"

"She wants her stuff before she moves next month," Chris said simply.

"When is she coming?" Laurie asked, already thinking about how she needed to tell Penny and Halsey and William and somehow circle the wagons for this grumpy, prickly guy.

"She says this weekend," Chris said.

"Okay, we'll be ready." Laurie kept her hand on Chris's shoulder, even after he kept shrugging and until he finally gave up and let her keep it there. They stood quietly looking at the screen—Laurie managed to read a few lines that involved words like *closure* and *loose ends* and *goodbye*—and Chris slowly and lightly put his hand on top of his sister's.

"Thank you. I'm sorry I'm being a jerk. I'll call Trevor later, I promise."

Laurie left her brother's room and went back to the desk. She ignored a handful of work emails as she drafted a new message.

To: Penny, Halsey, William
From: Laurie
Subject: Chris/This Weekend
Time: 11:35 AM EST

Message: That jerk Alison is coming this weekend to collect a box of items she left here when she abandoned Chris and stole his heart. I know things have been tense up here as we figure everything out, but we need to rally. Halsey, can you host dinner on Saturday? I'll supply the food and we can keep raiding Uncle Harry's wine cellar. As soon as Alison leaves, we'll come over. I don't want Chris to have to do this alone. LMK.

Love, Laurie

To: William, Penny, Laurie
From: Halsey
Subject: Re: Chris/This Weekend
Time: 11:40 AM EST

Message: I'll host, yes! Fuck that girl—we never liked her. She always pretended to be that country-club type and I doubt she even plays golf. William will bake his bread and everything. Family is everything.

Halsey

P.S. My friend Heather might join too, with her son. You'll like her. She's one of us but funnier and lives down the hill.

To: Halsey, Penny, Laurie
From: William
Subject: Re: Chris/This Weekend
Time: 11:45 AM EST

Message: Let's not make judgments so easily, dear family. There are two sides to every story.

In love and light,

William

To: William, Halsey, Penny
From: Laurie
Subject: Re: Chris/This Weekend
Time: 12:05 PM EST

Message: We know the story. We know enough of one side to know we don't care about the other side. Hals, excited to meet your friend. We'll bring lots of wine!

Laurie

To: Laurie, William, Penny
From: Halsey
Subject: Re: Chris/This Weekend
Time: 12:06 PM EST

Message: Dearest brother, please don't mistake us for your fans from social media. We can judge whomever we'd like. Please bake your bread as discussed.

HALS

CHAPTER SIXTEEN

Penny had been looking forward to her best friend's bachelorette for months. There would be ten of them, most friends from college and now all over the hump of thirty, all devoted to the bride, Isabel. Penny and Isabel had been best friends in college and become even closer as roommates in New York in the years directly following. That Isabel would marry her college boyfriend, Daniel, was only a matter of time, the delay driven mostly by Isabel's brief foray into feminist history and politics. Twenty-six was too young to marry, but thirty was just fine.

And while any good feminist would push against the objectification of women, Las Vegas seemed like a pretty fun place for a bachelorette. They descended on the city in April, when the weather was fresh from winter and still far away from the dry desert heat.

Penny was the first to arrive. It was a quick flight from San Francisco, and she rode the complimentary shuttle from Las Vegas Airport to the Venetian, her eyes two saucers as she took in the spectacle of the Strip. She'd been to Vegas before, but the constructed mecca of it all always took her breath away. Like a group of men had said, *Let's build what our wives won't give us*, and Vegas was the result.

The other girls trickled in, and the three-bedroom suite with panoramic views was soon overrun with all the stuff that accompanied young women, and Leigh flew with a cooler that had IF FOUND, RETURN

TO THE VENETIAN, ISABEL WARREN written in black Sharpie on the top. It was filled to the brim with cans: beer, Red Bull, Diet Coke, and sparkling rosé.

"Should we get ice?" Annie, one of the girls from college, asked, already picking up the phone to order. "Buckets and buckets of it, please!"

Penny looked on from the couch, a beer in one hand and a Red Bull in the other. This would be a good weekend.

She needed this to be a good weekend.

"How are you?" asked Lucy, one of Penny's favorite friends from college but also someone she was a little afraid of, because there were moments she thought that if she had to pick one of her friends to sleep with, it would be her.

"I'm good, yeah," Penny said, taking a sip of Red Bull.

"Have you heard from Jason at all?" Lucy asked.

Jason had been Penny's boyfriend for three years. She had wrongly assumed they'd get married, and he'd wrongly dangled the carrot of marriage when he kept asking her what kind of diamonds she liked. Their ending came out of nowhere and felt like a bullet that shot right through Penny's body. It hadn't helped that she'd moved across the country for him or that he picked the night before her birthday to break up with her.

"I haven't," she said, looking around for the bottle of Grey Goose. Jason had broken up with her in the parking lot of Bowl Time. They'd been on their way inside, supposed to go bowling with friends, and instead he'd said he couldn't go through with it.

"With bowling?" she'd asked, reaching for the door.

"With us," he said, his voice grim. His hands were stuffed in his pockets and he'd stopped walking.

She looked at his sandy-blond hair and how his chest perfectly filled out the T-shirt under his jean jacket and thought he'd never looked so handsome.

"Oh," was all she could say. "What about bowling?"

But Jason had already turned around and started walking back toward the car. The car they shared, the car they'd driven from their home to the bowling alley. She just stood and watched as he got inside, turned the ignition, and drove away.

Penny found the bottle of Grey Goose and poured it directly into the Red Bull can.

"I always thought Jason was a bit of a blowhard," their friend Julia said. She turned up the speaker for Rihanna's new song.

"He was a total dick," Annie said.

Penny drank deeply.

She loved Jason so much that sometimes she held her own hand and pretended it was his.

"I think we should talk about something else," Lucy said, getting up and taking Penny's hand in hers and guiding them both to the middle of the hotel room. She started to dance, and Penny awkwardly followed suit. But Penny couldn't dance. She could barely stand. Jason had broken up with her only a month earlier, and in that time, they'd oscillated between not speaking and speaking so much, they didn't know whose words were whose.

This weekend was a weekend where they weren't talking, though Penny kept checking her phone in case. He might have texted. He might have called.

"Stop looking at your phone," Julia said.

Julia was a devotee of tough love.

Penny drank again from the can and decided the least she could do was not get too drunk this weekend.

~

It rained on Saturday, something that never happened in Las Vegas, and the girls started jumping in the fountains outside the Venetian. They were soaking and shivering, and Penny felt alive in the discomfort, her teeth chattering against her jaw.

Julia's friend arrived with an eight ball of coke just in time for the bachelorette games, and Penny stationed herself behind the desk in the living room, like Al Pacino in *Scarface*. She was having such a good time, she didn't notice that nearly all the cocaine was gone by the time they left for dinner, twenty legs tottering in high heels down the Las Vegas Strip. She pulled out her phone and boldly texted Jason, You are overrated! Her friends cheered her on.

No one ate at dinner, except for Claudia, who didn't do cocaine. Penny decided it would be fun to play a game: everyone kiss the person on their left. Lucy was on her left, and Penny closed her eyes as she went in.

~

"I need you to wake up," Annie said, shaking Penny. At first, the shake felt far away, almost like another body was shaking on another bed, but the shaking and the soft words continued, slowly making their way into Penny's consciousness.

Penny opened an eye, and it was so bright, she shut it again.

"Mm?" she said, both eyes still closed. She burrowed under the pillow. Annie didn't move.

"Penny." Annie said her name gravely, and Penny felt fear and shame shoot down her spine, shocking her body into alertness. Penny opened her eyes properly and saw that it wasn't just Annie on the bed. Lucy and Julia and Isabel were there too, sitting around her.

"What is it?" she asked, now in a seated position against the bed frame.

"Who did you bring back last night?" Isabel asked.

"Bring back? What are you talking about? I slept here," Penny said, gesturing to the bed. She realized she couldn't remember anything after dinner. There had been the food nobody ate. There had been the kissing game. And there were images that didn't go together: strobe lights, a woman laughing, old hands fumbling over playing cards, a man sitting at a table, a glass with ice clinking another glass. Penny felt like a ball of thread trying to tie them together.

Annie cleared her throat before speaking. "You brought someone back here around six this morning. He took all our electronics. My computer. Isabel's phone, her iPad. Julia's computer. Claudia's phone. Do you have your phone?"

Julia and Lucy and Isabel nodded along with Annie. She wasn't lying, Penny knew this, even if she could hear the ding of an elevator but couldn't remember going inside.

"The electronics are gone?" Penny asked. She was about to cry; she could feel the tears forming, her throat closing around a sob, and she was very afraid that if she cried right now, her friends would leave her.

Isabel nodded.

"The others are with security right now, watching footage. Claudia woke up when you guys got here, and she heard him scuffling around. He gave her his real name, the idiot," Isabel said. "*And* he said he was staying at the hotel."

"So maybe we'll be lucky," Penny offered.

The girls bristled around her.

The feeling when you realize you've blacked out is this: imagine every event in your life rushing before your eyes, but you know none of those events happened the night before. The events you want to remember, the events you are desperate to remember, live behind a film you can't touch or see through. You get the reflection of a light against a dark glass without knowing where the light is coming from. The truth is the light source. Penny had blacked out before. Many times. Too many times. But she'd never been caught. Not like this.

"Was he cute, at least?" Penny asked. Sometimes humor worked.

Isabel was the first to loudly exhale, and the other two followed suit. Penny felt like her blood was suddenly a wave in her body, making its way up from her legs through her stomach, coming right for her lungs. She'd drown right there on the bed.

She tried desperately to remember something from the night before. The strobe lights were there; she could see them in the side of her mind, and she could see a body in front of her that she was following. The body was wearing sequins, which meant it was Tara, one of Isabel's friends from work. The strobe and the sequins went together.

"We were in a club?" Penny asked.

Annie furrowed her eyebrows and cocked her head. "Yeah, we went to XS."

That was the club in the Encore, Penny remembered, farther down the Strip from the Venetian.

Penny nodded and opened her mouth, hoping very much that someone else would say something. Part of hiding a blackout was fooling other people into repainting the night for you, so you never technically asked what happened. The girls stayed silent, though, their eyes darting between each other. Penny had been here before. With Leigh. With Annie. With all of them. Going out and drinking too much and not remembering the next morning. They were tired of this trick. She would have to ask.

The door to the hotel suite opened with a bang, causing each girl to flinch.

"We got them!" Claudia shouted as she walked inside, her arms overflowing with electronics. Lucy followed suit, holding two phones and a large coffee.

"That's amazing," Isabel said, getting off the bed and helping Claudia put the devices on the table under the television.

Penny moved to get out of bed, attempting to go help sort the devices but instead tripping over the sheet and falling onto the ground, shoulder first. The instant pain was almost relieving because it distracted her from the rest of her body. She scrambled to get up.

"Typical," Claudia said, not hiding the sneer in her voice.

"*Claudia,*" Annie said. "*Stop.*"

"It's fine," Penny said, standing.

"It's actually not fine," Claudia said. "I'm worried about you, okay? Are you just really upset about Jason? What happened—"

"Nothing happened. I just lost control a little, I think—" Penny said, her voice tight.

"Are you sure?" Claudia cut her off. The other girls stood on either side of them, flanking the bed.

"I should go," Penny said. She felt the tears stinging behind her eyes. There wasn't any oxygen left in the room, Penny was sure of it, as her throat constricted, and she waited for the others to start collapsing. They didn't move. She tried to take a deep breath and felt a bruise under her rib. She graced her finger over her hip and up her stomach to see if anything else hurt. Her hip was also bruised. She felt a low throb in her ankle. When she pushed her heel into the ground, she could feel it sharply. Had she been walking last night?

"I don't know what you want me to say," Penny said, mostly to herself. The tears had come, and they freely fell down her face. She kept waiting for someone to give her a hug.

Isabel stepped over to Penny with her arms outstretched, and Penny thought she wanted to hug. Penny put her arms out to meet her, and instead Isabel put her hands on Penny's shoulders and leaned into her ear.

"I love you," she whispered, "but you scare me sometimes, and you scared these girls, and you do need to go, if only to press 'Reset.'" Isabel pushed back and smiled without opening her mouth. Penny felt gutted.

"Let's go get breakfast," Isabel said to the group, stepping toward the door. Penny realized that everyone else was dressed. They'd been up since she came home with that man, concerned and scared and furious.

Isabel looked at Penny as the other girls trailed outside. "I'll call you in a few days, okay?"

Penny knew this meant she needed to be gone before they got back.

~

Penny had nowhere to go but the airport, and so she arrived with three hours to spare. She sidled up to a bar called Red Star Lounge and ordered an IPA.

Beer was safer at airports.

It was foamy and cold, and Penny drank the pint in no more than three sips, her head even tilted back on the last one. She signaled to the bartender for another. She wouldn't see those girls again, she thought. She couldn't possibly see them again. The way they'd looked at her, dripping with judgment, like they'd never had a few too many or gotten carried away at a party. She personally had carried Leigh away before, dragging her up the stairs from the bar they went to every Thursday night in college. And there was Isabel in that hotel room, whispering that she should go.

She could not see those girls ever again, nor could she see anyone they shared: friends, acquaintances. Penny needed to disappear and vow to never play the name game ever again.

Some friends they were.

Penny signaled for another beer.

It took nearly a minute of generic melody for her to realize her phone was the one ringing. It was her brother, Chris. She pressed "Ignore."

~

The airport was bustling, a whir of white noise and variously paced walkers, and as Penny rounded toward the ladies' room, it was like her ears turned back on and she heard the final boarding announcement for her flight to San Francisco. The voice over the loudspeaker was tinny and far away, but Penny followed the sounds toward the gate, handing over a printed-out ticket to the flight attendant and making her way down the jet bridge.

It was only when the plane was in its final descent that Penny woke up, realizing she was on a plane and that she'd peed her pants and that she had no bag. She slowly turned her head without moving her body to see if there was anyone sitting next to her. There was. An older gentleman who wore glasses and happened to turn his head as she turned hers and he looked down at her lap and then at his and she saw that he'd fashioned a series of blankets between them, clearly trying to keep the urine at bay.

Penny closed her eyes and cried silent tears as she prayed for the plane to crash.

CHAPTER SEVENTEEN

Halsey and Chad had been divorced for a year. It started out as Chad's fault—cheating will do that—but ended up really Halsey's fault, because in Chad's mind, Halsey offering him little more than blanket rejection and dismissiveness for five years drove him to cheat in the first place. With someone she'd gone to college with, no less. A woman named Sara, who wore an awful lot of popped collars given she couldn't tell you where Fairfield County was. Or Winnetka. Or Short Hills. Yes, they'd tried couples therapy. No, it hadn't worked. Yes, Halsey felt guilty all the time for upending her son's life. That Adele album helped.

The coffee machine beeped and pulled Halsey out of her reverie. She was thinking about Chad because he had Miles, and they would be arriving here any minute. It was her week with him—Chad lived in town, so they traded Miles every week and didn't have to pretend that nothing had changed when they divorced. Everything changed, but no one left, and Miles was able to step into two households with impressive dexterity. Halsey poured a cup of coffee, topped it off with enough half-and-half to color it light brown, and inhaled. Her phone buzzed and a text came through.

Is it time for that playdate yet? Jeremy is asking.

Heather. Halsey caught herself smiling. The boys had played together the week before, going so far as to build a fort down by the woods, and the women didn't stop talking the entire time. Since the first playdate, Halsey's phone had become even more of an appendage than it normally was. They texted all day and most of the night. Even Miles had started to notice that Halsey's phone was constantly beeping. She'd finally had to put it on silent.

Miles gets dropped off here any minute, and I could make his day with the news that his friend Jeremy is coming over.

Outside, the dew made the field glisten, and Halsey had a flash of the four of them building a fort down by the pond and eating brownies after.

Shoot, Jeremy has soccer today. Will the peewee season ever end? It might not, Hals, it might not.

Halsey's stomach sank a little. She could still take Miles down to the pond and make brownies, she thought, overly bummed out that the playdate that was never an actual thing was canceled. As she started to draft a response, another came through:

Victory! I had my days mixed up. How's noon?

Halsey smiled as she typed out that noon was perfect.

"You look awfully happy," Chad said, startling Halsey enough that she physically jumped at the sight of him. He put his hands up. "Whoa, sorry. Did not mean to scare you."

Miles was like a breeze through the kitchen, around her waist for a hug, and back out the door to his clubhouse.

"Hi—hey, how are you?" Halsey said, trying to regain her composure. "Sorry. I definitely didn't hear you two come in."

Chad let out a polite laugh. "That much is clear. Who has your attention?"

Halsey cocked her head, confused.

Chad pointed to her phone. "Someone is in there."

"Oh, that." Halsey put her phone on the counter. "Just a playdate for Miles."

Chad put his hands in his pockets and leaned against the fridge. Was he staying?

"What's up, Chad?" Halsey asked. She had learned recently that she did very well with ten minutes of Chad, and then anything after was too much.

"Well," he started, looking everywhere except at Halsey, "I wanted you to hear it from me and not from Miles that . . ."

Halsey waited for him to continue. When he didn't, she said, "Is this a 'help me help you' moment? Can we move this along?"

If she had a timer, she knew it would read five minutes and ten seconds.

"I'm seeing someone," Chad blurted out. Halsey's eyes widened and she could feel her pupils exposed to extra air. "We've been seeing each other for a little while now. Her name is Ashley. She lives in town. She's a ski instructor actually."

Halsey considered this. Ashley in town. Chad was forty-four years old. Ashley in town was either a washed-up fortysomething ski instructor or she was a recent graduate unsure what to do with her life.

"Where's she from?" Halsey asked, her voice impressively even.

"She's from outside Boston. She actually went to school up here and now she lives here. In Stowe," Chad said. He was rambling.

Ashley was a recent graduate unsure what to do with her life.

"Where'd she go to school?" Halsey asked next.

"UVM."

Halsey exhaled. Ashley was a recent graduate of *college* unsure what to do with her life. Ashley was in her *twenties*.

The relief was brief. Once Halsey registered that Ashley had gone to college, and thus her ex-husband was not openly dating a teenager in front of their son, she registered that her ex-husband was dating someone at least twenty years younger than her. She almost preferred the affair with her college friend. At least that was an even playing field.

Halsey realized Chad was desperate for her to say something. She stayed silent a few moments longer, watching him squirm.

"How'd you meet?" she asked.

"Out one night," Chad said. That meant either Chad was out drinking with his buddies—the majority of whom had never grown up—or they'd met on an app. Inexplicably to Halsey, she wanted it to be the app. It somehow felt more mature.

"Things are getting serious, then? If Miles has met her?"

"Oh, Miles *loves* her!" Chad said, clearly not thinking. Halsey felt like the air evaporated from her lungs. As she clenched her jaw, Chad's eyes became saucers, and he blurted out, "I mean, they've met a couple of times. She's a really nice girl and great with Miles. And yeah, I just wanted you to know."

Halsey moved her head up and down like a nod and glanced at the photographs hanging in the hallway outside the kitchen. She hadn't taken down their family photos, even the ones with Chad, because they looked so happy in them. Even if the day surrounding the photo was filled with fighting, or even if in one of them it was obvious Halsey had been crying. She didn't want someone else in those photographs. She didn't want family photographs with Miles that didn't include her. In an instant, she'd been replaced by recent-college-grad Ashley.

"Okay, thank you for telling me!" Halsey said too brightly. She picked her phone back up and pretended to check something. Heather had texted, which made Halsey smile without meaning to as she thumbed out a response. Ashley came flooding back and she remembered her frustration. She looked up. Chad just stood there. "Listen," she said, regaining her composure, "we've got stuff going on today. Miles has a playdate. Thank you for bringing him home. We'll see you next week?" As she said all this, she lightly guided Chad to the front door, ushering him outside and closing the door without letting him respond. She could feel him standing outside, confused, facing the closed door in front of him as she walked through the kitchen and out onto the terrace, where Miles was playing. Her phone vibrated in her hand. Heather.

Chad has informed me he's dating a recent college grad who Miles "loves!" she typed.

I'll bring enough wine for four people, then, Heather responded instantly.

She will officially be known as "recent college grad Ashley" and please bring enough for six, Halsey typed back.

She stood on the terrace and called out, "Hey, buddy, guess what!"

Miles looked up.

"Jeremy is coming over here in a little while!"

"That's awesome!" Miles said, wielding a play sword at a pretend predator.

Halsey crossed the lawn to Miles's clubhouse. "Miles, Dad told me about his new friend, Ashley."

"Yeah." Miles kept sword fighting with the air.

"What do you think of her?" Halsey asked. She knew she was digging for dirt with a six-year-old. She knew God was rolling his eyes at her. She fully expected to be struck down by lightning for this.

"I don't know. She smells weird and she wears a lot of makeup."

Halsey let out a murmur. Miles was a pretty good spy.

"How often is she around?" Halsey asked.

Miles looked up and tried to count in his head, but the numbers tumbled out of his mouth anyway. "Sort of all the time, I would say.

She's there a lot. But she does not do anything in the kitchen. Not one thing." He said this emphatically, nodding as he said it.

"Not a cook, I guess."

"No," Miles said loudly. He put down his sword. "Mommy, one time, she made me a peanut butter and jelly and it was entirely wrong." Miles confessed this like a secret, and Halsey knew in this moment, her son would always love to gossip.

"What was wrong about it?" Halsey asked, genuinely curious. By now they were sitting together on the grass.

"Mommy, the question should really be what was right about it."

Halsey laughed at her son. "What was right about it, then?"

Miles looked his mother square in the eye, his mouth a thin line, his hands in his lap. Very calmly he said, "Nothing."

CHAPTER EIGHTEEN

They decided using the hot tub outside as a temporary bathtub was the most efficient. Halsey and Heather stood waiting with towels. But then Miles and Jeremy decided it would be more fun to see if they could make it all the way down to the pond in their underwear without, in Miles's words, "freezing our tushes off."

"Miles, not by the jumping rock!" Halsey shouted down the hill, laughing as she tried to catch up with him. Heather was right behind her, chasing Jeremy, but tripped and took Halsey down with her. The women fell onto each other with enough momentum to roll down the hill, and at one point Halsey actually thought about that famous scene in *The Princess Bride*. The main difference between two grown women falling together down a hill and the movies is coordination. They were two pillows pressed between elbows and knees, and no head was spared by an accidental slap. It was at once faster and slower than expected. At one point, Halsey noticed a modest rock on the ground, and in their spinning, she had plenty of time to move the rock out of the way. That was the moment she realized just how ridiculous they probably looked.

"Shit, I'm sorry," Heather said, laughing and scooting herself off Halsey, whose back was wedged into the tall meadow grass.

Halsey tried to pull herself up by grabbing onto Heather's belt loop, but instead of getting herself up, she pulled Heather down on top of her again. Both women were laughing too hard to talk, until they realized that Heather was lying on top of Halsey, and their faces were suddenly touching nose to nose, and like a light switch, the laughter ended and neither woman knew what to say next. Halsey could see everything about Heather's face right there in front of her, and looking directly into her eyes was like looking at the sun. Blinding but impossible to look away from.

"Now I'm sorry," Halsey all but whispered. She realized her fingers were still in Heather's belt loop and pulled them away. Heather smiled without opening her mouth, and for a second Halsey thought she was about to kiss her, and in the split second where that was a possibility, Halsey had no idea whether she wanted her to kiss her or not, and in the split second after, when Heather moved her face just enough to get her bearings and it was clear she was not going to kiss her, Halsey felt a watermelon seed in her stomach start to bloom. She had wanted her to kiss her.

"I get it—you wanted me on top of you," Heather said easily, using her knees to hoist the rest of her up.

Halsey let out a laugh. "No, I wanted to stand up," she said.

"Why are you wrestling?" Jeremy asked from the pond. The women looked at their sons, pickled and shivering from their hot-tub escape.

"Sometimes adults wrestle too," Heather said. Somehow, through this entire exchange, she had managed to hang on to the towels, and now she held them open and commanded each boy come to her at once. They had no choice but to follow her orders. Halsey took one of the towels and hugged Miles with it.

"You should probably wrestle somewhere else," Miles said. Jeremy nodded in agreement.

"Where else should we wrestle, buddy?" Halsey asked. The foursome had started walking back up to the hill toward the house. Halsey noticed that her cousins were on their porch looking out, and she held up an arm to wave. They waved back.

"Probably the couch," Miles said. Halsey and Heather exchanged a look.

"The couch?" Halsey asked.

Miles nodded. "Heather is a little bigger than you, Mommy, so if she's going to be on top, then you need to be somewhere soft because you're always complaining about your back hurting, and the ground is hard."

At this, Heather let out a loud-enough laugh that Halsey saw her cousins peer over to see what was happening. Heather's laughing was contagious; first it spread to Jeremy and then to Miles and then to Halsey, and Halsey was laughing harder than she had laughed in years. Certainly since Chad left, and probably a few years before. Heather's hair caught the late-afternoon sun and Halsey could swear she saw strands of gold among the brown. She was beautiful, and Halsey noticed herself noticing it, but not in the way she noticed other women's beauty. This wasn't magazine beauty. Or someone recognizable. This was a beauty she noticed in how all the parts of Heather worked together to build *her*, this person laughing and walking up the hill to the house.

~

Two hours later, the boys had eaten, bathed, and fallen asleep in the bunk beds in Miles's room upstairs. Halsey and Heather found themselves in the kitchen, everything quiet except for the fall noises outside. More owls than you'd expect. A little wind against the chimes.

"Should we watch a movie?" Halsey asked, suddenly desperate for this evening to stretch on forever. She didn't need to be nervous; the boys were upstairs, asleep. There was no reason for Heather to leave before the morning. And yet. Halsey couldn't bear the idea of Heather walking upstairs too, finding her way to the guest room and closing the door behind her, leaving Halsey alone in the primary downstairs.

"Only if we can have more wine," Heather said, smiling. Halsey smiled back.

Halsey pulled a bottle of Chardonnay out of the wine fridge and two glasses from the bar above it. The women made their way into the living room and sat on the couch facing the television. Halsey wasn't sure how close to sit, so she chose the far corner, only to feel a wave of disappointment when Heather chose the other corner. She should have just sat in the middle. It was too late now. Halsey tried to move into a more lounging position in hopes it would cut the distance between them.

"What should we watch?" Heather asked as she filled their wineglasses.

"Definitely a comedy," Halsey said, now elated because she realized she would need to get up to get the remote. She could sit back down closer to the middle of the couch.

But Heather was still at her corner. Would it be weird for Halsey to come sit closer to her? Halsey realized she was standing in the middle of the room with the Apple TV remote in her hand and not saying anything. Heather was looking at her carefully.

Halsey meant to suggest they watch *Tommy Boy*. Instead, she said, "I don't know where to sit."

As soon as the words came out, she dropped the remote and put her hand over her mouth. Heather's eyes widened just enough to tell Halsey she'd registered what had been said. It was official. Halsey was a creep. Heather didn't care where Halsey sat. She was a grown woman— a grown, *straight* woman—happy to have a new friend who happened to also be divorced. They were divorce friends. That's what this was. Halsey wondered if she could die of mortification.

"You could come sit by me," Heather said, her lips stretching into the subtlest of smirks.

Maybe they weren't just divorce friends.

Halsey nodded and bent over to pick up the remote, but she was so nervous, her fingers kept fumbling around the rug. It was like her fingers were cased with butter. Finally, she made contact between fingers and remote, but only after whispering to herself, "For the love of God, woman, you've got to pick this thing up or you'll die out here." She stood up, victorious. Heather's smirk had faded, which sent Halsey into another tailspin in which she feared in fact she'd sent a mixed message, and by fumbling the remote she had said, *I do not want to sit by you, but instead of saying anything I'll simply stand here silently.*

The night sounds outside were not loud enough to drown out Halsey's heartbeat. She took a deep breath, gripped the remote, and walked back to the couch. Heather moved slightly to the left and patted the fabric next to her. Halsey sat down.

The women sat facing the television, even though nothing was on.

"I want to kiss you," Heather said quietly. Halsey's insides warmed from head to toe. She wanted to kiss her too. After the playdates and the banter and the texting and the wine and the pasta and the easy way Heather moved around her, she wanted to kiss her too.

Halsey turned to face her.

"Have you ever kissed a girl before?" Heather asked.

Instead of answering, Halsey tipped her head to the right and kissed Heather on the lips, softly, tentatively at first, and then with a little more pressure. Heather kissed back, and soon they both explored the other's head and face and shoulders and arms with their hands. It was at once alien and familiar. Heather's lips were so soft, so different from Chad's, but of course everything about Heather was different from Chad. Halsey was excruciatingly present, overtaken with joy but sick with nerves.

What did this mean? To kiss a woman this way, in her living room, with their sons sleeping upstairs? All Halsey knew was this felt incredibly natural, like she'd been doing this all her life, or like she and Heather had known each other in another lifetime. Before long, they were fluent in the other's body, and after, when even the owls were turning in, Halsey didn't know if she'd ever been so happy.

CHAPTER NINETEEN

The snow came early in 2005, and by the time mid-November arrived, the hill was primed for sledding. The Nolans and the Ridges gathered on the Wednesday before Thanksgiving, with so many extra family members and significant others, Shaw Hill literally overflowed with bodies.

Penny was in charge of hors d'oeuvres. She was nineteen and finally old enough to take something like hors d'oeuvres seriously. Her mother gave her a mandate, not a budget.

"Let's have a collection of bites that will make everyone feel at home," Bea said, flitting around the kitchen like preparing a meal for twenty was a dance. Penny tried to mimic her mother's movements, but she didn't have the grace to take a plate out of the dishwasher and spin around and gently place it in the cabinet. Penny needed to isolate each movement in order to get it right: lean over into the dishwasher, extract the plate, hold the plate with two hands, turn on one foot and then the other toward the cabinet, step and then step again and then stand before placing the plate down. Her mother was a ribbon and Penny was a box.

~

"Let's get dressed up tonight," Bea said to her children on Thursday morning, their eyes still crusty from sleep. She'd been up for hours, transforming the dining room into a blend of fall harvest and holiday cheer. Their father came in from the side door, stomping his boots on the mat to shake off the snow, his arms filled with firewood.

"Did I hear an opportunity for formal wear?" he asked when he reached the kitchen.

"It wouldn't be a Nolan holiday without a tie," Chris said acerbically. Frank continued through to the fireplace.

"Who wants to do a pre-Thanksgiving ski?" he asked once the wood had been neatly stacked.

Laurie and Chris murmured various excuses and Bea reminded him she had a meal for twenty to prepare. Frank looked at Penny hopefully.

"We could squeeze in a few runs," Penny said to her dad.

"Yes!" Frank said, clapping his hands together. "To the mountain we go! Liftoff in twenty."

~

By six, the Nolans' house was crowded. Uncle Harry and Aunt Jean had invited their best friends, and Halsey and William both brought whoever they were dating. Penny's grandparents came too, and her mom's sister and her husband. Penny displayed her hors d'oeuvres proudly: smoked salmon with hardboiled egg and minced red onion, a baked brie on water crackers, hard and soft cheese and salami with cornichons and olives and cheese knives with festive handles. She did pigs in a blanket for Chris and sun-dried tomato and Parmesan for Laurie. The baked brie was for Halsey, and the salami was for her father, who sneaked so many pieces, Bea refused to put out more.

The dining table stretched from wall to wall, and the cousins huddled around the kids' table in the living room. Penny's place setting was the only one without a wineglass, and Halsey had been the one to conspiratorially fill her water glass instead.

"Stick to white and it'll look like water. And if you add ice, no one will think twice," she said, winking at her youngest cousin. Penny swelled with pride to get this kind of notice from Halsey.

Penny looked around the room. Their downstairs was one giant open floor plan, and she could see her mother at the head of the table, talking animatedly to her sister. Penny turned to see Laurie, who was quiet beyond a steady stream of one-liners mocking whoever was speaking. Even at nineteen, Penny knew there was such a thing as too much sarcasm.

"What do you think of all this, little cous?" William asked, knocking Penny out of her revelry.

"I love it here," Penny said almost automatically. She did love it here, she thought to herself, looking past William to the window, which at night was one gigantic mirror of the inside. This was a party, full stop, with music playing and conversation flowing and laughter cutting through every couple of seconds.

"I love it too," William said. "And you know what?"

"What?" Penny asked.

"It's all going to be ours someday," William said.

Penny had never considered this before. She was young enough that her parents were immortal, she and her siblings perpetual children. How would it be theirs someday?

"Hey, you guys," William said, knocking the table lightly with his knuckles to get the kids' table's attention. He knocked the table again, slightly louder. "Guys."

Everyone looked up.

"What's up?" Chris asked, his smile slightly goofy from too much bourbon.

"You know this place will be ours one day," William said.

Chris considered this. "I guess it will be, yeah."

"Isn't that cool?" William asked. It was like he was also realizing this for the first time.

Halsey and Chris and Penny all nodded. Halsey raised a toast. "To the hill!"

"To the hill!" the cousins called back.

"We will definitely need to put in a new kitchen," Laurie said, her stream of one-liners still in full effect.

No one paid her any attention, and after a while, her one-liners dwindled.

~

A few hours later, when the cousins and the adults had more or less separated for the night, Chris suggested they all go sledding. He and William had built a jump the day before, and they wanted to race when the track was fully frozen. Penny stood at the top of the hill, her legs a little wobbly from the wine, and she watched the boys barrel headfirst in sleds down the tracks. She felt the cold air hit her face, and she liked how it pricked at her skin, making her feel vulnerable and alive.

The sky was so dark, her eyes got lost in it, the stars so far away, they looked more like sprinkles. She leaned back on her hands—thankfully in mittens—and soon on her back, the cold ground slowly breaking down her jacket's barrier. She could hear her siblings and cousins sledding, but it was muffled, like the earth itself wanted her to focus on looking up. She belonged on this hill, Penny thought, thinking again about what William had said, that this place would be theirs one day.

CHAPTER TWENTY

Penny's phone buzzed.

Your chariot awaits.

She looked outside the large window at the front of Harvest Market and saw Andrew sitting in his Subaru. Phish—definitely live, definitely bootleg, definitely a sign she was really dating a Phish guy—seeped through the car all the way to where she stood by the door.

"Hi," she said, getting into the passenger seat. They kissed quickly on the lips.

"Howdy." Andrew flashed her his goofy grin and she leaned back, sighing out the energy of the day.

"Where to?" she asked. Andrew had only mentioned date night, nothing beyond that.

"Well, Penny Lane, I've met your world. It's time for you to meet mine. We're going to Zenbarn."

~

When they arrived, there was already a group clustered by the bar. Penny took in a range of ages and backgrounds as Andrew squeezed her hand and introduced her around. She was dating a real local, and for a moment, it made her feel local too.

"How about a beer?" Andrew suggested, nodding between Penny and the bartender.

"Sure, yeah," Penny said, feeling the nerves take root in her stomach. She hadn't been in a bar in a long, long time, and she hadn't been in a bar with friends, or friends of a boyfriend, in an even longer time. Bars and Penny did not really mix: too many options, too steep a descent from the first drink to the last. Penny counted to ten in her head, willing her thoughts to calm down so she could at least pretend to be a good-enough girlfriend for this adorable boy standing next to her.

"David!" Andrew exclaimed. And turning to Penny said, "This is David! From college."

Penny stuck out her hand.

"I'm a hugger—get in here," David said, simultaneously patting Andrew on the back. They had the physical shorthand of lifelong friends. "Andrew tells me you're a real foodie."

"That's one way to frame it. Are you talking about Harvest Market?" Penny was suddenly self-conscious not to have a *job* job, the kind with bonuses and stock options.

"More like you know every single kind of produce that grows in the state of Vermont?" Andrew cut in, squeezing her hand and smiling in a way that said, *You are enough*.

"Remind me where you went to school?" David asked. At the same moment, a woman came up behind David and hugged him. He turned around and kissed her head, bringing her into the fold. "This is Caroline."

Andrew and Caroline hugged, and Caroline and Penny shook hands.

"I went to Colby," Penny said.

"No way—what year did you graduate?" Caroline asked, perking up.

"2010?" Penny didn't know why she answered it like it was a question.

"Did you know Isabel Warren, by chance?"

Penny's heart sank. Her brain turned into a forest and then a forest fire. She bit her lip. Maybe if she bit hard enough, it would turn the flames in her mind into smoke.

"Yeah, yeah, I did, for sure, for sure," Penny said. "I guess you know her." She was rambling. "How, how do you know her?"

Caroline cocked her head to the side. "We met on the trading floor of Morgan Stanley. God, she was my ride or die for those early associate years." She shook her head at the memory.

"That's amazing!" Penny said way too brightly.

"I just saw her, actually. I can't believe she's got two kids. Two!" Caroline said.

Penny couldn't tell if she was walking a plank, about to free-fall, or already free-falling. Isabel had two kids. Penny had missed so much that life had literally spread around her. When friendships fade, it's easy to believe that the people fade too, their lives frozen in time until you reconnect. And yet. Isabel's life had continued. Penny was the one whose life was frozen.

"I need, like, one single second of air," Penny eked out, the sweat already forming on her brow. She knew this person would call Isabel, saying, *You'll never believe who I just ran into*, and Isabel would say, *Wow, I can't believe she's still around; you won't believe what she did at my bachelorette*, to which Caroline would turn around to David and say, *Are you sure your friend should be dating this person?* To which David would call Andrew and say, *Hey, buddy, we heard some things we think you should know*, and then Andrew would have to call Penny, abruptly and out of the blue, and cancel whatever plans they had because that's what you do when you learn that your girlfriend is not at all who you think she is.

Penny pushed the door to the outside too hard, and it swung dramatically on its hinge. She counted in a loop, *one two three four five six one two three four five six*, even putting her hands on her knees and bending over, anything to get more oxygen to her brain.

"Pen?" Andrew's voice cut through the noise in her head.

"Hey."

"You okay?"

Penny swallowed, took in a breath. Looked right. Looked left.

"Yeah, sorry, I think I just got tired all of a sudden?" she said.

Andrew nodded. "Totally. These days on my feet kill me. Should we get out of here?" He put out his arm for Penny to move into his nook.

"Let's get out of here," Penny said.

They started walking toward the parking lot.

"Do we need to say goodbye?" Penny asked, already nervous to see Caroline again.

"Nah, I told them you were beat after a long day and that we'd catch up with them soon," Andrew said. He was so nonchalant, so unconcerned by Penny, she couldn't help but feel soothed. Maybe Caroline wouldn't call Isabel. Maybe Isabel wouldn't tell Caroline the horrible thing Penny had done. Maybe Caroline wouldn't tell David, who wouldn't tell Andrew, who wouldn't have to break up with her. Maybe. Maybe. Maybe.

CHAPTER
TWENTY-ONE

They were due at Halsey and William's at six. Really, it was Halsey's at six. Penny couldn't remember if Miles would eat with them or if he would eat before, and she couldn't remember if William was back or if he was still in Hudson. Neither of those things mattered, not really, but she was aware enough to connect her nerves around the family properly meeting Andrew and her attention to detail.

"Hey, Laur," Penny called from the Birds Nest.

"Yeah?" she heard Laurie shout from her own room down the hall.

"Does Halsey drink red wine?" Penny shouted this. She looked at herself in the full-length mirror. Was the dress trying too hard? She liked that the red fabric hung on her frame in a way that made it look like she wasn't trying too hard. She'd salvaged the dress from the back of her closet, trying to strip it of all the memories still hanging to its threads. She'd been a different person when she bought this dress, she thought, rubbing her thumb and forefinger over the hem. She'd had friends then. A job. An apartment in New York City.

"Why do you care if Halsey drinks red wine?" Laurie asked from behind her, knocking the memory right out of her head. Penny turned around and looked at her sister, who looked adorable, in a word.

"You look great," Penny said.

Laurie cocked her head. "What?"

"The cream jeans. They look great. And the blouse," Penny said. She wasn't telling the entire truth. Laurie looked thin, and the jeans fit her well. But her complexion was ashy, and she looked exhausted. Penny knew how to mention only the good part.

"I don't know if Halsey drinks red wine," Laurie said instead of answering Penny's compliment.

"Andrew wanted to know. He's bringing something for dinner," Penny said.

"So we finally get to meet him?" Laurie asked. The two women walked out of the Birds Nest and down the hall toward the stairs.

"It seems that you do," Penny said.

"Is he your boyfriend?" Laurie asked.

"I think so. Maybe? Yes? I can't believe it, but I like him a lot," Penny said, the words sort of tumbling out of her. She *did* like him a lot. That petrified her.

Chris was already in the kitchen waiting for them.

"Shall we get this over with?" he asked, smirking out of the side of his mouth. Ever since Alison had emailed that she was coming to get her stuff from the hill, Penny and Laurie had treated Chris like he was made of glass.

Chris and Laurie left the kitchen while Penny put a dish back in the fridge. She looked down at the counter and saw the telltale signs of mouse droppings. Penny opened the cabinet next to the fridge and saw there were enough droppings to suggest a modest colony living in the drawers. She could hear her brother and sister talking outside and knew she did not have "calling an exterminator and dealing with the mice" in her right now. Instead of saying anything, she simply grabbed a paper towel and sprayed the entire area with Windex, trying her damnedest to erase the evidence. Let someone else discover they had a mouse problem.

~

The three siblings walked across the driveway together, the sun long since dropped behind the ridge in front of their property. Daylight savings had been weeks earlier, and they all hunkered down for the long, often sunless winter. Halsey had been texting almost frantically for the past three days, determined to present Chris with his favorite foods and drinks, and Penny remembered how much she liked this side of her cousin. The connector, the bon vivant. The one who had convinced them to go midnight sledding as kids and the one who had figured out how to sneak out to the Rusty Nail as teenagers.

"Hey, you guys!" Halsey yelled out from the front door. She was standing with a tray of what looked to be Dark 'n' Stormies. "Cocktail time!"

Halsey seemed overly excited for the occasion. She wore an olive-colored sweater over dark jeans and little booties. Her hair was blown out, showing off just how blonde and just how full it really was. Even the diamond studs were out. Penny half expected to see her sporting her family sapphire and old wedding bands.

"Thanks, Hals," Chris said easily, taking a glass from the tray and drinking deeply. Penny and Laurie made eye contact and knew what the other was thinking: it would be that kind of evening. They took a glass each as well and drank deeply. Chris was best joined in his drunkenness.

Inside, William and Miles were debating the merits of chicken fingers versus chicken nuggets, and Penny almost dropped her glass when she saw Andrew sitting in the living room.

"Well, hi," she said, walking over as he stood up and clumsily kissed her cheek. "You're here."

"I am here," Andrew said, grinning. He pointed to the bar by the kitchen. "There you will find that, after being unable to decide on the appropriate beverage, I brought a collection."

"Your boyfriend brought enough booze for a convention," Halsey said from across the room. Her own Dark 'n' Stormy was nearly gone.

Andrew shrugged. "A guy can't come empty-handed."

Penny gave him a side hug. She was so happy he was here already. "You've met everyone?"

"I have met Halsey, Miles, William, and Heather," Andrew said a little proudly.

"Heather?" Penny asked.

"Halsey's friend?"

Halsey perked up at her name just as a woman walked out of the bathroom and into the living room. Penny watched Halsey lightly touch the woman's lower back.

"Hey, I'm Heather," the woman said to Penny, sticking out her hand. "My son, Jeremy, is somewhere around here with Miles."

Penny shook Heather's hand. "Penny," she said.

Heather was beautiful, Penny noticed. Her hair was shorter, chestnut brown, her eyes big and matching. She wore clothes like they were meant to be worn, almost perfectly filled out yet still relaxed. Even her sneakers, simple lace-up Keds, looked cool.

"I've heard a ton about everyone," Heather said, smiling, her eyes looking directly into Penny's. It was piercing, and Penny had to look away first. She felt hunted all of a sudden.

"Well, I can't imagine what you've heard," Penny said, trying to be light and willing Andrew to come stand next to her.

"It just sounds like you all have your work cut out for you with the property," Heather said. "I can't believe this is yours." She gestured outside to where the moon had risen and shone its light over the pond. The meadow and the trees and the mountains in the distance were outlined in black and blue. Mountains at night looked like promises that hadn't been broken yet. Penny sipped her drink and agreed with Heather. They were incredibly lucky.

Andrew came up next to her and gave her shoulder a squeeze. "How do you fit in to this group?" he asked Heather.

Penny could hear laughter punctuating the din of conversation around her, and she couldn't remember the last time her cousins had interacted so easily. Did the property decision have to be so hard? This was a group of people who loved each other—a family—and they shared the kind of history worth hanging on to.

"Miles and my son, Jeremy, are new best friends after meeting at gymnastics," Heather said.

"The old 'somersaulting to find friends' trick," Andrew said. "I did that in my day too."

Penny leaned into him. "Whatever it takes, right?"

Heather laughed and Chris came up next to them. Penny could tell he had already refreshed his drink. His khakis—folded deliberately at the ankle to show off his newest sneaker—might have had a wet spot on the front.

Andrew stuck out his hand before Chris had a chance to say anything.

"Andrew," he said.

Chris took his hand and said his own name out loud. "You and my sister?" he asked, looking between Andrew and Penny.

Andrew let out a soft chuckle. "If she'll have me," he said. Penny's stomach did a flip.

"Well, don't let her change her mind," Chris said. Penny could see now that he was rocking unsteadily from foot to foot. He must have started drinking in the afternoon when she and Laurie had been distracted. Andrew opened his mouth to respond, but Chris put up his hand. "They change their minds, you know. Nothing you can do about it."

Chris was drunk. Penny couldn't believe it had taken her two full minutes to see it.

"Should we get a snack?" she asked, going so far as to touch her brother's elbow. He stepped back dramatically.

"I do not need a snack," Chris said. Andrew and Heather looked at each other and both took a quiet step back. Chris didn't notice. "I do not need a snack," he said again. "In fact, I will go outside and wait for the sunset."

Chris found his way to the sliding doors and helped his way into an armchair on the porch. Penny didn't want to point out that the chair was actually facing away from the sunset and that the sunset had taken place nearly two hours before. If Chris didn't notice, then he wasn't meant to notice. Sometimes not noticing is its own form of survival. She quietly followed him outside with a glass of ice water.

"We love you, bro," Penny said quietly, putting the glass on the table next to him. Chris kept looking not at the sunset. He was looking so intently, she wanted to ask what he thought he was looking at, but she knew it was not the time to poke the bear.

"I could have just sent her stuff to her. In a box or whatever. Why does she need to come all the way here? And why couldn't she have come today, like she said she would? Even in a post-Alison reality, the world still revolves around her," Chris said, his voice sounding faraway.

Penny let out a sigh.

He continued. "She left, then Mom left, then Dad left. They all left."

"Laurie and I are still here," Penny said softly. "William and Halsey and even Miles too."

Chris nodded but didn't look at her.

"I didn't want a single one of them to go," he said, so quietly that Penny almost didn't hear it. She walked over and stood by him and squeezed his shoulder with her right hand. She didn't say anything; there weren't words for a broken heart, only time and the gradual belief that the holes would be filled one day. After a few minutes, Chris's hand found Penny's on his shoulder.

~

Penny found Andrew and Heather back inside. Halsey was now corralling the group to the large dining table in the middle of the main room, and there was a brief discussion of where everyone should sit.

"What did I miss?" Penny asked Andrew, putting her hand on the small of his back.

"You missed nothing. And I . . . missed you," Andrew said. He smiled, and Penny melted.

She bit her bottom lip and looked in his eyes.

"How's your brother?" he asked.

"His fiancée, his mom, and his dad all left abruptly around the same time, and none of them left a note," Penny said.

"And it all feels knotted together?" Andrew asked. They were in the corner of the living room, letting Halsey seat everyone else.

"I guess so." Penny nodded. "I hadn't thought about it before, to be honest. No wonder he's so crabby. Everyone has left! Except his two sisters, who, I hate to say, he would have probably given up to keep the other three." Andrew furrowed his eyebrows. "I didn't mean it like that; I guess I'm just thinking about how he's feeling. I'm not sure I've done that before."

Andrew scooped her into a hug and kissed her forehead. "You have to be one of the most thoughtful people I've ever met," he said.

Halsey's voice broke their trance. "Chris! Inside! Where the life is!" she called out, going so far as to knock the wall behind him.

Penny watched him begrudgingly get up and come inside.

"Andrew and Penny, you take those two side chairs," Halsey said, pointing. "And, Laurie, how about you sit next to William on the other side, and then Chris and I can take the heads."

Heather raised her hand like a student. "Excuse me, Ms. Ridge?"

Halsey looked up and Penny felt the two women exchange something she couldn't identify.

"You sit next to me at the head," Halsey said.

~

Dinner was a cornucopia of fall dishes: pan-seared pork chops, roasted carrots with parsnips and herbs, cheesy potato gratin, a kale salad with butternut squash and ricotta salata, skillet corn bread, even a cannellini bean–and–spinach dip with toasted baguette for dipping.

"Halsey, this looks *amazing*," Laurie said, her typical sarcasm and wit put aside.

"It's nothing," Halsey said, helping herself to a pork chop. "It's all from Daedalus in town."

Laurie shot Penny a look that she knew meant, *Do we think this will be charged back to the property account?* As their mother had always said, it was easy to spend other people's money.

"Well, it's delicious," Andrew said, squeezing Penny's thigh under the table.

"So, Chris," Halsey said in a tone that made everyone stop what they were doing. She waited for him to look at her across the table before continuing. "That woman will be here in the morning. Do you want us to greet her with a true Vermonter's welcome?"

"What, mistake her for a deer?" William asked, making everyone laugh.

"At least her car," Halsey said quickly. "We don't need to confuse *her* for anything besides a pathetic loser."

Chris cracked a smile.

"What if we left her stuff at the mailbox with a sign that said, *Nothing here to sell?*" Laurie asked.

"What if we just unpacked the boxes item by item and left them like a treasure hunt down the road?" Penny asked, envisioning Alison finding a shoelace, then a stained T-shirt, maybe a sock.

"What if we sent her on an actual treasure hunt?" Heather asked, clearly enjoying herself. "She gets to your door, you hand her a clue that leads her down to the pond, then a clue that leads her to the barn, and so on. All the while, we put her stuff in her trunk so when she comes back, we can say, *Hope the soul searching was worth it.*"

By now, everyone at the table was several drinks in, and Penny felt the warmth of the alcohol working its way through her body. Her tipsiness always started in her legs and worked its way up, landing in her head and giving her entire body a fuzzy feeling. She didn't even mind that Chris's head was bobbing, his eyes glazed over. The night felt like it had when they were younger, squeezed together at the kids' table while their parents shouted stories at each other. And Andrew fit in perfectly. She'd never brought a boy home before. Penny was overcome with joy.

"We should keep the property as is," Penny blurted out. Her statement immediately sucked the air out of the room, and she was surprised she and her chair weren't sucked out with it. Laurie furrowed her brow and William grimaced and Halsey looked away. Chris's head was still bobbing.

"I don't think now's the time," Laurie said. Her cousins didn't say anything.

The warmth Penny had been feeling throughout most of her body went cold. Her gut sprouted a peach tree.

"I just meant we're having such a lovely time. There's history here." Penny said this quietly, and she felt Andrew reach over and touch her shoulder. She was humiliated. And mortified to have ruined the moment.

No one said anything for a few seconds. Heather finally tapped her glass. "Well, clearly, there is a lot at play. But I will say, as a new friend on this hill, you have a beautiful spot and I'm honored to be here."

Halsey raised her glass. "Hear, hear!" And everyone raised their glasses in unison, toasting the hill.

Penny leaned back in her chair and wished she could disappear. Sometimes it felt like she had been born with a foot in her mouth; no matter how hard she tried, she always managed to say the wrong thing. Did people ever really change? she wondered. She'd been trying for years, but she was the same old girl, wasn't she?

CHAPTER
TWENTY-TWO

Laurie looked at her phone again and winced. How many people got fired—as a partner, a role that usually involves an entire board voting on a dismissal—via email? Her supervising partner hadn't even been the person to write it; someone named Lucinda from human resources had sent the email. Sweat formed on Laurie's brow as soon as she started to read.

Laura Hancock Nolan
41 West 68th Street, Apt. 2F
New York, NY 10023

November 22, 2021

Dear Laura, it started.

Laurie cringed at seeing her legal name.

> I regret to inform you that your employment with
> Howell, Columbus, Plymouth & Rodgerton is ter-
> minated effective as of November 22, 2021 (the
> "Effective Date").

This was both a surprise and not a surprise. When communication with Paul had first dwindled, Laurie leaned in harder to the texting, going so far as to *sext*, an act she hadn't considered in her purview. But then Paul had disagreed with her in a meeting. It was a Zoom, Laurie and a few other sad souls in boxes on a screen against a conference room filled to the brim with lawyers. Laurie had been updating the firm on a case and Paul interjected.

"I believe you're confusing Morris with McAllister," Paul said, looking up from his notepad. They had never acknowledged each other at work before.

"I am well aware of McAllister, Paul, and I'm not confused. Morris is holding to close on the thirtieth, whether Kevitch comes through on the terms or not," Laurie said, her cheeks heating up under the skin. She hated Zoom. To glare at Paul was to glare at the entire company. She sat there and forced a smile.

Paul nodded as a way to show he was contemplating. "Very well," he finally said. By now the other partners were shifting in their seats, clearly uncomfortable with an associate calling out someone senior. "Perhaps we should confirm all this with Parsons?" Paul suggested, turning his head toward the firm's senior managing partner, Liam Parsons.

Laurie hadn't texted Paul again.

Five days later, Tom had made his cryptic, opaque phone call. Two days after that, someone who was not Lucinda from HR had informed her she was the subject of a sexual harassment investigation. The proceeding interview had been as brief as it had mortifying.

~

As you know, an Associate filed a claim against you on September 22, 2021.

He was like the unnamed assassin here.

Since our investigation, we've concluded that this claim was substantiated, and in fact, there was a nonconsensual relationship between you and an Associate.

Paul had turned her in and pretended that she'd taken advantage of him. She felt her stomach at her ankles. Seeing it written down like this in legalese made the whole room start to spin.

As our firm's policy states, we have zero tolerance toward any workplace harassment. As of November 22, 2021, your employment and partnership with Howell, Columbus, Plymouth & Rodgerton are hereby terminated. As you are terminated with cause, you are not eligible for severance.

Within ten days of the Effective Date, you must return all Company documents and property. Please arrange to return your company-issued laptop and accompanying equipment no later than December 6, 2021. Failure to do so will result in the Company charging you for the equipment.

Could you mail a laptop? Couldn't the laptop be a parting gift after ten years of service? What happened if she forgot to include the charger? What about the mousepad? How far would they go to charge back the "accompanying equipment"?

After the Effective Date, you will no longer accrue or receive vacation benefits. Your final paycheck will be paid on November 30, 2021, and will include any unpaid wages, salary, overtime, accrued vacation, sick leave, and other amounts owed to you by the Company. Your health insurance will end November 30, 2021. You may maintain this coverage at your own expense if you notify us of your intention to do so within ten days of the Effective Date. Your life, personal accident, and long-term disability insurance coverage will stop on the last day of the month of the Effective Date. Any shares due you by the company will be paid out in accordance with your severance agreement no later than December 31, 2021.

All confidential information you received during your employment at the Company must remain confidential.

Our policy is to give information only about job title and employment dates to companies checking references. We can assure you that the details of your departure will remain confidential unless we are required by law to reveal them. In the case of the employee complaints, should any of the employees filing complaints decide to press charges, we will be required to share the basis of their complaints and the findings from our internal investigation.

Laurie had a flash of throwing a stapler at an especially dull associate named Lauren. But that had been years ago. When Laurie was actually much angrier as a person. Before the life coach and the executive coach and even the stint in anger management. What was the statute of limitations on stapler throwing?

> Please sign, date, and return a copy of this letter as confirmation of your receipt and acknowledgment of this letter.

> Thank you for your time at our company. We wish you success in all your future endeavors.

> Best regards,

> Lucinda Moorehead

> Human Resources

> Howell, Columbus, Plymouth & Rodgerton

> Read and accepted:

> Employee's Signature: _____

> Date: _____

Laurie reread the letter several times. Would she risk the humiliation of having this printed at the UPS Store in town, or would she just buy a printer to print the document in private? Would she contest the investigation's findings, even though she knew it was all true? She'd knowingly started a relationship with a subordinate. Even if he had pursued her. Even if she'd hoped it would turn into something real. She knew Paul had traded her for fleeting power at the firm. It broke her heart, and it made her hate him.

She did a quick calculation. She had one more paycheck coming; that would cover her mortgage and her latest AmEx bill. Then nothing. Firing for cause meant no severance, which meant that all her leverage in how they would handle Stowe went out the window. Now Chris was the only one of them who had any financial leverage, and he wanted to sell. She was also unemployable. That was worse than being fired. She had no prospects, not nearly enough savings. No friends to speak of. She had this land and this family, both hanging together by a thread. What happened when they were all ready to move on? What would she do?

She looked up from the desk and out the window that faced Camel's Hump. Two figures were walking by the tree line, and as Laurie studied them, she could see it was Halsey and her new friend, Heather. Halsey wanted to keep the property; she'd maintained that since the beginning. But without a job, Laurie knew her only option was to sell. Her family could not know what had just transpired—if Penny could lose all her friends overnight and never tell them why, Laurie could bring this to her grave. The only way to do that would be to walk away from this property.

Halsey's resolve to keep her family and her family's land intact was only getting stronger. Laurie could sense it in her, and she could sense that even Chris was warming up to their cousin's constant ruminating on how they could make Shaw Hill work. And yet, Laurie knew enough about negotiation to know that keeping the opposition close to you was as valuable as surprising them entirely. She walked downstairs to the mudroom and put on her sneakers, grabbing a baseball hat on her way outside.

By the time she was halfway down the hill, Halsey and Heather were on the trail that went into the forest. Laurie loved this trail: it spanned the entire property, winding its way up and down hills and past caves that housed black bears all winter. There was the family chapel built into the hill and a neglected shooting target from when William went through a brief rifle phase. As kids, they had sailed down these hills on sleds, dive-bombing for cover before hitting the trees. There were rusted, disintegrating old cars from a hundred years ago and even a sugar shack that had been vaguely operating when Laurie was little but now was no more than a heap of old wood and nails. At a certain point, the trail sloped up a steep hill and then opened to a massive field, untouched by anything human. In the summer, the grass was so tall, you could barely wade through it, and by the fall, you could disappear completely.

Laurie was halfway through the field when she saw Halsey and Heather stop walking. She held up her hand to wave, prepared to shout a "hello!" when she saw Halsey grab Heather's hand and pull her close. Then they were kissing, wrapped in an embrace, and Laurie had to cock her head to the side and squint to make sure she was really seeing this. This was not a first kiss, of that Laurie was certain, and as she watched Halsey weave her fingers through Heather's hair, she realized this was also much more than a kiss. They kissed like they were making up for lost time or trying to cram in enough life with each passing minute. They kissed like teenagers who had just figured out how intense kissing can be. Laurie realized her mouth was hanging open when she felt a bug fly inside.

Halsey kissing a woman was not something Laurie had ever expected to see. It was weird. Not because there was anything wrong with women kissing, of course not, Laurie thought, she had a handful of gay friends and she'd even kissed a girl in college. Granted, the kiss was a dare and she hadn't felt much, but she could recognize another girl being attractive. It was weird because Halsey was not someone Laurie had ever imagined kissing with . . . passion. Even on their wedding day, Halsey and Chad had stayed at arm's length, their kiss at the altar nothing more than a quick peck on the lips. Before Chad and after him, Halsey had dated a little, but never in a way that suggested desire. Plus, Halsey still made gay jokes sometimes, ones that caused everyone around her to roll their eyes. When Laurie had once brought a lesbian couple up to the house for a long weekend, and Halsey had been across the driveway with Chad and an infant Miles, Halsey had spent an entire dinner asking increasingly inappropriate questions of the women. One, Andra, was bisexual, and this fascinated Halsey. She could not let go of the technicality of it.

When Halsey asked, "If you're bisexual, wouldn't it be easier if you just dated men?" Laurie had to properly intervene. Her friends barely talked to her after that.

Laurie silently turned around and started walking back toward the woods. Was Halsey a lesbian now? Had Heather always been a lesbian? Was this a fluke, or was Halsey acting on something that had always been at the surface? Laurie picked up her pace once she crested over the hill and was fully out of view, not that either woman had noticed her in the first place. But if they were out here kissing, as opposed to in the house, or by the pond, or anywhere in the open, that meant they were keeping this a secret. Which meant that Laurie had something on Halsey. Which finally gave Laurie the leverage she'd always wanted.

By the time Laurie got back to the house, both Chris and Penny were sitting on the porch reading. A baseball hat on one of the chairs suggested Andrew was around somewhere. Laurie kept the news about Halsey to herself.

CHAPTER
TWENTY-THREE

A major benefit of dating your son's best friend's mom is the ease in aligning schedules. Halsey and Heather had taken to rendezvousing at school drop-off and spending the morning together, often at one of their houses, though sometimes they didn't quite make it out of the car. The parking lot by the bike path was blissfully unpopulated during the off-season.

Today had been a car morning. That they both drove SUVs was not lost on them. Car mornings were not meant to be spent in a Prius.

Halsey glanced at the clock: 12:30. They had two blissful hours until pickup. "Sandwiches?" she asked.

Heather was refastening her button-down shirt. "Is there a stronger word for 'yes'?" she answered.

~

They crossed the street from the parking lot under the church to Black Cap Coffee & Beer and went inside. Heather had her arm outstretched over Halsey's shoulder, and Halsey had her hand on the small of Heather's back. Halsey felt as safe and at home nestled in Heather's nook as she did anywhere in the world. She leaned in to inhale Heather's scent. They met eyes and smiled.

"Share a sandwich and share a soup?" Heather asked as they both looked up at the menu on the bulletin board.

"Is there a stronger word for 'yes'?" Halsey parroted back to Heather.

A bell chimed and signaled the front door had opened. Halsey looked behind her and saw William walk inside with a brunette woman who looked strikingly like her cousin's ex-fiancée at his side. She instinctively threw Heather's arm off her and took a large step to the left, creating ample space between them.

"William, hey, what are you doing here?" Halsey said, almost like she was talking to an old acquaintance, as opposed to her younger brother. She tried to get a closer look at the woman with him, but he kept moving into Halsey's eyeline.

"What up, sis?" William said easily, though before he took another step forward and introduced this new woman, he murmured something in her ear, causing both of them to turn around.

Halsey opened her mouth to say something.

"We're not feeling sandwiches. I think we're feeling more Mexican," William said, holding up his hand for a little wave. "But we'll catch you two later."

With that, they turned around and left, the woman still under William's arm, but no more familiar to Halsey than she'd been a minute ago.

"What was that?" Heather asked, her eyebrows raised.

"That was so weird. Who was that, and why did they leave so quickly?" Halsey asked, her mind racing through memories to see if this woman popped up in any of them.

"No, why did you suddenly act like I was flammable when your brother walked in?"

Halsey looked at Heather. Now she saw that her raised eyebrows were not out of shock but out of hurt. Maybe even annoyance.

"You know we aren't telling people yet. And my brother has never met a secret he wanted to keep."

"Except for whoever that was," Heather said. She seemed annoyed.

"There's no way William would do that to Chris," Halsey said, mostly to herself. "It couldn't have been her." She tried to take Heather's hand in hers, but Heather bristled and dug her hands into her pockets. "Do you want everything out in the open?" Halsey asked.

"I think there's a difference between not wanting a parade in your honor and making someone feel like a dirty little secret," Heather said.

Halsey looked down at the floor. It was weathered and had been buffed too many times. She looked around at the café. Besides the staff, they were the only ones in there. She looked out the glass door and windows and saw the sidewalks were basically empty. She looked at Heather. In a moment of deductive reasoning, she knew to kiss her right now would fix the moment entirely, and she knew they wouldn't be caught.

She leaned forward and kissed Heather on the mouth. "You are not a dirty little secret."

Heather smiled back and looked like her regular self again.

"Let's get that sandwich," Halsey said, squeezing Heather's hand.

CHAPTER

TWENTY-FOUR

It rained on the Fourth of July before their mother, Jean, died. She'd had breast cancer twice. The first time it went away, but the second time it came back in several places at once. William decamped to Stowe, refusing to leave his mother's side for the last year of her life. They were all in the big house that year: Jean and Harry and William and Halsey and Chad and Miles. Somehow it worked. Somehow it was the best year of William's life.

"We should throw a barbecue," Jean said in late June. She was sitting on the covered porch looking out at Mount Mansfield.

William was sitting next to her, a paper open in both their laps. They'd been out there all morning, reading articles aloud and then analyzing them, Jean's absolute favorite pastime. Halsey was chasing Miles around the house.

"At the house?" William asked. He considered the logistics. His mother was ill, visibly so, and she did not host lightly. To Jean, hosting was a sport.

"Of course at the house," Jean said, smiling. "Either in the yard up here or down by the swimming pond."

"Should we have people over for the Fourth?" William called to Halsey, who was now trying to convince Miles to keep his diaper on.

Harry walked outside holding a tray of glasses with ice and a pitcher of iced tea. Lipton, the powdered kind, Jean's favorite.

"So we're throwing a party?" Harry asked, putting the tray down on the table by the couches. He picked up the empty mugs by his son and wife and put them on the tray.

"Don't worry, Wills, it'll be fun," Jean said to her son, wiggling her eyebrows for effect.

~

Ten days later, they awoke to rain. The kind of summer downpour where you layer up and stay indoors, the clouds so low, you could go outside and touch them.

"Do we cancel? I can send an email out to everyone," William asked his father in the kitchen.

"Absolutely not," Harry said, shaking his head. "Your mother wants to host. Let her host. We'll move it indoors."

And so, later that afternoon, when the clouds had risen a few feet higher in the sky but had not stopped releasing moisture, a crowd of twenty or so helped the house teem with life. Jean sat in her favorite armchair in the corner, a blanket over her lap, a glass of wine with ice on the little table with a lamp. She managed to host without ever standing up, and William and Halsey both made sure the guests were never without drink or food.

Chris and Laurie walked across the driveway, both of them soaking wet by the time they made it to the living room. Penny was up in Burlington, unable to miss work for the party.

"Aunt Jean, how are you feeling?" Laurie asked, pulling a chair next to her. William sat on Jean's other side.

Jean smiled without opening her mouth and squeezed her niece's hand.

"It's great that you're here," she said. Laurie squeezed back. Their own mother had died the year before, and Jean did everything she could to step in.

The guests were mostly locals, people Jean and Harry had known for decades, many of them neighbors on Shaw Hill. Chris and Halsey were mingling, but William felt like he was frozen in place next to his mother. He kept watching her breathe, as if she might stop at any moment, even though she was fine, sitting up, even taking sips from a drink. But that was terminal illness, wasn't it? The accordion of waiting: every moment matters, but time slips through like sand in a palm. He was desperate for his mother not to die, and he was equally desperate for the death to come so he could stop waiting for it.

"Wills," his mother said, breaking him out of his trance.

He looked at her. "Mm?"

"You can leave my side and go have some fun, you know," she said, smiling while she spoke.

"This is fun," William said, probably too quickly.

His mother lightly shook her head. "Go. Mingle. Please. Laurie and I need to talk over here anyway."

His mother and Laurie immediately got to talking, and William took his cue. He didn't know his place in this room: sometimes the trouble with a room full of people who have always known you is you have no chance to be anyone other than the person they believe you to be. He felt awkward in chinos, his polo shirt suddenly too snug. He watched Halsey telling a story to a small group in the kitchen and decided to sneak down the hallway, slipping into his parents' bedroom and then out their sliding door to the terrace.

It was still raining when he got outside, but he didn't care. He needed the fresh air to tingle against his skin.

CHAPTER
TWENTY-FIVE

"So," Trevor said, in an attempt to break out the chatter in the conference room. Halsey was murmuring with Laurie; Chris and William were in the throes of a sports conversation Penny couldn't begin to care about. Penny looked at Trevor and they made eye contract. The chatter continued.

"So," Trevor said again, now also hitting his papers and folder against the table. This was the problem in taking over the family business: the kids stayed the kids. No one paid him any attention, Penny knew, because no one wanted to discuss what needed to be discussed.

Penny hit her fist on the table and said, "Okay, team, let's do this! Remember we pay by the hour here." Her voice was just high enough to get their attention. She gestured to Trevor that he should begin.

"We all know why we're here today," Trevor said, to which Halsey abruptly put up her hand.

"*Do* we know why we're here today? I'm not sure your email actually specified that," she said.

"You know why we're here, Hals," Chris grumbled.

"Well, Chris, considering none of us has seen you in the past two weeks, and you're the main conduit between us and Trevor, and we all got an email yesterday that we needed to be here today without saying why, in fact, no, we don't know why we're here. We also don't know where you've been, but that's a topic for another day." Halsey sat back and crossed her arms, proud of herself. Penny sank back in her chair and inwardly groaned.

Chris had been in an Alison-size hole of depression for the past two weeks, hunkered down in their basement and refusing to come up during daylight hours. She and Laurie took turns bringing him food and making sure he was still breathing. He'd been fine, and everything up to actually putting Alison's stuff in her trunk had gone off without a hitch, but then he'd suggested they grab a drink and talk, and she admitted she was with someone and that spending time together wasn't the best idea. To add insult to injury, when he'd said at least this guy was a stranger—he knew none of his friends would ever go near her—she had winced.

"Do I know him?" he'd asked. Penny and the rest of them were eavesdropping from the front door.

Alison nodded without saying anything.

"Do I know him *well*?" Chris asked. Spittle had collected on his lips.

Alison nodded again.

Chris walked back inside, past Penny and Laurie and Halsey, down the stairs to the basement. He hadn't been upstairs since.

Trevor furrowed his brows and leaned forward on his elbows. He nodded a few times before starting to speak. Trevor was well aware of the Alison Hole but far too polite to cross that boundary here. He briefly met Penny's eye before looking away.

"We are here because it's been almost four months, just over a fiscal quarter, since the preliminary reading of the will, and based on the contributions and deductions of the property's shared account, we are in a place where a decision needs to be made on whether the property will remain in the family or whether the family will move to sell the asset." Penny was impressed by how authoritative Trevor sounded. It was almost like he'd deepened his voice by an octave.

"Contributions and deductions?" William asked. He was dressed in clothing that could only be described as what someone might wear while selling goat milk at a modest farmers market. His hair was coiled into a loose bun. He squinted instead of wearing glasses. Alison had mentioned that she was seeing someone very invested in yoga. For a moment, Penny wondered if it could possibly be William, but she batted away that thought as soon as it hit her. Impossible. William couldn't possibly dip that low.

"As of last week, the property's shared account held a balance of two thousand, two hundred and fifty-six dollars. Given that the last contribution was from an account ending in 9045 of ten thousand dollars on September 15, the account will be overdrawn at the next maintenance and tax cycles," Trevor said, using a pen to keep track of the numbers he read aloud.

"Well, whose account is 9045? I know I contributed our family's share when it was our turn," Halsey said. Penny knew it was Chris's account, but she also watched Laurie staring intently at the floor, refusing to make eye contact with anyone. Penny made an internal note to ask about it later.

"My account is 9045, obviously," Chris said, sitting straighter in his chair. "And the thing about contributions, Halsey, is we are all meant to contribute every quarter."

"I contribute every quarter, *obviously*," Halsey shot back.

Chris turned his body toward Trevor. "When was the last time another account contributed to the shared account?" he asked.

Trevor used the same pen to track data on the page. "It looks like there was a five-thousand-dollar deposit from an account ending in 7875 on December fifth."

Chris turned to Halsey expectantly.

"Things are tight with the divorce," she all but muttered. William let out a soft whistle.

"Are you really whistling right now?" Chris asked him, incredulous.

William put up his hands in mock surrender. "Don't come after me, man," he said.

"Where the hell are you, *man*? Halsey is your sister. You're just leaving her out to dry? What, hoping none of us call you out on the fact that you're happily up here doing your little yoga in the back without actually lifting a finger?"

Penny hadn't heard Chris unleash like this before. He was venomous in his anger, ready to stand up, and she could tell Trevor was about to fall over with anxiety.

Laurie hit the table with her knuckles. "Let's take a step back here," she said, her voice calm and even. "Trevor, you said we had a year to figure this out, and that the account will be overdrawn if we don't start contributing. When do we need to contribute, and when do we need to decide?"

"You want my opinion?" Trevor asked.

"Yes," Laurie said on behalf of everyone.

"You need to deposit another twenty grand in here now. Like, right now. Whatever this is"—Trevor gestured to the room—"shouldn't cost you the ability to decide what you want to do. If you let the account go and don't pay the taxes and continue to bury your heads in the sand, then you're going to lose this property. And that will happen *before* the year is out." He said this emphatically enough that Penny knew they were all listening. "Then, after you deposit the money, we are going to meet back here on December thirty-first, New Year's Eve be damned, and you're going to tell me your decision."

"What happens on December thirty-first?" Penny asked.

Trevor inhaled and exhaled before responding. "Nothing, but I grew up with you guys. Our parents were best friends. *Best* friends. I can't watch this anymore. Whether you keep the Compound or not,

I can't watch you just slowly disappear because you don't know what you want."

Penny twisted the ring she always wore on her right ring finger up and down between her knuckles. Her mother had given her this ring, a silver one with mountains etched into it, after her first summer at sleepaway camp. Penny had been eleven, gone for a whole month at a camp only an hour from Stowe but worlds away. Her mother had found the ring in a store in Cambridge and declared it was Penny's ring for bravery. "Because you can do hard things," she said, sliding the ring onto Penny's finger.

"We can do this," Penny said, nodding and standing up as she said it. She looked at her cousins, who all seemed like they'd been in a battle. "We can do this," she said to them directly, but like a coach, trying to convince them that they really could.

CHAPTER
TWENTY-SIX

Laurie still called it the big house in her head because she couldn't bear to call it Halsey's house or William's house or even Halsey and William's house. Their parents had always called it the big house, not because it was so much larger (it was a bit larger) but because Laurie's aunt and uncle had built a new house over the old one first. Each child did it: Harry surprised Jean with plans in 1995, and then Laurie's dad surprised her mom a few years later. It seemed awfully chauvinistic, Laurie thought, at the same time realizing the books that sat near the fireplace hadn't changed since she was a child.

"Why haven't these books changed?" she blurted out, even breaking her own daydream into the odd way both her aunt and her mother had simply waited for their husbands to build them nicer houses.

"Don't fix it if it ain't broke," William said. Halsey rolled her eyes at him.

"Don't you want this house to look like yours?" Laurie asked.

"You do realize we were in the middle of a conversation, right?" Chris asked, his arms crossed and his brow furrowed. A scotch with condensation rolling down the glass rested near him. He'd moved on from beer, then, Laurie noted and let out a small sigh. Chris was easier when he stuck to beer.

"Were we, though?" Laurie asked, shifting which leg was crossed over the other. "I can't even remember what someone said last."

Chris ignored her and carried on. "We're going to vote, right here, right now. On the count of three. Those in favor of keeping the property, raise your hand. Those in favor of selling, don't."

"And the anticipated sale is?" Halsey asked.

"Ten million," Chris answered quickly. Two million a cousin. Laurie knew she could use the money. She also knew the property would continue to appreciate if they hung on to it. Plus, selling this meant never re-creating the magic they all shared.

"Okay," Chris said, "one, two, three."

Penny and Halsey and Laurie all raised their hands. Chris did not. Neither did William.

"You want to sell?" Halsey asked her brother, incredulous.

"Not necessarily," William answered.

"So you want to keep it?" Penny asked.

"Not necessarily," William answered again.

"Not raising your hand in the vote was the same as saying you wanted to sell," Chris said, sounding smug. Laurie shot him a look. He was still outnumbered; what was there to be smug about?

"Then we should have had a third option. The truth is, I see merit in each scenario, and I see disaster in each scenario. We keep the land, we have to maintain it. It's not 1950 and we aren't slowly buying parcels of land from farmers while our partnership stake at the country's largest ad company keeps growing. And our land isn't the easiest sell either. It's two houses, each on five-acre plots, plus the two five-acre plots that don't have houses on them yet, plus the other one hundred and thirty, which are all protected and in trust, by the way, and people buy on convenience. These houses all need updates. They all need repairs. The land needs a ton of upkeep. That isn't convenient. That isn't a ski house for some family living in Connecticut." William finished speaking and took a sip of his vodka.

No one said anything for a minute.

"Have you been studying property law or something?" Halsey asked, perhaps the most incredulous of them all. "Is that what you're doing all the time?"

William smirked without opening his lips.

Chris turned to Halsey, Laurie, and Penny. "You three want to keep it, right?" The three of them nodded and shrugged and agreed. "Say I walk away with my hundred bucks. And William walks away or stays, it doesn't really matter—how will the three of you keep this going?" He gestured around toward the field and the woods.

"We've got Laurie," Penny said. "Aren't you always telling me that she's the superior sister?" Both Laurie and Chris winced because they knew it was true.

Chris looked at Laurie. "You're ready to float this thing?"

Laurie thought about the termination letter, about how any day a box of her things from the office would arrive. Her last paycheck had come and gone. She had not one single idea of what she was going to do, and no one here had any idea.

"If that's what I need to do, yes," she said, pushing the truth all the way down to her feet. She sat up straighter. "Plus, if you are gone, and one day we do decide to sell, we all get your share." She flashed him the same smile she flashed opposition during arguments when she knew she was right. Chris bristled and leaned back, crossing his foot onto his knee.

Halsey leaned over and rubbed Laurie's shoulder. "I knew we could work this out!"

Penny was the first to stand, ready to leave.

"I need to go," she said and turned toward her brother. "For the record, I don't think you should walk away for one hundred dollars." She left before he or anyone could contest or ask her to stay. William also got up and walked outside, grabbing his jacket hanging on the hook by the front door.

"Don't wait up!" he said as the door closed behind him.

Laurie, Halsey, and Chris were left.

"I need to find Miles, and I need to feed him, because he is my son," Halsey said to no one in particular, almost like she'd just remembered herself. She was gone like a shadow, calling out for Miles as she stretched through the hallway.

"Isn't Miles with Chad?" Laurie asked her brother.

"I hope so. Otherwise, where has he been for the past hour?" Chris said. He hadn't meant to be funny, but Laurie laughed, and then Chris laughed too.

"Did Halsey just pretend her son was here so she could leave?" Laurie asked, realizing her cousin had gone to yet another height in displaying passive aggression. "She could have just said she was tired. We would have left!"

"Well," Chris said, picking up his glass and putting his legs up on an ottoman, "now we don't have to."

"That's a fair point." Laurie leaned back into the sofa.

Chris looked at his sister and back at the fire.

"Do you want to talk about Alison?" she asked him. Instead of answering, he got up and left, not bothering to bring his glass to the kitchen or even say goodbye. "So Halsey pretending she has to get dinner for her kid does not send you the message to leave, but my question about your very real pain does?" Laurie said to no one.

Laurie realized for the first time all night that music was playing. It wasn't even all that quiet, a reggae mix she'd heard in this house hundreds of times before. Halsey was the one who loved reggae, inexplicably so for a girl from Vermont, but over time they'd all gotten so used to hearing it, Laurie loved it too.

She looked at the books again and saw most of them were photo albums, all put together by her aunt Jean, filled to the brim with their childhoods. Laurie reached down and grabbed one off the shelf, opened to a page, and traced her fingers over the faces. This particular camera roll was from a spring break in Boca Grande, back when Laurie's grandparents had a place. Laurie was five or six, the other cousins spread out around her, with their parents looking as young as the cousins were right now. They'd had their whole lives in front of them. One photo showed nine-year-old Halsey holding a milkshake, sporting an ice-cream mustache and two missing front teeth. Her hair, a combination of blonde wisps and curls, was held precariously together with a single plastic butterfly clip. Laurie closed her eyes and remembered that day. Halsey seemed so big, and Penny still in diapers seemed so small. Laurie couldn't imagine being anything other than four, riding on top of her father's shoulders as he walked them into the ocean.

Laurie opened her eyes and saw the fire was nothing more than embers. She could hear the hushed talking of Halsey to someone. Clearly, she had hoped her guise about Miles had emptied the house. It was dark out, dark enough that she would turn on the flashlight on her phone to walk home. At this point in the year, the coyotes were bold in their packs, fearless as they patrolled for food before winter really took hold.

She didn't want those coyotes to study the mechanics of another family. They had been on this hill for sixty years, long enough to cycle several generations of that pack. She wanted Miles to tell his younger cousins about them one day. Hearing the coyotes howl down by the pond was as comforting as hearing the reggae come through the speakers. It wasn't time to lose this place, not yet.

CHAPTER
TWENTY-SEVEN

Christmas arrived at the hill like a sneak attack. One day Halsey was driving Miles to school and making playdates and generally avoiding the other house and then suddenly it was Santa's Day, when even the tensest families put aside their differences for caroling and eggnog. They had a week before Trevor would say it was finally and truly time for them to decide what to do. The twenty thousand they cobbled together—thanks mostly to Chris—bought them another quarter of operating expenses, but they needed that time to either take the property over in earnest or prepare it for a sale. She knew he was right: the only thing worse than indecision was losing this land to an auction. After all that, no land, no sale, no $100.

Heather texted her, as if reading her mind. The idea that it's Christmas in two days scares me. Jeremy is with his dad for a father-son ice-fishing day. What are you and Miles doing?

Halsey smiled. Miles is with his dad, but definitely not for ice fishing. Probably screen time while his dad plays cards online.

She started to get dressed—a simple athleisure outfit that allowed for whatever Heather suggested next. Over the past six weeks, Halsey had been equally addicted to the three dots that signified Heather was sending a text and actually kissing her, which continued to be odd not because it felt odd but because it felt so normal. By now she could barely remember how Chad's lips would always be a mix of chapped and rough, his stubble sometimes making its way to her mouth. Heather was all smooth and gentle, like each kiss was the politest question that had ever been asked. Halsey felt hugged in those kisses.

Halsey looked down at her phone and was surprised that Heather hadn't texted back. She checked her signal (strong) and her emails, in case Heather had switched avenues on her. Nothing there either.

Was the idea of me being unencumbered by a child too exciting to bear? she sent, too confused to overthink her own eagerness.

Halsey stared, waiting for the three dots to appear. Nothing.

A car started loudly across the driveway, and Halsey walked to the window by the front door. Laurie and Chris were in some sort of fight, she could see. Chris was standing by the driver's side door and Laurie was shouting from the steps leading down from the side porch.

"Don't back me into a corner here!" Chris shouted, stepping up to get into the car. Laurie took quick steps down from the porch to get closer.

"Don't just drive off!" she shouted back. "You put yourself in a corner! It's lonely on an island, isn't it?"

Chris said something back Halsey couldn't hear and drove down the driveway. Penny was now standing at the door, and when Laurie turned around and saw her, they immediately started talking. Halsey bit her lip as she tried to read theirs—not that she could. Penny had always been a mumbler, and Laurie really only made sense in little spurts. But Chris driving off was intriguing, she thought, walking back to the kitchen island to check her phone again. Still nothing.

Maybe Chris was getting worn down from being the only cousin who really wanted to sell this place, she thought. What would that do? Halsey tried to visualize Chris actually walking away, Laurie Venmoing him the $100. Would he still come up for holidays? Or did walking away from here mean you also walked away from your family? Halsey couldn't imagine it: couldn't imagine Chris walking away, couldn't imagine her walking away herself. Wasn't that what made a family? The inability to ever truly leave?

A knock on the door startled Halsey so abruptly, she felt her heart jump into her throat.

"Jesus Christ!" she yelled instead of saying hello, expecting it was one of her cousins on the other side of the door.

Heather was standing on the welcome mat, a picnic basket packed to the brim at her side. At first glance, Halsey could see crackers, a bottle of wine, and several different types of cheese. She opened the door, suddenly speechless.

"Hi," was all she said, looking between Heather and the basket.

"Hi," Heather said back, stepping forward to kiss Halsey on the lips.

"Hi," Halsey said again, this time as much to herself, because it felt like Heather's kiss woke her up. She guided Heather inside. "What is all this?"

"We're two grown women without anything to do today. It's almost Christmas, so I thought we might have an indoor picnic," Heather said.

Halsey could feel herself smiling ear to ear. Gestures were not something Chad had ever prioritized.

Despite it being Halsey's house, Heather led them into the living room and started setting up. Johnny Mathis played on a portable Bluetooth speaker, and Heather laid out a blanket with an actual picnic basket filled with goodies: soft cheeses, a fresh baguette, cornichons, some sliced charcuterie.

"You're absolutely spoiling me," Halsey said, taking a perfect bite of brie and fig and soppressata.

"I absolutely love spoiling you," Heather said, taking her own perfect bite of cheddar and apple and bread.

They leaned in for a kiss.

"To spoiling," Halsey said.

"To spoiling," Heather said back.

When the Johnny Mathis Christmas album started from the beginning, Halsey suggested a walk.

"I can't believe it's sixty degrees on December twenty-third," she said.

"Let's go on our favorite loop," Heather said, standing and holding her hand down for Halsey to grab.

Halsey swooned at Heather saying *their* favorite loop. She couldn't remember the loop before Heather.

~

The women walked down the path hand in hand. Halsey glanced over her shoulder once to make sure they didn't have an audience but could see that even if Laurie and Penny were home, they weren't outside. No one knew about her and Heather yet, and she wanted to keep it that way, at least until she really knew what she and Heather were. Or how to explain it. Heather was her first anything since Chad, forget that she was also a girl, and Halsey hadn't totally figured out what dating post-divorce really was.

By now, Heather had been in these woods enough to lead the way, and Halsey noticed how she had her own preferred route now. Instead of rounding past the old cars and the decrepit sugar shack, Heather liked to cut through the woods, bushwhacking their way up the hill before the trees opened onto the meadow.

"I've never gone this way," Halsey said to Heather's back.

"The best part about bushwhacking is you never really take the same path twice," Heather said, stepping hard on a branch to snap it in half.

Halsey noticed something shadowy near a fallen tree to their right. "You aren't afraid of critters, are you?" she asked, a little mortified to seem so untough in front of Heather.

Heather stopped walking and turned around. She put her hands on her hips and waited for Halsey to stop in front of her. "For the record, I'm incredibly afraid of critters."

"You are such a liar!" Halsey said, laughing. "No one who willingly bushwhacks is afraid of anything."

"Not true. I once saw a mouse in our kitchen, and I told Henry if he didn't get rid of it, we had to move. He had to show me video evidence that all signs of life for that mouse and any of its colony had been destroyed."

Halsey laughed at the image of Heather trying to seek shelter on top of her kitchen counters. She put her hands up and lightly pushed Heather up the hill and said, "Come on, fearless leader, get us to the meadow." But Heather stumbled moving backward and pulled Halsey down to the ground with her.

They were kissing and trying to get back up in one motion, which wasn't working, and it caused them to keep getting as high as leaning on their elbows and then falling back down again. It didn't take long for the snowy ground to seep through their clothes.

~

They reached the meadow, dead and overgrown and dusted with wet snow, and Halsey reveled at how different it looked through each season. In August, the grass shimmered in the high sun. In April, the grass was barely high enough to create a covering, every day a battle between green and mud. They'd come to a group of rocks all large enough to perch on, their surfaces warmed by the sun. God's lawn chairs. The sun was just warm enough that they could sit without shivering. A light wind played its soundtrack in the background.

"I think we should tell your family about us," Heather said plainly.

Halsey felt like something had zapped the air right out of her lungs. "So soon?" she asked. "What would we tell them? What is there to tell?" She felt frantic. Clammy. Like the ground might split open at any moment.

Heather cocked her head to the side.

"Why not start with the truth? That we're spending a lot of time together, and that we care about each other, and that our children are fast becoming best friends."

Halsey bit her lip. It was true; all those things were true. But they didn't tell the whole story. Halsey didn't know the whole story, and that's why she didn't want to tell it yet.

"They aren't going to understand," she said, shaking her head as she spoke.

"How do you know that?" Heather asked. "Your cousins seem pretty open. As does William, for that matter."

"What even are we?" Halsey asked back. "What is there to tell?"

Heather furrowed her brows.

"Are you embarrassed by me?" she asked.

Halsey put up her hands. "I didn't say that."

"So what did you say?"

"That it's not time. Why can't we keep going like we have been? Where it's no one else's business?"

Heather leaned back on her hands. "Because I don't want to keep declining dates by saying I'm not ready. I want to decline dates because I have a girlfriend."

The word 'girlfriend' echoed in Halsey's mind at full volume, and she put her hands up to her ears in an attempt to make the sound go away. *Girlfriend, girlfriend, girlfriend.* Halsey was not a girl who dated other girls. Halsey was a girlfriend; she did not have a girlfriend. 'Girlfriend' was all wrong.

"I can't do this," Halsey said. Heather looked like the words had impaled her. She didn't say anything back; her eyes were searching Halsey's.

Halsey looked down.

"I'm going to go," Heather said. Her chin was trembling, and Halsey knew she was holding back tears. Halsey was too.

"Okay," Halsey said. It came out as a whisper. She stood up so Heather could fold up the blanket.

"I'm sorry," Halsey said.

Heather looked at her. "What are you sorry for?"

Halsey shook her head and shrugged. "I don't know."

Instead of saying anything, Heather sighed and started walking back the way they came. Halsey watched, not knowing what else to do. She wanted to chase her down, touch her shoulder, swing her around and kiss her and take everything back. But then they would be girl-friends. Halsey didn't realize she was crying until she tasted snot on her upper lip. It felt like her stomach was trying to digest plain acid.

She leaned over to catch her balance. It wasn't fair of Heather to back her up against the wall like that. To rush her.

Halsey started the walk back to the house, relieved that Miles would stay with Chad tomorrow. Then it would be Christmas and she could put everything else out of her mind. She didn't know who to talk to about this. How could she? As she walked down the path, she caught a glimpse of something shadowy by a rotting log and realized all too late it was a snake. It wasn't until the snake had successfully bitten into her leg—a few inches above her ankle, where her calf muscle ended—that she knew it was a snake at all. Registering the rattle came right after.

She instinctually took several steps in the opposite direction, fran-tically searching her mind for what to do in this exact situation. The only thing that kept popping up was that in a state that had exactly one incredibly endangered species of rattlesnake, what were the chances one was here, on her property, *in December*, hanging out waiting to bite her? It didn't seem right, and as she slid to the ground, somewhere between a lying and sitting position, she laughed at the absurdity of it.

Halsey fumbled to the side pocket of her spandex where her phone was. She prayed Penny was not only up at her house but up at her house with her phone as she texted. Help. Trees by the bottom of the hill right after the bog bridge.

She added, Hurry

And realizing she hadn't ever texted Penny before, she added, Halsey.

She put her head down on the ground and looked up at the sky. All she could hear was the wind jostling the leafless branches.

CHAPTER
TWENTY-EIGHT

Despite Stowe, Vermont, being a booming, year-round attraction, complete with the largest ski mountain on the East Coast, the nearest hospital was twenty minutes away from the Compound. And despite Halsey's objections, Penny sat perched in the ambulance transporting them to the hospital. Her mind jumped between Halsey's leg—a swollen beast of a leg—and what Halsey had been doing down by the bog bridge in the first place. While Penny and Halsey had very little in common, they did share an aversion to most forms of exploration. If Penny was a house cat, Halsey was a small dog who preferred to go out on a leash. It made no sense that she'd been down there all by herself, roaming around the woods.

She used her thumb to navigate a call to Andrew.

"You won't believe where I'm going right now," she said after he picked up on the first ring.

"I'm guessing it's not that you're already going to the Bench?" They were supposed to meet there for dinner that night.

"As lovely as sitting on the sidewalk waiting for a bar to open sounds, try again."

"You are going to hike Camel's Hump."

The memory of their first date made Penny smile. "Better."

"There is nothing better than a late-afternoon hike to Camel's Hump in the summer," Andrew said plainly.

"Are you asking me out on a hiking date for six months from now?" Penny asked.

"Only if you tell me where you're going now," Andrew said.

"I'm currently in an ambulance that contains Halsey, who was out wandering the property and was somehow bitten by the only rattlesnake to ever slither north of Rutland County," Penny said.

"I told you not to tell anyone!" Halsey cried out from the gurney.

"Relax," Penny said to her. "You know no one can actually keep a snakebite a secret."

Halsey let out another low cry-howling sound.

"Holy shit," he said quickly, almost stammering. "Is she going to be okay?"

"The EMTs say she'll be fine," Penny said, looking at the EMTs while she said it. "But her leg looks pretty bad."

"Stop talking about me!" Halsey cried.

"Listen," Penny said, knowing she had only a few seconds before Halsey really blew a gasket.

"Yeah?" Andrew said.

"I'm in the ambulance with Halsey, which means I have no car. And while there is literally no way that the rest of the family won't find out about this"—she looked at Halsey while she said that part—"I can at least delay the inevitable by having you come get me. Copley Hospital. We should be there in ten minutes, and as soon as she's stable, we can go," Penny said.

Andrew said of course and that he would call once he arrived, and Penny hung up her phone. Halsey was breathing with an oxygen mask. Her skin looked like a coat of white paint that hadn't come all the way out. Her leg, propped up by one of the EMTs, was continuing to swell.

"Hey," Penny said, reaching out and taking her cousin's hand. Halsey looked at her. "You're going to be okay. They don't think the snake got too deep in its bite, and the timber rattlesnake's venom is pretty slow-moving."

Halsey had started to cry, which unlocked a part of Penny she hadn't felt in a long time. She stroked Halsey's hand with her fingers. Halsey cried harder. The EMTs kept checking her vitals. Penny squeezed her hand a little harder.

~

By dinnertime, Halsey was stable, though she would be in the hospital for at least a couple of days. The doctors had administered enough antivenin to flush her system, and her leg was already looking less swollen. Andrew arrived not long after Halsey had been wheeled into the ER and found his way to her room. Penny was almost overcome with excitement to see him.

"Did you bring"—she looked again at the bags he carried—"apple cider doughnuts and gas station hot dogs?"

Andrew shrugged. "It's my first snakebite. I also brought Gatorade, an AriZona Green Tea, some weed gummies, and a gas station doughnut."

"Gimme," Halsey said from the bed. Penny and Andrew both looked over at her.

Andrew stepped toward her and held out the bags like a waiter. "Madam, what can I bring you this evening?"

"Gummies," Halsey said without any fanfare. Andrew's eyes fell when she didn't play along.

"I highly doubt we should be giving you weed gummies in the hospital. Who knows what's coursing through you right now," Penny said, feeling a little authoritative.

"Oh relax," Halsey said, sitting up a few inches taller and holding out her hand. "You weren't bitten by a rattlesnake today and you aren't spending Christmas in the hospital. I was and I am. And I need something for the pain."

Andrew handed her half a gummy and gave Penny a look that said, *What do you expect? She scares me.* Penny sighed but understood. Halsey scared all of them.

~

Thanks to the gummy combined with whatever the hospital was giving her, Halsey was sound asleep within an hour. Penny left a note saying she'd be back in the morning with fresh clothes and followed Andrew out to his car.

"Should we have stayed?" she asked. "Isn't that what people do?"

He shrugged. "Maybe? But she's out cold."

"But I'm her cousin."

"Didn't she have to sign her name after she texted you? She's lucky you were by your phone," he said. Penny laughed.

"Fine. Maybe I'll just come back after dinner. Or tell Chad to go."

Andrew put his arm around her shoulder as they walked through the hospital doors.

"Is that a new Phish sticker?" Penny said, pointing to the rear left bumper.

"You do realize they continue to tour, right?" Andrew said, smirking.

"The question is not whether they are; it is whether they *should*," Penny said, getting in on the passenger side. They clicked their seat belts in at the same time.

"Jinx!" they both said, and Penny felt a warm flow through her body. She still felt like a stranger to this kind of earnest flirting. As if reading her mind, Andrew linked his hand with hers and squeezed.

"So, where should we go?" he asked, pulling out of the hospital and heading back toward Route 100.

Penny looked at the clock.

"Wasn't our reservation for eight thirty?" she asked.

"It was," Andrew said.

"Well," she said, nudging him and pointing at the clock on the dash, "you've got fifteen minutes before we're late."

Andrew gunned the gas for effect. "The Bench, wait for us! Wait!"

~

The Bench was on Mountain Road, a hipstery place that served things like wings and wood-fired pizzas but also a honey-miso salmon and a zoodle dish, so tourists from New York and Boston could eat too. The restaurant was crunched between the church and Trevor's law offices. It made Penny feel like she should whisper. They ordered matching whiskeys and split a pizza and wings.

Penny dug into the food and remembered she hadn't eaten all day. She was starving.

"Stop watching me eat," she said in between bites.

"It's cute," Andrew said, taking a large bite of pizza himself.

Penny shook her head. "Don't be gross."

"So," Andrew said.

"So," Penny said back.

"I'm having fun with this. With you," Andrew said. He let out a small cough at the end.

"I'm having fun with this and you too," Penny said.

"I'm glad to hear that. But we never talk about your plans," Andrew said.

Penny could feel her eyebrows furrow. "My plans?"

"With Stowe. With the Compound. With anything, really." Andrew gestured around to prove his point.

"Maybe I'm in a transition," Penny said a little sharply. She took a sip from her whiskey glass and moved her plate around, trying to center it with the candle in between them.

"Even in a transition, it's okay to say what you want to do next," Andrew said softly.

"I'm open to ideas," Penny said, crossing her arms over her chest. The last thing she needed was Andrew to sound like Chris or Laurie.

Andrew looked everywhere except at her as he decided how to answer.

"What about . . . anything?" he finally said.

"Anything?" She could feel the blood boiling in her.

Andrew looked at her, and she could see he was exasperated. "You don't do anything! Since we've met! I suggest everything we do together, I pick you up, I come to your family dinners, I bring you things. What are you doing when I'm not around?"

Penny didn't realize she was standing until she was pushing her chair into the table. Andrew was standing too, but she put her hands up to stop him.

"What I do when you aren't around doesn't matter to you. And after all this, all those *things* we wouldn't have done if you hadn't suggested them, I still thought somehow you wouldn't be like everyone else. I'm trying to figure it out, *Andrew*, and I can tell you right now, you aren't helping."

She stormed out of the restaurant before he could catch up, and she ducked into the alley between the Bench and the law office. She walked to the end and then down the hill to the parking lot under the church, where the bike path started and snaked its way through town. The path was barely lit at night, but she walked on it anyway, letting the stars guide her. After a few minutes, when enough sounds made her jump out of her skin, she started running, pumping her arms harder when her legs wouldn't move fast enough. She felt like she flying, sweat pouring down her face and her body, her wallet and phone clutched in either hand. When she moved like this, her thoughts washed over her, playing out like a movie she could tune in and out of.

For a moment, she almost felt free.

CHAPTER
TWENTY-NINE

"You said all creatures great and small," Miles said. He was perched on the hospital bed, curled up next to Halsey and staring at her intently. He looked so much like her father. Chad was sitting on a chair with one knee crossed over the other, clearly playing a game with himself in which he tried not to check his phone. He was losing this game.

"Well, that's a song, M-dog," Halsey said.

"It's a hymn," Miles corrected.

"It's a hymn. And all creatures great and small, God *does* love them one and all," Halsey said.

"Then why did the snake bite you?" Miles asked.

Chad had given up his game and was just texting now.

"I think I startled the snake while I was out walking," Halsey said, debating how she could explain a snakebite—one that landed her in the hospital for two days with a lower leg the size of a missile—without giving her son a serious phobia of snakes.

"Mommy, I get startled all the time and I do not bite." Miles said this emphatically. He paused for a moment, looked between Halsey's leg and her face. "I want to know, where was this snake's mother? She never should have allowed her snake son to bite you."

"Chad?" Halsey said. "Do you want to take a stab at this?"

Chad looked up from his phone and furrowed his brow. "Sure, what's up, buddy?" he said to Miles.

Miles rolled his eyes. "Forget it."

Halsey laughed without meaning to. It was like Miles summed up their entire marriage in that one moment. This made Chad shift uncomfortably in the chair and finally put the phone in his pocket.

"Are we talking about the snakebite?" he persevered.

Miles huffed before answering. "Yes, Daddy. I want to know where the snake's mother was, because let me tell you, if I tried to bite some-one at the playground, Mommy would be over so fast, pulling me away from that. We do not bite."

Halsey felt a swell of pride. She could claim credit for her son's lack of biting.

"I don't think the snake meant to bite your mom," Chad said.

"You can't bite someone by accident," Miles said.

Halsey and Chad traded a look. Miles was more upset by the unjustness of a bite than the idea of a snake biting him. She patted the bed for Miles to snuggle up closer to her.

"Come here, buddy."

Miles burrowed into her shoulder.

"You know how sometimes we do things we don't mean?" she said to her son.

"Like when my pee-pee goes on the wall?"

"Sure. Yes. The snake didn't mean to bite me. I bet he feels pretty bad about it, and I bet he told his mom later that he bit someone. But what do I say after we've done something we don't mean?"

"The snake is going to tell you he's sorry?" Miles asked, a little hopeful.

"In his own way, sure," Halsey said, envisioning the rattlesnake slithering up to her and giving her a nod.

"I hope you aren't scared of the woods now," Miles said.

"Your mom can take on the woods," Chad said, looking up from his phone again and putting it back in his pocket. He checked his watch—a completely unnecessary action, given that he was glued to a screen with a clock on it. "Buddy, we should get you some lunch and let your mom here rest." He stood up and held out a hand for Miles.

Miles looked between his parents but didn't move.

"When are you coming home?" he asked his mom.

"Tomorrow!" she said, maybe too brightly.

Miles's face got very serious. He looked between his parents, causing Halsey and Chad to lock eyes and make a wordless promise to take whatever Miles said in stride. It was Miles. He could say anything.

"Did you say tomorrow?" Miles asked gravely.

Halsey nodded, a little afraid to speak.

Miles started shaking his head back and forth. "I've always wanted to see one, but I wasn't sure I would," he said.

"What, buddy?" Chad asked.

Miles took a deep breath before exclaiming, "A Christmas miracle!"

Chad smirked and looked at Halsey.

"You know what else about tomorrow?" Halsey asked. Miles looked at her. "Santa said he'd be willing to drop by a little later, so all three of us, you and Mommy and Daddy, can open presents together."

Are you sure? Chad mouthed over Miles's head. It was supposed to be Halsey's holiday.

Halsey nodded and mouthed, *I sure am.*

Chad held out his hand again and stepped toward the bed.

Miles held out his hand but stopped inches from his dad's. "Can lunch be pizza?" he asked.

Chad nodded.

Miles allowed his hand and his dad's hand to clasp. "Then we should go," he said.

Chad leaned down to kiss Halsey on the cheek.

"Feel better, champ. I'll bring Miles over tomorrow once you're home," he said. She wanted to laugh at "champ." Was it worse when your husband or your ex-husband called you "champ"?

Halsey mustered a small smile. "Thanks, I should be home midday. I think Penny is going to come get me. Then we can do Christmas with everyone. Laurie is making stuff, I think."

"You sure you don't want us to get you?" Chad asked.

"God, no," Halsey said too quickly. She followed up with, "I don't want Miles to spend more time at this place, and you know how long discharging actually takes."

"Okay," Chad said, walking out.

Halsey laid her head back on the pillow. She and Chad communicated like old friends who had gone to summer camp together but hadn't had a thing in common for fifteen years. A connection, yes, a shared history, but nothing tying them to the present moment. Even Miles, who they managed to trade seamlessly every couple of days.

~

Miles and Chad had been gone only a few minutes before there was a light knock on the open door. Heather stood in the doorway with flowers and a bag from Four Corners of the Earth, arguably the best deli in the entire state of Vermont.

"You brought sandwiches?" Halsey said, immediately mortified. She'd meant to say *hello*, or *I'm so glad you're here*, or *thank you for coming*, or even *Merry Christmas*. Instead, "sandwiches."

"I brought sandwiches," Heather said, not missing a beat. She crossed the room to where Halsey lay and kissed her. "I came as soon as I heard."

Halsey was so incredibly happy to see her. Heather was wearing a simple navy top and jeans that hit the exact inch over her ankles that made her look long and lean, and her hair was down, luminously so. Halsey couldn't remember noticing women like this before, but with Heather she could only notice her. She noticed everything: the way her brows arched over her eyes as she spoke and the way her neck had a vein that popped slightly when she laughed. Her eyes told a story without meaning to, and her hands could paint a picture in their movements.

"I can't believe you're here," Halsey whispered. They kissed again.

"I'm so sorry for leaving you. I never should have done that," Heather said, seeming to mean it.

Halsey shook her head. "I'm sorry. I shouldn't have let you leave like that." What Halsey couldn't quite say was that she was scared, and that every ounce of desire was matched with an ounce of fear. It didn't feel fair to experiment with such high stakes.

"Should we both just keep apologizing? Really duke it out as overly apologetic women?" Heather asked, smirking. Halsey smiled too.

"A rattlesnake bit me after I said I wasn't ready to tell my family about us." Halsey hadn't said that out loud before. Karma really was a bitch.

"One could argue that a rattlesnake bit you after your girlfriend was insensitive to how big of a deal this is and left you alone in the woods."

"Girlfriend?" Halsey looked at Heather and swore she could feel the butterflies in her stomach warming her entire body. Maybe it was time to get more comfortable with this word.

"If you'll have me," Heather said. Halsey felt tingly through her whole body. She closed her eyes, and it was a three-second montage: giggling over glasses of red wine; the light dimming in the living room as they got more comfortable; outside at some sort of barbecue, people around and mingling; holding hands as they walked on the stone path leading away from the party. It was perfect, and it felt completely out of reach.

Heather pulled a small box out of her purse.

"I never gave this to you yesterday. Merry Christmas," she said.

Halsey took the box and slowly unwrapped it. She untied the gold ribbon first, then the red-and-gold paper. Inside was a long box, and when she flipped it open, there was a watch.

"Look inside," Heather said, and Halsey flipped it over. It was inscribed:

No Rush

HNR

"It's perfect," Halsey said. She took a deep breath. "I don't know if I'm ready to tell everyone." She took another deep breath to continue the honesty. "And I don't know when I will be. Or if I will be. It feels like too much to navigate with Miles and Chad and everyone."

Heather was quiet, but she kept stroking Halsey's hair.

"Like the watch says, no rush. But what if we both just try our best to get ready?" Heather said. "You consider a world in which you get to be yourself with someone you care about, and I'll practice patience as a reminder that not everything can happen on my timeline?"

Halsey nodded without saying anything. It sounded so reasonable. So fair. Discussions with Chad had never been like this.

"So then, girl . . . friend?" Halsey said. It was like she was just learning how to speak.

"If you'll have me," Heather said again.

They kissed, and Halsey lost herself in the feeling of Heather's lips on hers.

"Girlfriend," Halsey said again, this time the whole word together and looking right at Heather as she said it.

CHAPTER THIRTY

The news of Halsey's snakebite fell over Stowe like a good rain: within minutes, everyone knew. The town was respectful on Christmas, but as soon as Boxing Day hit, their phones didn't stop ringing. No one had ever been bitten by a rattlesnake in Stowe, Vermont, before, and they were curious. The news was alarming and quickly blown out of proportion. There was talk of locating the snake; there was talk of teaching children about having a snake plan. It was ridiculous, as far as Laurie was concerned, even if in the few days since the bite, she had taken to walking around with tall boots and thick pants.

Halsey's leg was still swollen, and as soon as the big house emptied out and it was just her and Miles, Halsey called Laurie in tears an hour later.

"Chad is gone, obviously, and I'm walking with a cane. How on earth am I supposed to parent alone?" she said. Laurie moved the phone off her ear to confirm it was really Halsey on the other end of the line. She was not the type to ever sound frantic.

"Where is Miles now?" Laurie asked.

"He's watching *Cars* again. In the living room," Halsey said. "If I hear that theme song one more time . . ." She trailed off. Laurie could hear Halsey's jaw clench.

"How about I come take him for a few hours? I can cover until he goes to bed; then we can grab Chris or Penny for tomorrow," Laurie said, already putting on a Patagonia puffy jacket to walk across the driveway. Winter was no joke in northern Vermont, and the warm spell from a few days earlier was now a distant memory.

"You'd do that?" Halsey asked. She meant the question.

"Of course," Laurie said. "We are family after all."

The comment sounded so obvious, Laurie thought, and yet she wasn't positive she'd ever said something like that before. Proclaiming the importance of family was Halsey's lane.

~

A few minutes later, Laurie found Miles in the living room, fully engrossed in *Cars*. She took off her jacket and hung it up in the coat closet. Halsey and William hadn't gotten rid of their parents' winter garments yet; they lined the walls, and Laurie caught herself inhaling the scent still attached to one of her uncle's Carhartt jackets. It smelled like pine and Old Spice, with the faintest hint of tobacco. They hadn't gotten rid of their parents' clothes yet either, Laurie mused, giving the jacket a tug and closing the closet door behind her.

"Hey, Miles," Laurie said. He didn't look away from the television. His mouth hung a few inches open. "Miles," she said again.

"Aunt Laurie, you'll see I'm watching *Cars*. It's my favorite movie. Can we talk after the movie is over?" Miles said.

"Of course, little man," Laurie said, biting her cheek so she wouldn't laugh. She knew adults who couldn't communicate their needs so clearly.

"Thanks, Aunt Laurie," Miles whispered, his eyes back on the screen.

~

Halsey was sitting with her leg propped up at the kitchen island, thumbing through an *US Weekly*.

"At some point, Disney Plus is going to start sending us the babysitting bills directly," Laurie said, breaking the silence. "Miles asked me in a complete sentence if we could please talk after the movie."

Halsey shook her head and rolled her eyes. "I will give my ex-husband credit for one thing and one thing only and it's teaching our son about hypercommunication."

"For today, let's take it," Laurie said. "You want some wine?" she asked, already opening the refrigerator door to see what was cold.

"Is there a stronger word for 'yes'?" Halsey said from her perch.

They both sipped a Sauvignon Blanc with a few ice cubes.

"We are nothing if not classy," Laurie said.

"We're going to be a lot less classy without this place," Halsey said, gesturing around.

"You really think we should keep it?" Laurie asked. She wasn't asking it as a trick question.

"You know I do," Halsey said a little sharply, a cross between offended and afraid.

Laurie shook her head and the ice in her glass at the same time. "I didn't mean anything by it."

Halsey waved her hand to signify it was nothing and Laurie let herself breathe. She took a sip of wine. Looked out the window at the snow falling next to the outdoor light off the roof.

"Don't you think we should keep it?" Halsey asked.

"What do you mean?" Laurie asked back, trying to hedge.

"We know where Chris stands. We know William will do whatever. Penny wants to live here. I want to live here. That leaves you. Are you with Chris or are you with the rest of us?" Halsey said all this matter-of-factly, a device she'd employed all her life. It was effective: Laurie hung on every word, and her insides were immediately a mess in trying to figure out how to answer.

For every second Laurie didn't answer, Halsey's squint grew more pronounced.

"I don't stand where Chris stands on this," Laurie finally said. That was true. She did not want to sell this place. What was not true was that Laurie could even afford to have an opinion. She was nearly a month post her final paycheck and a lifetime before she could ever find work again.

"Do you want to keep it?" Halsey asked.

"I know this place is important," Laurie said. She was hedging and Halsey knew it.

"So you want to keep it, because it's important?" Halsey asked. By now, her squint was so severe, her eyes were reduced to lines drawn on a canvas.

Laurie shook her head slightly and stared into the fire. "This place is incredibly important to our family," she said in a whisper.

Halsey let out a small cough and sat up straight. She had a look about her just before an attack, and Laurie was all too familiar with it.

"Why are you so positive we shouldn't keep it?" Halsey asked. Her eyes were narrow, and her body language was tilted forward, like she was ready to pounce. Laurie felt her tongue go dry. No matter how old they got, she was still five-year-old Laurie to ten-year-old Halsey, being pushed down the slide before she was ready to go. It didn't help that this time, Laurie really was hiding something, and Halsey was the last person she wanted to find out.

"I didn't say that," Laurie said.

"You know, Laurie," Halsey said, her voice strong and authoritative, "you could go so far in this world if you learned how to say what you mean, instead of sending everyone running around in circles to try and guess."

The words were thrown like little pellets, strong enough that Laurie almost put up her hands in defense.

"I do say what I mean," Laurie said, preparing to pounce. Fighting with Halsey was never about the fight in front of you; it was about what had happened years ago or what might happen years from now. Halsey fought outside of time, and she used everything in her arsenal every time. Laurie had been getting schooled by Halsey her entire life, and no matter how many times it happened, she was never, ever prepared. Until tonight.

Halsey took Laurie's pathetic rebuttal in stride. She'd been waiting for it. "You don't say what you mean. That's the problem, right? And it doesn't make any sense. You're a lawyer; you're successful, at least allegedly, but then you're alone. You linger up here like you're waiting for something. At least the rest of us are trying to figure out our lives."

Laurie was on the verge of tears, but she took a deep breath, that day near the woods playing like a short film in her mind, watching Halsey and Heather embrace. Her whole life, she'd been waiting to fight fire with fire.

"Would you argue that you say what you mean? That you live out in the open?" Laurie asked. She stood up while she spoke.

Halsey cocked her head and let out a little laugh. "I'm nothing if not direct."

Laurie smirked and crossed her arms. "Then when are you planning to tell us about Heather?"

Laurie saw Halsey's eyes widen slightly. She saw her take in a strong, quick breath. She saw her shoulders stiffen under her sweatshirt. Laurie had Halsey on the defensive, and for a moment, right before she knew she would scale back, because attacking someone's love was past her own boundary, Laurie understood why Halsey went for the jugular. It was as powerful as you can be over someone without lifting a finger.

Halsey opened her mouth slightly and then pursed her lips. Laurie was ready to throw up her hands in surrender before Halsey spoke. Fighting fire with fire felt horrible. Laurie's knees almost buckled with the regret of ever holding something like love over her cousin.

"You mean Miles's friend's mom? What would I tell you about her?" Halsey said, her tone perfectly mimicking genuine confusion. Had Halsey gone after a business degree instead of social status, she would have taken over the world; she was that good.

Laurie's compassion evaporated with the lie.

"Deny all you want. I saw you by the woods a few weeks ago. It was not an accidental embrace. Nor was it the first. And I would bet good money that you weren't alone in the woods when that snake bit you. I would also bet good money you'd said something to make Heather go away, leaving you alone and forcing you to call Penny." Laurie had moved closer to Halsey so she could keep her voice down. She wanted to teach her cousin a lesson, but not at the expense of her six-year-old overhearing something he didn't need to. Halsey remained seated and staring at her.

"Say what you want about me. But tread carefully," Laurie said.

Halsey shifted in her seat. "What do you want?" she asked.

"You can't push me, or any of us, around anymore. We aren't in a position to keep this land; you know that as well as any of us," Laurie said. "If you want your thing with Heather to stay between us, it's time for you to get on board."

For a moment, something flashed in Halsey's eyes, and Laurie thought she was going to come clean, which meant that Laurie could then let this termination-size weight off her shoulders.

"Don't go to war with me, cousin," Halsey said, her voice brittle and even. "I don't know what you think you saw or why you think it's relevant now, but usually when we expose someone else, it's only because we're desperate not to be exposed ourselves. So what I might ask you is: What are you hiding?" Halsey dared to smile as she finished speaking. Laurie's breath caught in her throat and she willed her body not to cough.

Halsey continued. "This land has been in our family for sixty years. It's where Miles is growing up, and there's no other place like it. I will be *damned* if I let some snobby, ill-spoken hobbit woman get in the way of that. I will find out what you're hiding, and you better believe I'll use it against you, just like you're trying to use some fantasy romance against me."

Halsey stood up and leaned on her crutch.

"Get out of my house."

CHAPTER THIRTY-ONE

The week between Christmas and New Year's is a whole lot less exciting if you still have to work. Penny had put in for the day before Christmas Eve and the day after Christmas, but Harvest Market was in full force in the days leading up to New Year's. No matter that there was not a ton of local produce to speak of; Penny was put on wine-stocking duty.

She'd stocked two cases of the Brunello when her phone buzzed.

A text from her brother on the family chain: Trevor meeting pushed to January 31st, but seriously fam, we can't push it again. Coffers are L O W.

Penny closed out of her texts when the phone buzzed again.

Andrew. If we switch it to the 12 Days AFTER Christmas, can we pretend we're still in the holiday spirit?

"Ugh," Penny said, loud enough that a customer turned around. "Sorry! Don't mind me; it's just, this is the best Brunello I've ever tasted and we're down to our last case." The customer took note and picked up a bottle.

Penny gave her head a shake to try and get back into the task at hand. Her family was driving her crazy. Andrew was driving her crazy.

More specifically, her family was running around like a bunch of chickens with their heads cut off, and Andrew's unrelenting kindness made her so uncomfortable in her skin, she wanted out.

She texted the family chain that she was in for January thirty-first and ignored Andrew.

~

A little before closing, her manager, Jake, came to find her.

"Can you do me a favor, Pen?" he asked. She hated it when he called her Pen and he knew it.

"What's up, J-man?" He hated it when she called him J-man and she knew it.

"We need to organize the stockroom. Any chance you can do it now and I'll pay you overtime? It shouldn't be more than a few hours," Jake said.

Penny didn't respond immediately, causing Jake to keep talking.

"I have plans tonight. Or I would do it myself. But I promised my family I'd be home, you see." He was rambling.

Penny was tempted to let him keep going—what else could she push here? A raise? A promotion? But he was awkward and gangly and a few years younger than her.

"No problem—I can do it."

Jake held up his hands in a prayer position and mouthed, *Thank you.*

Penny went into the back room to assess. The shelves were piled high with a random assortment of items definitely for sale, and Penny immediately started piling them into potential gift bundles. She loved putting things together—unexpected pieces of produce with cheese and a fig butter and small bottle of wine—and watching to see which customer would pick it up.

For the first bundle, she stayed with the shelf-stable items: a fig candle, a stone flour cracker, a Vermont cheddar sealed in wax, two mini bottles of Prosecco, and a tube of salami. The perfect winter basket.

She did five bundles and then actually got to work organizing the shelves. This was one of the rare times Penny felt comfortable in her skin. She was good at putting things away. It was methodical, and it was instant gratification. Assess, categorize, organize, move on.

Four hours later, Penny headed out. The store had been closed for two of those hours, and she had to shimmy through a back door that didn't totally lock but also didn't really open. As she was leaning sideways to make her body as flat as possible through the barely open doorway, her jacket got caught on the hinge and pulled back. Somehow in the shuffle, a folded piece of paper fell out of the jacket's breast pocket.

Penny leaned over in the dark and fumbled for it, picking it up between her fingers. She walked out into the parking lot, looking for a stronger streetlight to see what was on the paper, mostly expecting some long-forgotten receipt.

Instead, she recognized her father's handwriting. The note was dated in July, just a few weeks before he died.

Tiger, I'm proud of that garden we built. I don't have a green thumb to save my life, but you've got two of them. Should we start planning next year's harvest? I think it's time you start really using our garden.

Penny held the note to her chest like a hug, closing her eyes and inhaling the air, desperately missing her dad. She read the note again and again and clutched it in her fist as she drove home.

She'd ignored the garden entirely since he died. It was way too painful to even go near it, and she couldn't fathom planting anything. But maybe that was the point of her finding this note now. He'd clearly tucked it into a jacket during the summer—she wasn't meant to find it when he wrote it.

~

Chris and Laurie were both at home when Penny got back.

"You won't believe this note I found from Dad," she said, walking through the front door.

Laurie and Chris met her in the kitchen and each took a turn reading it.

"That's cool that you found that," Chris said. "Dad wasn't really a note leaver."

"Definitely not a note leaver," Laurie said, laughing a little.

"He loved a formally written email, though," Chris said, which made Penny laugh at all the times he'd signed off "Regards, F. Nolan."

"Think you'll go back in the garden?" Laurie asked, touching Penny's shoulder and then moving in for a full hug.

Penny shook her off as kindly as she could—she felt too brittle to touch anyone right now, even her sister.

"Sorry. I just . . . The note sort of hit me," Penny said in a whisper. She walked away from her brother and sister to the sliding door that led to the porch and the field. Even though it was nearly ten, the full moon cast an impressive light on the field, gifting Penny a clear path to the garden. She walked all the way to the wooden fence, determined to go inside.

But she couldn't. The hinge was frozen, and the door wouldn't budge, and Penny took it as an omen. Of course she couldn't go back in there. Her father had died in that garden, and it had been her fault. For lemonade! No one even likes lemonade. She could kick herself, she thought, walking a lap around the fence.

She didn't deserve to garden. How could she?

CHAPTER THIRTY-TWO

Halsey checked her phone for the hundredth time, even though she still hadn't responded to Heather. Every time she tried, Laurie popped back into view.

Hiya, girlfriend.

Heather had texted her that morning, in the minute between Miles calling from his room asking for *Paw Patrol* and Halsey listening for the ding that said the coffee was ready. Now it was nearly eleven, three hours later, and Halsey had no idea what to say back.

"Mommy," Miles said, breaking her trance. They were driving to peewee ice hockey at the rink.

"Miles," Halsey said back.

"If we do tuna fish for lunch, I think it would be best to cut my sandwich into triangles," Miles said.

"Okay, buddy, we can do that. Crusts on or off?"

"Off, Mommy."

Halsey nodded without saying anything. She could feel Miles staring at her.

"Mommy," he said again.

"Miles," Halsey said again.

"Have you ever put a potato chip into a sandwich?"

"I have done that, yes," Halsey said, flicking the turn signal on and turning right into the ice rink's parking lot. She could see a heated tent set up outside and decided immediately she would be ordering a hot chocolate with whipped cream. Parents of fellow peewee players milled about. The sight of a forty-pound little boy wearing little ice hockey equipment was too much to bear. She swooned at the sight of one, a gangly player named Harrison, who wobbled as he walked with his ice skates toward the ice rink doors.

"You have put a potato chip between the bread and then taken a bite?"

"You better believe it, buddy," Halsey said, gliding the car into a parking spot.

"Imagine the crunch!" Miles exclaimed, going so far as to throw his hands toward the roof of the car. "The crunch and the salt! Mommy," he said, leaning forward in his booster seat, "it is *brilliant*. We must try it."

Halsey put the car in park and turned around, though Miles was already shuffling across the seat so he could get out.

"Hey, Miles. What gave you the idea of a potato chip sandwich?" Halsey asked, genuinely curious.

"A potato chip sandwich!" Miles shouted, now laughing as he pulled his backpack from the car floor.

He was gone before Halsey really got an answer, already in the middle of the group of players by the time she had locked the car and started the twenty-foot walk to the heated tent.

~

"You're here," said a voice from behind her. Halsey looked around, even though she knew exactly who it was.

"I am here," Halsey said, smiling but not turning fully around. Heather was standing with two iced coffees and handed her one.

"Half-caf, almond milk, extra ice?" Heather said.

Halsey took the cup. "I am—"

"Incredibly impressed that I remembered? Me too," Heather said. Halsey took a sip and nodded at the same time. What about the hot chocolate? She debated whether she could drink this really fast and move on or quietly let this one go. What were the rules with girls? If it were Chad, she wouldn't have thought twice; she would have thrown the thing out as soon as he handed it to her. She would have made him throw it out.

They stood side by side a few feet apart from the rest of the parents. The coach, a young man aptly named Coach Blue, sent the boys on a series of low-impact drills. Miles was struggling to master a proper dribble with his hockey stick but did manage to hit the puck in a sort of pass to a teammate named Caleb. Heather's son, Jeremy, was openly distracted by a bird flying near the hockey rink.

"That bird must be freezing," she heard Jeremy say to no one in particular.

"I'm sorry I haven't responded to your text," Halsey said, nervous. "It's been a crazy morning."

It hadn't been a crazy morning, not at all. Miles had watched *Paw Patrol* and played blocks and Halsey had leaned over the kitchen counter staring at her phone.

"Totally get it," Heather said. Her voice was sweet and understanding, and it made Halsey want to run away or cry. She was used to Chad, who declared things that made no sense and walked away when Halsey was midsentence. Laurie's thinly veiled threats echoed in her mind. So did visions of her being ridiculed for being with Heather. The entire thing was petrifying, and Heather just looked at her with the sweetest eyes she'd ever seen. She didn't know if her insides were swooning or repulsed. Sometimes love can feel like lust and disgust at the same exact time.

"What are you up to later?" Halsey asked, refusing to let herself look at Heather. She knew if she did, she would lose her resolve.

"Jeremy is going to his dad's house, if you want to watch a movie or something after Miles goes to bed?" Heather answered. She answered so simply, like making plans with a woman you were dating was no big deal.

"I can't," was all Halsey could say. She could feel the tears welling up inside her, starting in her thighs and moving up. *Do not cry. Don't you dare cry.*

"Okay, well, maybe tomorrow?" Heather asked. This time, she sounded more concerned.

Halsey took a step to the left, so her arm wasn't brushing against Heather's.

"I think we need to cool things off, actually," Halsey said, begging herself to keep it together until this conversation was over. She could not bear it if Laurie told everyone her secret. She could not bear it.

"Are you sure?" Heather turned her body to face her, and when Halsey looked up, she could see Heather's eyes were two saucers.

"I'm sure," Halsey said, nodding.

"Halsey," Heather said in a whisper, reaching out and touching Halsey's lower arm. "What happened between yesterday and today? Was it something I said? Was it that text? It was too bold, wasn't it?" Halsey was watching Heather process this, and she was watching Heather get hurt, and it gutted her. This was not what she wanted to do to Heather—sweet, funny, unbelievably caring Heather. Heather, who had brought sandwiches to the hospital and promised to take things at whatever pace Halsey needed. Heather, who had looked at her in a way she didn't even know someone looked at another person.

"It wasn't anything. I just need space. From this. From you. It's too . . . it's too much," Halsey said. She took a pull on her coffee in hopes of stopping her chin from trembling, but it didn't work, and Halsey knew she was about to cry. Then she was crying, wiping the tears with the back of her hand like a child, and standing with her back to Heather, hoping her shoulders weren't moving.

"Halsey, I know you can be brave. I've seen it. I promise you; this will be okay," Heather said quietly. Halsey wanted to turn around and tell her about Laurie and that she didn't mean a single word of this. She could feel Heather standing there and looking at her. And she could feel Heather turn around and walk back toward the rest of the hockey parents.

Halsey pulled her phone out of her pocket and pulled up Heather's name.

I'm sorry. You're too good for me.

Send.

She stared at her phone while the message went through and watched three dots appear. Heather was responding. She held her breath while she waited, letting in oxygen, and crying out a sob in the moment when the dots went away.

CHAPTER

THIRTY-THREE

Penny didn't totally register she was going to Palm Springs until she was in Palm Springs, checking in to the Holiday House with a haphazardly packed bag and sunglasses on inside. The trip had been on a lark. Or Instagram advertising. She'd been scrolling through pictures—the most passive way possible to marginally interact with the world—and right there, between a photo of an old friend's toddler and another old friend's sunset, had been a photo of Holiday House, a boutique midcentury hotel in the heart of Palm Springs. She didn't think twice clicking on that photo, or putting in dates a few days later, or even getting out of bed to find her credit card to finish the transaction. Then suddenly she was on Delta.com, booking a three-stop flight from Burlington to Palm Springs International.

She texted Andrew: Going to Palm Springs for a few days. Maybe we can talk once I get back.

She left a note on the kitchen counter: *Gone for a few days. Back soon. No need to worry.*

And here she was now: pale, skittish, and probably in need of a real meal. Neither Laurie nor Chris quite processed the news of her departure. She was there in bed, and then she was gone without any fanfare. Her phone had several unread texts from both of them. But she was here to get her head on straight, and she knew she needed to be off the hill and away from her family to do that. She especially needed to be away from Andrew, even if she still couldn't tell him exactly what he'd done wrong. (He kept asking with increasing desperation.)

Penny would stay at Holiday House for six days. She was in room 202, just above the pool, with a kitchenette and round table and a porch with two chairs on it. The decor was uplifting: bright whites and blues and that shade of wood that doesn't darken against the wall. She felt it was a good sign that she even noticed the decor. There were enough wreaths and trees around—artificial, of course—that she remembered it had just been the holidays. She expected it to be hotter, even though it was December, and even though she had taken a few courses about climate in college and was well aware how it worked in the desert. Even still, she was surprised when the sun went down before five p.m., and she took that surprise as a good sign: She was interested in the sun! That meant she was interested in potentially being outside!

Before the pool, where she would go with a sun hat and a linen cover-up and lie under an umbrella and appear to be a woman in from LA, she crossed the street to a block that had both a liquor store and a bodega-type place. Supplies. The convenience store was easy: crackers, a cheap cheese, a bag of potato chips, Twizzler Bites. These were not snacks she was positive she'd eat, but she felt safe that they were not trying too hard. Had this been a health-food store, Penny would not have gone inside. The last thing this particular anxiety attack needed was kelp. That's the funny part about anxiety: sometimes it comes with inexplicable self-awareness, like a wave you don't know if you're riding or being pummeled by.

The liquor store demanded a social narrative. Penny started with the mini bottles. These she liked to keep in her bag. Vodka, gin, and mescal. She then moved to the midsize bottles. These were for cocktails in the room. Vodka again, bourbon, rum. She found a premade cosmopolitan mix and then a bottle of already chilled rosé. The hotel room had beverages like ginger ale and Coke and club soda.

"Having a party at the time-share?" the clerk said, eyeing Penny's selection.

"You bet. We just got to town; I'm buying the booze while my husband buys the food," she said, looking him straight in the eye. She'd been prepared for this.

The clerk smiled.

"Well, enjoy it," he said. She paid and left, her steps just a little lighter with the lie. She loved the idea of a husband buying food somewhere. It was so collective, so rational.

Penny crossed the street back to Holiday House, lugging her purchases. Her phone beeped as she made it to the hotel's main door.

If I call, will you pick up?

Andrew.
She hadn't responded to his last five text messages.
I just need a few days to think, she typed back.
I'll be here whenever you're ready, he responded seconds later.

The kindness felt like staring into the sun. She didn't know how to hold it inside her.

Upstairs in her room, Penny lined up the liquor and snacks. She could be regimented here, rationed again, safe from the eyes of her siblings. This was where Penny went when the world became too much to handle. She felt something akin to relief as she took a sip from one of the mini vodka bottles. The burn felt like running into a friend in town, familiar and surprising at the same time.

~

What Penny didn't expect was to see Lucy Breen at the pool. She was there with her husband, Tim, and Penny saw Lucy before Lucy saw Penny, but it was still too late to dart out of view.

"Penny Nolan, is that you?" Lucy said from her pool chair. She was in a white bikini, her skin flawlessly tanned. Next to the chair were a fashionable tote and leather sandals. She also wore an oversize hat. Penny felt like Tinker Bell, not in a good way.

"It is I, Penny Nolan," Penny said in the bravest voice possible. There was a chair open next to Lucy, and Penny wanted to die at the idea of taking it.

No such luck. Lucy patted the empty seat. "As I live and breathe. Sit! Here!" she said with too much excitement.

Why was Lucy being so nice? Lucy had been at that bachelorette party in Vegas. Penny had left Las Vegas disgraced and never talked to any of them again. That had been five years ago. She'd skipped weddings, baby showers, group chats. The shame was too much to bear.

Lucy motioned to the seat again and Penny realized she'd just been standing there without saying anything. The pit in her stomach had grown into a bowling ball. She put her bag down on the chair.

"Let me go find a towel," she said.

"Hurry back. I can't wait to tell everyone we ran into each other," Lucy said, still too excited. Her husband was either playing dead or napping. Lucy noticed Penny noticing him. "Tim has been working nonstop on this deal that just closed. The poor guy needed a rescue mission for some rest."

Penny grabbed two towels from the station and set up her chair, utterly unsure about how she would survive this day. Lucy Breen was not part of the plan. Speaking to other humans wasn't part of the plan: Penny was here for solitude. To go through her rations and try to find the part of herself that knew how to function in this world. It was all too much.

"So," Lucy said before Penny had even lain down, "tell me everything. Where are you now?"

"We're in Stowe, figuring out what to do with the hill," Penny said.

"We?" Lucy said, the excitement creeping back into her voice.

"Just Laurie and Chris. And then Halsey and William. My dad died last year, so the land is ours now, and my grandfather wrote this ridiculous trust where all of us have to be in perfect agreement. You can imagine how that's going," Penny said.

Lucy rolled her eyes in commiseration. Penny's hands were sweaty enough that she kept checking the towel for wet marks. She reached quietly into her bag and thumbed around until she felt the pill bottle, expertly unlocking the cap with two carefully positioned fingers. She shuffled two pills—they were blue and they were Xanax—into her palm and carefully and in one motion put her palm to her mouth and chewed the pills in a quiet grinding motion that really just looked like she was listening to Lucy, who was about to finish her statement about Connecticut in the winter and ask her a question.

Penny loved the bitter, metallic flavor of chewed-up pills. It lingered on her tongue and behind her teeth, and she could swear that flavor made the pills do their job faster. She waited for that telltale sign that her bloodstream was about to slow down, her heart finding its way into its cavity for a stress-free nap. The backs of her eyes, normally filled to bursting with pressure, slowly relaxed, and right before the world got fuzzy, she could see it perfectly.

"So where did you go?" Lucy asked, five seconds before Penny was ready.

"I'm sorry, what? What do you mean?" Penny tried to ask casually. Would Lucy notice that her shoulders were starting to slump into their Xanax position?

"No one has seen you since 2015. Since Vegas. I know the girls will die when I tell them I ran into you."

Penny had known this question was coming; she had known it as soon as she saw Lucy Breen lying on a pool chair. And yet. She would have done anything for Lucy not to ask that question. What would she say? That she'd left Vegas a changed person? Forever ashamed and forever scared of her past? That she was like a tumbleweed up and down the East Coast, constantly moving but unable to feel control in motion?

"I got so busy with work," Penny said. There was a woman walking by each chair and taking drink orders.

Lucy's brows lifted behind her sunglasses. "I guess that's exciting. What are you doing now?" she asked, playing along with Penny's lie.

"I'm actually in advertising now," Penny said without missing a beat. "I'm at Chiat\Day in their food-and-beverages division."

"That's amazing! Have you done any ads I'd recognize?" Lucy sat up and leaned a little forward as she asked this.

"You know that food-delivery service Blue Apron?" Penny asked.

Lucy nodded. "Of course—Tim and I had it for a little while."

"I created the apron part of the brand. I do the visual graphics behind the copy." The lies poured out of Penny, fueled by the Xanax variety of lowered inhibitions. She had no idea about Blue Apron, not their ad spend and certainly not the connection between who would have ever drawn that little blue apron by the words. But Lucy wanted an answer—any answer—and Penny knew without knowing why that the truth, that Penny was a shell of her former shelf, stuck between hating who she was and afraid of who she could be, was absolutely not the answer to give.

"That's just awesome, Pen," Lucy said, shaking her head for effect. She waved her hand to the female server. "Hey, excuse me! Could we order some drinks?" she said, louder than necessary.

The woman approached.

"I'll do a glass of the rosé," Lucy said before turning to Penny.

Penny quickly scanned the menu, debating how exactly to deviate from her rations.

"Rosé works," she said.

"Should we just do a bottle, then?" Lucy asked. The server nodded, and Penny found herself nodding too. "Can you also get an IPA for that one?" Lucy said, motioning toward a still-sleeping Tim. Penny braced herself for when he finally woke up.

~

Two hours and two bottles of rosé later, Tim was awake, and Lucy and Penny were trading college stories. Penny had eaten two more Xanax to take the remaining edge off. She could do this, hanging out with college friends! She felt bold. She felt a little like Gumby. Her mouth was dry, but that could also be because her tongue wouldn't stop licking her teeth.

"The girls are just going to die that we're here," Lucy said. Her voice sounded a little farther away than it had a few minutes ago, and Penny stared at her mouth, in case she was still speaking without any sound coming out. Lucy laid her head down, face up toward the sun, and Penny did the same, the world spinning ever so slightly around her.

"How did I get here?" Penny said to the sky.

"You probably flew," Lucy said and then laughed. Penny hadn't meant to ask the question out loud. She hated the part of drunkenness when she got overtly self-reflective. It was way too dangerous.

Penny rolled over to her side and faced Lucy. Tim had gone swimming, and she watched him glide through the water, his arms effortlessly crawling from one end to the other. He was not a guy who thought much about his movements. He was not someone who understood what it meant to try to take up less space.

"I need a nap," Penny said a little too abruptly. She climbed up to a standing position and shuffled her feet to where her sandals were.

"Nap here," Lucy said. Was her voice farther away, or was she speaking softer?

"I need a bed," Penny said. "I'll call you later." She said this with zero intention of calling Lucy later. She had zero intention of getting out of bed.

Lucy waved from where she lay without moving her head.

"It was so good to see you; I just can't wait to tell everyone that I, Lucy Breen, was the one to rediscover Penny Nolan. Like finding an endangered species in the wild." Lucy said all this to no one in particular, her words falling one into the next.

Penny walked carefully up to her room, counting the steps to stay balanced. The room was cold, perfectly air-conditioned, so Penny could get under the blankets. As she got into bed, she remembered her rations, the rations that were supposed to structure this trip. The rations were what allowed Penny to get her head on straight.

She got out of bed and walked to the kitchen. The rations were evenly divided, and she took the portion intended for today. She lined up the mini bottles and walked down the hall with the ice bucket. The rations were how she was going to climb out of this.

Much later that night, when the rations were finally finished and she had been reduced to a crawl across the floor, Penny got into bed, laid her head on the pillow, and fell into a very deep sleep.

CHAPTER

THIRTY-FOUR

If you had told Laurie that one day she would be sitting in the parking lot of her late father's late lawyer's son's law office, hoping very much for a job but scrolling through Facebook while she waited, only to scroll past a picture of what could only be described as an extremely drunk Penny in Palm Springs with two people Laurie was sure Penny hadn't spoken to in at least five years, she would have reminded you that she was a proud member of the partnership at Howell, Columbus, Plymouth & Rodgerton. But there she was, doing exactly that, caught between mortification and pride in her resourcefulness.

Trevor had seemed a little surprised to hear from Laurie when she'd called two days earlier.

"I'd love to meet with you one-on-one," she said, her hand shaking slightly as she held the phone.

"If this is about the land, you know I'm representing you as a group—" Trevor said, his voice uncertain.

"It's not about the property," Laurie cut him off. "It's about me, specifically. As an individual. Just me!" She ended on too high of a note. She could hear Trevor shift in his seat. He let out a little cough. Was it a good cough, a "you caught me by surprise but all good" cough? Or was it a "you caught me by surprise and I'm going to have to call your brother because he's my boy" cough?

"Cool," he said.

Cool? She rolled her eyes. He really was a boy.

"Okay . . ." She didn't know what else to say.

"Why don't you come by around one on Tuesday? I've got a meeting out of the office at eleven, but I'll be back by then. We can discuss whatever you've got going on," he said. Laurie immediately exhaled.

~

Two days later, and here she was at 12:45, watching the clock in the car, watching the clock on her phone, and scrolling through apps.

The photo looked innocuous at first. Penny was in a bikini Laurie hadn't seen before, and she was lying on a chaise by a pool. It was clearly a hotel pool, with the matching towels and umbrellas in the background. She had sunglasses on, and she was smiling, but as Laurie peered closer, she saw the smile was slightly crooked, the smile Penny gave when she was down several drinks. It was just Penny in the picture, but the detritus around her suggested she wasn't alone. Plus, Penny was not giving the crooked smile of a drunk person who had asked someone to take their picture.

Laurie looked at the caption. *Can't believe I ran into this one in PS! Such a fun surprise @PennyLaneLikeTheSong #PalmSpringsGetaway #LoveyaTim #Sooooohot* Posted by @LucyInTheSky

What were the chances of two people with Beatles nods in their social media handles, Laurie thought, clicking on Lucy's profile to see if there were more pictures from the day.

Laurie knew Lucy. She was one of Penny's best friends from college, though Penny had stopped talking to her entire group of girls after a bachelorette weekend six years earlier. Penny had never said why; she'd never even said they weren't friends anymore. But Laurie remembered the shift from Penny having friends to Penny not having friends, and that no one in the family was supposed to talk about it.

She took a screenshot and sent it to Chris.

I guess Penny is in Palm Springs?

He typed back immediately.

She's not with you in Stowe?

Chris had gone back to New York for the two weeks in January after the holidays. He would get organized, which meant time away from the people who drove him the craziest, before they all reconvened for Decision Day. Neither Chris nor Penny had any idea she'd been fired, and the silver lining of having one sibling who hadn't worked in an office before and another who worked for himself was that no one was curious as to why Laurie was able to simply exist in Vermont while being a partner at a law firm.

Laurie felt like an idiot telling her brother that Penny had left abruptly five days before and she hadn't bothered to track down where her younger, volatile, highly emotional sister was going. Was it horrible to say she was exhausted by it? The spectacle of Penny? She needed a job, for Christ's sake, not a needy sibling.

I thought she was going back to the city or something, Laurie typed spinelessly.

～

Trevor drove into the parking lot, gravel crunching under his car and snapping Laurie up from her phone. He drove a Volvo station wagon, a car that screamed middle age or at least father of two girls. Trevor was neither. He waved from the driver's window. Was he wearing a driving glove? Laurie waved back and dropped her phone into her purse and got out.

"Howdy," she said, immediately mortified. Howdy?

"Howdy," Trevor said back. He smirked but accidentally opened his mouth, making it a proper smile and showing Laurie that he had even less cool than she did. "Let's go inside," he said.

They sat in the same conference room Laurie and her family filed into every few months. Trevor sat across the table from her.

"What can I do for you?" he asked. He had a pad of paper and pen at the ready.

"Well, as you know, we're still sorting through Shaw Hill, but I'm also trying to figure out my place here," Laurie said. Trevor nodded along. "And what I might do, you know, to fill my time."

What she didn't say: *I was fired two months ago. Nobody knows. I'm out of money. I need help.*

"Are you thinking of moving up here permanently?" Trevor said. Were his eyes brightening at the prospect of her moving up here?

"I'm not sure," she said, meaning it. "But I'm also not sure I want to go back to New York." She crossed her arms and leaned back in the swivel chair.

"The pace up here beats New York; I can promise you that!" Trevor said. "I went to NYU Law School, you know." She didn't know. She envisioned Trevor navigating Greenwich Village in his docksiders and it made her smile.

"I guess, then, it's a matter of what to do up here?" she asked. She was beating around the bush; she knew this, but she could not muster the strength to say, *I need a job; can you give me one.*

"Oh, for someone like you? Anything you want," Trevor said emphatically. He even hit his fist lightly on the table for effect.

"Any suggestions?"

Trevor looked around and bit his lip.

"Maybe something in Burlington? Or even Morrisville? Whatever it is, you'll do great," he said, nodding along as he spoke.

Laurie looked across the table at Trevor and decided: this man was a loser. He wasn't; Laurie shook away the thought. She was the loser.

The rest of the meeting was a blur. Laurie got up too abruptly, and then Trevor tried to save face by sticking out his hand, but Laurie thought it would be more personal to go in for a hug, and instead their bodies crashed together in such a way that it was clear both of them wanted to die. Laurie almost stumbled to the car, her feet not going nearly as quickly as she needed them to. Trevor awkwardly watched her walk, but as if he didn't want her to know, he stayed behind the closed office door, which then made him look like he was spying. By the time Laurie was safe inside her vehicle, the heat at full blast, Cool 102.7 playing a song that was far from cool, she felt like she'd aged five years.

She looked at her phone and saw ten missed calls and as many text messages from Chris.

He answered before the first ring even finished.

"We need to go to Palm Springs. I booked my ticket. You book yours. It's already two; I leave at five. Book whatever you can and we'll meet there."

"Slow down," Laurie said, holding up her hand in the car. "What are you talking about?"

"It's Penny. I called Lucy and they're at this Holiday House hotel, and Lucy and Tim are there, and they saw Penny at the pool, and that's where the photo is from," Chris said. He was talking so fast, his mouth couldn't keep up. "Penny left and said she was going to get something from her room and that she'd call Lucy later, but Lucy never heard from her. That was, like, three days ago."

"You called Lucy?" Laurie asked, feeling stupid immediately after. Who cared if he'd called Lucy?

"We were sort of friends," Chris said, way kindlier than Laurie deserved. "When I saw her post, I called without really thinking about it."

"Did Lucy ask the hotel to check on her?" Laurie asked, her own blood pressure rising.

"I don't . . . I don't think so. I mean, it's Lucy. Remember Lucy? She slept with my friend Jimmy in the hot tub and Dad made me drain it after." Laurie laughed at the memory. "Anyway. I called the hotel. She's booked through Friday, but she's had the 'do not disturb' up on her door the whole time, so no one has been in. But when someone knocks on the door to check on her, she answers and tells them to go away, so we know she's alive in there."

Laurie nodded.

"Hello?" Chris said.

"Sorry, I was nodding and forgot you couldn't see that. Okay. I'll book now. I might be able to get there tonight, but probably tomorrow."

"Just text me your flight info. I'm guessing you fly tomorrow morning. I can pick you up, and then we'll go find her."

They hung up and Laurie felt her stomach fall through the seat. This was what they were scared of with Penny, that sweet, fragile Penny would go too far one day, to a place they couldn't reach her. They were harder, better at either absorbing the pain of the world or blocking it out entirely. Laurie didn't know which was better, because at least Penny felt stuff. She and Chris went through the motions, seemingly waiting for something else to come along.

~

Two stops, $2,000 she didn't have, and a four a.m. wake-up later, Laurie was on her way to Palm Springs. Chris had kept his word and picked her up at the airport, his car like the poster child of a Hertz economy vehicle.

"Where'd you stay last night?" she asked him, getting in the car.

"The Parker."

"When Penny is at Holiday House?"

Chris shrugged. "I didn't know the etiquette of running into someone you're in the process of rescuing."

Laurie considered it. He made a good point.

"But you called the hotel to make sure she still has a pulse?" Laurie confirmed.

"That I did."

~

They drove the rest of the way in silence, punctuated only by one of them pointing out something obvious. Palm trees. A line outside a popular brunch spot. The thermometer reading seventy-five degrees. "How hot do you think this place gets in August?" they asked each other at the same time.

Palm Springs is many things at once. It's a gay mecca and a midcentury architecture fantasy and also a bit of a meth depot and a giant desert wasteland of forgotten dreams and forgotten people. You can come to Palm Springs with one dollar or a million and fit right in. Laurie looked at her brother driving. His golf shirt tucked into khaki shorts. Lace-up navy Vans with barely there socks. A hat from Maidstone. She looked down at herself in an equally preppy outfit. She looked up as they passed a pristine golf course. Even the WASPs had a place here.

~

Chris drove up to the front of Holiday House and parked in a valet spot.

"Are you sure?" Laurie asked, looking around for an attendant.

"Don't we have a sister to save?" he said, kidding but also serious.

The front desk was already expecting them. Chris had called earlier, confirming Laurie's arrival, saying they'd be there by one, and if Penny surfaced before then, to please call him.

"Any word from her?" Chris asked.

"No, sir," a woman wearing a name tag with "Henri" on it said.

"Thanks, Henri," Chris said. "What room is she in?"

Laurie wasn't used to her brother being so observant. Or assertive. Or *nice*.

"Room 202. Housekeeping is nearby if you need anything," Henri said.

The siblings headed upstairs, equally nervous about what they would find. Penny had done things like this before: she would push everything down until it was too much and then combust. Before, their parents had largely handled it. Their mom especially would track down Penny and bring her home, often wrapped in a blanket. When their mom died, their dad picked her up once from a hospital in New York City. And now it was their turn, Laurie thought, following her brother up the stairs.

"Pen," Chris said, knocking on the door, "it's C and Laur; we're here." He looked at Laurie and gestured she should knock too.

"Penny, it's us; let us in," Laurie said, knocking a little softer than Chris.

Inside, the room was silent.

"Seriously, Pen, open up," Chris said, louder in both voice and knock. Laurie followed suit.

Still nothing.

"What do we do?" Laurie asked her brother.

"Keep trying," he muttered. His hand never stopped knocking.

"But what if she doesn't answer?"

Chris turned his head to face her.

"We stand here, and we knock, and we call until she lets us in. End of story. This is what family does."

His knocking took on a new ferocity, and Laurie blinked back tears watching her brother fight for her sister with an energy he hadn't shown in years. He desperately wanted Penny to be okay. And she did too, she realized, knocking now alongside him with just as much verve.

"Penny!" she shouted. "We love you!" Her voice cracked but she didn't care.

Finally, they heard rustling inside. A few steps. Perhaps a bathroom door closing. And then the steps got closer to the door.

"What do you guys want?" Penny asked faintly.

"Just want to see you, is all," Chris said. His forehead was resting lightly against the door. Laurie found herself gently stroking his back. He didn't shake her off.

"It's not a good time, guys," Penny said.

Laurie clenched her jaw and swallowed.

"Is it ever a good time?" she asked. She saw Chris was crying a little too. "What if we just come inside for a few minutes? Talk a little, then we can be on our way and leave you to it. Leave you to your vacation," Laurie said.

They heard the metal clang of the chain lock move to the side. The doorknob fidgeted and there was Penny, in a baggy T-shirt and wild hair. Her face pasty and blotchy.

"Hey," she said, turning around and leading them inside.

"Hey," they both said back.

The room wasn't as destroyed as Laurie feared, seeing a modest heap of clothing by the bed, but otherwise, that was it. And then she saw the empty liquor bottles on the table by the kitchenette and a few empty bags of chips. She imagined her sister coming in here, drinking the bottles one by one, methodically eating the chips, then getting into bed and not getting out for several days. The room smelled a little dank. Their mother would have said it smelled *fresh*.

The siblings sat on a built-in bench around the table, next to a window that overlooked the pool. Laurie wondered if Lucy and her husband were still here or if they were back to their regular lives, blind to all the pain Penny housed inside her. None of those girls ever called her again after that trip, Laurie realized. They thought Penny was too much. Not that she was in pain. Laurie shuddered at the realization that she was the same way. For years, she'd felt like Penny was too much, never focusing on the pain bubbling at her sister's surface.

"Thanks for letting us in, sis," Chris said. He was clearly nervous. Laurie was nervous too.

"Thanks for coming, I guess?" Penny said, smiling a little bit. Her skin looked sallow. Her hair was stringier than it needed to be.

"You could have put out a cheese plate," Laurie said stiffly. Chris and Penny both looked at her like she was deeply confused, until they realized she was joking, and Penny's laughter filled the room. It was the most beautiful sound she'd ever heard.

"I'm so sorry. For my next mental breakdown, I will be sure to plan ahead and provide snacks."

Laurie reached out and took her sister's hand, squeezed it, then squeezed it again.

"We love you so much, Pen. Whatever it is, we'll get through it together," Laurie said. Chris nodded furtively. She was positive the two of them had never gotten along so well before. Was this what healthy sibling relationships were like?

"Thanks," Penny whispered. Chris reached over and squeezed her shoulder. Penny started to cry softly, looking down at her lap. After a few moments, she leaned back on the bench. Chris and Laurie looked at her, both unsure of what to say next.

"What is it, Pen?" Laurie said after a while, her voice kind and worried. She didn't know how Penny was going to answer. She saw Penny was digging her fingers into themselves.

Penny shrugged. It was like she swallowed her words back down into her stomach.

"Was it running into Lucy?" Chris ventured.

Penny slowly shook her head. "Lucy was just a tree that fell onto a house during the storm."

"But the storm was already raging?" Laurie confirmed.

"I don't know where I fit, you know?" Penny said.

Chris let out a sigh that said he understood exactly what she was saying. Laurie sighed too, at first for show and then: her siblings still didn't know she was unemployed. She had nowhere to fit either.

"Should we get you something to eat?" Laurie said. "Room service or something?"

"I could eat," Chris said.

Penny looked at them blankly. "You really haven't done this before, have you?"

"What's that supposed to mean?" Chris asked, but he smiled while he asked it.

"Typically, we don't take a break in the middle of an intervention for a hot meal."

"And I'm asking you, Penny Nolan, why we don't?" Laurie asked in the best faux-reporter voice she could muster. All three Nolans laughed.

"Fine. For the purposes of this rescue, we can order room service," Penny said. Laurie got up to find the menu. "And you may order me a burger."

"I knew you were hungry," Laurie said. That was the thing about siblings: you can ebb in and out of emotion without leaving anyone behind. Laurie and Chris had flown all night to find Penny, and Penny knew that. She knew they were here to save her, and thus she was saved.

The food arrived on a wheeling cart from a service attendant who was clearly aware of the drama that had been Room 202. He gave Laurie a knowing look that said, *Are you sure everything is okay here?* And she returned his look with a look that said, *Maybe? For now? I'll call you if anything changes?* And Chris intervened with his own look that said, *I got this. I, Chris Nolan, am the man of this family.* Penny was the only person to audibly thank the attendant, receive the food, and sign the bill.

Laurie watched Penny come alive over the course of eating her burger. It was like the nutrients helped fill in the pockets under her eyes. Chris had opened the blinds, and after they finished eating, they went to sit on the porch overlooking the pool. Part of Laurie wanted to see Lucy and that husband of hers lying around, and the other part knew she did not need to cause a spectacle when she punched her in the face.

"Do you ever run out of room in your brain for more thoughts?" Penny asked, breaking a brief spell of silence. Laurie and Chris both considered the question.

"Sometimes I feel like the part of my brain that actually knows what to do is locked so far away, I'll never see it again," Laurie said. "Most of the time, I'm just trying to figure out what to do in the very next moment, but sometimes the moments don't string together, and I'm stuck feeling like I got lost in this maze other people knew just to walk around in." Penny nodded as Laurie spoke. Chris too was listening. She was finally telling them what had been going on all these years. That was Paul, wasn't it? A horribly wrong turn in a maze other people would have known to walk around in.

"Is that how it is for you?" Laurie asked her sister. Penny took in a deep breath. She was still twisting her fingers into each other.

"It's like I'm running, right? And there's a stick in the middle of the road. But I see a snake. And suddenly I realize I've gone running without my phone, and the snake has bitten me, and there's no way to call for help or even flag someone down, because the road is deserted except for this snake and me. And then when someone finally does come, an old woman walking her dog let's say, she turns to me and says, 'It's only a stick,' and all I can say is, 'But it could have been a snake.' The fear doesn't go away just because someone tells you it isn't real. Anxiety isn't a balloon you can pop. Anxiety is the air around the balloon."

Penny started to cry, and Laurie felt her own face get wet.

"I think I'm ready to try and stop feeling like this anymore," Penny said bravely.

"Let's go home," Laurie said. She looked over at Chris, and his eyes were shining.

Without saying anything, the siblings surrounded Penny and held her. Then they were holding each other, these three broken musketeers, holding on for dear life, hoping it wasn't too late to find their way.

CHAPTER THIRTY-FIVE

The birthday party was set to begin at two, and Miles was still deciding between the blue-checkered tie and the purple-checkered one. No matter that the tie was matched with a white T-shirt and khaki pants, with a red sweater to go over the white T-shirt and whichever-color-checkered tie.

"Miles, blue or purple, does it really matter?" Halsey asked, feeling guilty for asking but justified because it had been almost an hour since he first started this debate.

Miles stood at the mirror, holding one tie after the other under his chin.

"It matters, Mommy," he said, trading the purple for the blue. What did Chad do in these moments? The poor guy was color-blind and allergic to clothes that actually fit, and somehow their son was a preppy fashionista. Halsey counted to five.

"Well, I think this party is going to be fun. India's mom said she was bringing a special pizza chef to show everyone how to make their own personal pizzas and a—" Miles was now walking from one side of the room to the other. "What are you doing, buddy?"

"Seeing if one of them gives me more pep in my step."

"Pep in my step"? When did Miles start saying "pep in my step"? Okay, she was good with this. She'd read and listened and talked and prepared for this. She was going to crush this.

"And what do you think? Does one give you more pep?"

Miles stopped in the middle of the room. He closed his eyes and raised his arms up to the ceiling, like he was about to cheer or pray. Halsey waited, not breathing.

"We're going with purple."

"Purple! I love purple!" she said, genuinely unsure why she was so excited by the choice. Miles was pleased enough to formally apply the clip of the tie onto his T-shirt. He looked adorable.

"Mommy," Miles said, still staring in the mirror.

Halsey was scared to say yes. She met his eyes instead and raised her eyebrows.

"Now that we've gone with purple, we need a different sweater. Red won't do," Miles said.

"That's a very fair point," Halsey said, biting her lip to think of the fastest solve here. It was clear Miles would have better fashion sense than her within the year. "How about gray? Gray goes great with purple and white."

Miles looked at her seriously through the mirror. Halsey took a step toward his dresser, where the gray crew-neck sweater was folded.

"You might say, gray is the way?" Miles asked, his eyes lighting up every time he made a play on words.

"Gray is one hundred percent the way," Halsey said, laughing and handing the sweater to her son. Miles put his arms over his head for Halsey to scoot the sweater on. They both stood looking at him in the mirror.

"Should we hit it?" she said, guiding him out to the hall and down the stairs, grabbing her keys when they reached the front door.

"I like it better when there're two here, Mommy," Miles said, walking outside.

"Do you miss your dad, sweetie?" Halsey asked.

"I see Dad all the time. And he made me a room just like this one, so really, I have *two* bedrooms," Miles said. They both got in the car. Miles buckled himself into his seat in the back.

"What do you mean 'when there're two'?" Halsey asked.

"For you, Mommy. You're happier when there're two. Two adults," Miles said. She opened her mouth to ask more, but she could tell by how he was looking out the window that this conversation was over.

~

They pulled into a driveway fifteen minutes later. Miles's friend India lived just outside the town, on the other side of Route 108. She knew Jeremy would have been invited, which meant either Heather or Jeremy's dad would be here with him. Halsey prayed to all gods in the heavens that it would be Jeremy's dad. She wasn't ready to face Heather. She wasn't even ready to be on the same acre as Heather. She could barely stand knowing that Heather lived down the hill. They hadn't spoken since the ice hockey game three weeks earlier, and despite Halsey waking up every night in a sweat, her arm reaching for a body that wasn't there, she couldn't bring herself to call her.

"Jeremy is here!" Miles yelled from the back seat. Halsey followed his gaze. Shit. Heather's car. Heather's adorable, sunny, charismatic car. Even in the middle of winter, Heather's car looked like it was ready for a day at Lake Champlain. Halsey felt a bowling ball plunge down her throat into her stomach.

Halsey looked at her son as he wiggled himself free of the booster seat.

"Hey, kid," she said. He looked at her. "You look great. Plenty of pep in that step."

"Mommy, pep is private," Miles said, somehow rolling his eyes and getting out of the car and running into the party all at once.

She did not know what she'd done to deserve that child.

~

Nearly all birthday parties were the same, regardless of age, gender, and budget, Halsey thought, helping herself to a spritzer while she scanned the open-floor-plan living/dining/kitchen/extra room for familiar faces. Correction. All the faces were familiar. She was looking for faces that were not the single face she wanted to see more than any other face in the world. Chad was lingering by the sandwich station. She could see a chef complete with a little hat in the kitchen organizing large bowls of pizza ingredients.

"Hello," Halsey said as he lifted his gaze from a healthy amount of various meats between two slices of bread. "I didn't know you'd be here too."

"Hey, hey," Chad said, kissing her on the cheek. "Ashley told Miles we would go. She didn't realize it was your weekend, or she was just trying to be nice, or something. But yeah, we're here. I didn't realize the ratio of kids to adults would be so . . ." Chad gestured around the open-floor-plan living/dining/kitchen/extra room. "Slim." Halsey followed his gaze. He was right. For every adult, there were at least four kids. At what age were they allowed to just start dropping their kids off and wishing the party host a little luck?

"Where's Ashley?" Halsey asked, looking around.

"I think this is her first birthday party for kids?" Chad said and gestured with his shoulder toward a baby-fenced-off area filled to the brim with toys. Halsey looked instinctively for a toddler but saw only Ashley, inexplicably jumping up and down with no one in particular, a cross between a Playboy Bunny and Little Bo Peep. Halsey didn't mean to laugh, but one came out loud and hard. Chad first looked alarmed, his eyebrows all the way up to the sky, but then he laughed too, and soon they were doubled over, watching Ashley bopping around. Halsey couldn't decide if it would have been better if Ashley had been hopping around small children or if that would have been too dangerous to laugh at.

Suddenly Chad was waving. Halsey assumed he was waving Ashley over, and she straightened her hair and her top and did a little shrug into her black jeans. She took a sip of her spritzer and let out a breath and turned around—

"Ashley, hi!" she said before looking up, only to be met with Heather, who was embracing Chad and holding a plate of crudités. "Heather," she said unintentionally.

"Sorry, you two," Heather said once Chad released her. "Just dropping off this plate for the hosts!"

"Hey," Halsey said, almost reaching for Heather's arm. Heather finished putting down the plate and smoothly turned around in the direction away from Halsey.

"Hey, how are you," Heather said in one breath, not looking at her and not stopping to talk. She had her arm up and was waving to a group of women standing by a table set up as a bar. "Hilary!"

"That was weird," Chad said. He dug his hands into his pockets and leaned against the sandwich table.

"What was weird?" Halsey said, trying to sound nonchalant.

"Heather is usually so chatty. Especially with you," he said.

"I guess I've never noticed," Halsey said. She swirled the ice around in her glass. "Should we get more drinks? I'd love a Diet Coke." She started walking toward the table-bar.

"I'm surprised you didn't notice, actually," Chad said, following her.

"What do you mean by that?" Halsey asked.

"Just you two. I don't know. It seemed like you were becoming pretty good friends. Miles talks about Jeremy all the time. And he mentioned that Jeremy and his mom came over a lot. Even for sleepovers?"

Chad ended the question with an especially high-pitched inflection. Suggestive, even.

"Oh," Halsey said, collecting her words. "Yeah, they've been over a few times. Once we had some wine while the kids watched a movie, so everyone spent the night. Driving and all that." She was working so hard to sound breezy.

"Yeah, sure, well, maybe some people just aren't as warm when you really get to know them," Chad said, already moving on from the topic. Halsey bit her lip to stop from crying. She bit the insides of her cheeks as well. She clenched her jaw. She even put her glass down on an abandoned chair so she could wring her hands together. None of it worked, and she could feel the tears prick behind her eyes. If he only knew that Heather was the warmest, most generous person she'd ever met.

"Do you mind taking Miles home?" she asked Chad, fishing around her bag for her keys. "I realized I could use the afternoon to get some stuff done. And we both don't really need to be here," she said, begging her eyes to stay dry until she could at least get to the car. Chad cocked his head and squinted, clearly surprised.

"I guess so? Sure," he said.

"Thanks. So much," she said, walking away before Chad decided to ask what had just happened.

~

Halsey drove back up the hill a little distractedly, so much so that she clipped the turn into the driveway a little too close and may have nudged the other house's mailbox a little hard, sending it straight back into the ground.

"Good lord, can I catch a break?" she muttered, parking the car and getting out to assess the damage to the mailbox. The wood was splintered and nearly split in the middle. She turned around to the car and saw she'd dented the bumper. "Shit."

She looked behind her to see if there were people riding horses by the barn. Could she pretend it was someone else? Teens out with a baseball bat? Even in her desperation, she knew this was ridiculous. Why on earth would teens pile into a car and head up a dead-end dirt road? Could she blame the mailman? A delivery driver?

It wasn't until she was almost back in the car that she thought she should actually check the contents of the mailbox. That's what she would do. She would check the mailbox, take the mail, and then deliver the mail to her cousins, apologizing for being the messenger, but it seemed like a car had swerved, taking their mailbox down. It didn't matter what car. Just that it was not Halsey's car.

The mailbox was full to bursting, clearly forgotten about. It made sense; none of her cousins had ever used this house as their primary residence. Nothing of value would be sent here. She pulled out the envelopes, crumpled in with each other to cram as much as possible inside, and slowly started sorting them between junk and real. Nearly all were junk—did people get mail anymore?—except one, a large manila envelope addressed to Laurie. The return address said it was her firm. The front of the envelope said CONFIDENTIAL.

How much did a partner at a law firm make anyway? Halsey had some assumptions, but how much was Laurie putting away each year while pretending she was just like the rest of them? At least Chris was up front with his salary, $750,000 base with a guaranteed $350,000 bonus, thank you very much. Penny, she knew, was a tick above minimum wage. William was influencer gig by influencer gig. She knew she was nothing. The only mystery was Laurie.

But it was a felony to open mail. Was it a felony if it was within the family?

Her phone chimed from the console.

A text from Chris on the family chain.

Just heard from Trevor. We have two weeks and then it's decide or bust.

William responded in seconds.

Cous's! I'll be back in a few days and we can figure this one outttt. One love. One family.

Laurie responded next.

Thank you, William, for always being there and helping us navigate these waters.

Halsey laughed and typed out: At the very least, how about a New Year New You dinner party at my house?
Did you mean our house? William sent.
Only if you start helping me pay for the heat, she sent.
We're there, no question. Penny will bring the sparkling cider, Chris sent.
And Chris will bring Mom and Dad's old fondue set, Laurie sent.
Halsey put the phone down and stared back at the envelope addressed to Laurie. Now was her chance.
Laurie was pushing to sell, but Halsey thought she was just being selfish. Not paying enough homage to the family or history or even this hill. It wasn't fair that her selfishness was keeping them all from staying intact.
With a vigor that comes only with justification that is equal parts asinine and passionate, Halsey opened the envelope. Maybe it was a pay stub. Maybe it was her W-2. Maybe it was her contract-renewal notice. It could be anything, and Halsey's hands shook slightly as she unfolded the piece of paper. Her gasps couldn't keep up with her eyes.

Dear Ms. Nolan,

Further to your correspondence with Lucinda Moorehead and duly cosigned by Managing Partner Liam Parsons, Howell, Columbus, Plymouth & Rodgerton has denied your claim for a severance package. As detailed in the letter dated November 22, 2021, your employment with Howell, Columbus, Plymouth & Rodgerton was terminated with cause, consequently excluding you from severance eligibility.

Halsey read the rest of the letter in spurts, not totally absorbing anything beyond: Laurie had been fired. She was not a partner at a law firm at all. She was unemployed. And she was not telling anyone the truth. That was why she was here, suddenly around and available. Halsey had assumed it was some sort of leave. But no. Laurie was a liar. And she was threatening to expose Halsey and Heather. For what? Halsey slammed the driver's door and put the car into gear.

Laurie was a liar. And she was a blackmailer. And she was forcing them to sell the property because she didn't want to admit that her own life had fallen apart. Yes, three of the five needed to figure out a better long-term plan for life, but Laurie's lie could be the difference between losing the property or keeping it.

Halsey sped up the hill, gunning the gas and eyeing Laurie's car parked by the back door. Without consciously deciding to, she was driving around the tree in the middle of the driveway, speeding up and ramming into Laurie's bumper. She backed up and drove into it again just as Chris and Penny ran outside.

"What are you doing?" Chris shouted, waving his hands as if Halsey couldn't see Laurie's car. *"Stop!"*

Halsey put her car into reverse. She could hear metal grating on the ground. Chris looked at her with a mix of bewilderment and anger.

"What on earth?" he asked, slightly calmer but also panting.

Halsey rolled her window down. "Ask your sister."

She reversed all the way to her house, not bothering to line her car up against the snowbank like she normally did. She would have forgotten to turn the car off at all if it hadn't started beeping at her when she tried to get out.

Chris and Penny were still in the driveway, talking among themselves, wondering whether they should go over to Halsey. She didn't pay them any attention. She walked inside and locked the door, drawing the blinds in the living room and the entryway. Laurie had all but threatened her and Heather, and Halsey had fallen for it. She was furious with her cousin, furious with herself for taking Laurie at face value. What else were they all hiding? Her cousins were a bunch of liars.

CHAPTER
THIRTY-SIX

"What on earth was that about?" Chris said. He and Penny stood in the driveway, where moments before, Halsey had rammed her car into Laurie's.

Penny looked at Laurie's car, now desperate for a new bumper, and then looked at the other two black cars sitting beside it. "Why did she only attack Laurie's car?" she asked.

"Why can nothing be simple?" Chris whistled and groaned and looked up at the sky.

Laurie came outside to see what the fuss was about. Chris kept walking halfway to Halsey's house and turning around.

"What's up, guys?" Laurie asked.

Penny used her thumb to gesture to Laurie's car.

"Oh shit," Laurie said, walking around the car to survey the damage.

"Why did Halsey attack your car?" Penny asked her sister.

"I have absolutely no idea," Laurie said evenly, shaking her head from side to side. "Insurance better cover this," she said to herself.

"Don't you care why she did it, though?" Chris asked. He was still heated.

Laurie looked between her siblings before turning around and walking back inside. When she reached the door, she stopped. "It's Halsey—she has a lot going on right now, a lot more to lose than we do. She's probably just freaking out that I won't agree with her that we should definitely keep this place." She continued back inside.

Chris started to walk inside too. Penny kept staring at the car. Something wasn't adding up.

"Don't you think it's weird?" Penny said.

Chris shrugged.

"Why don't you care?" Penny asked.

"Honestly, Pen, we just got you home. I don't know if I have the bandwidth for a battle with Halsey right now." Chris said this so plainly, Penny let him go inside.

~

Without any cousin demanding explanation, there was no New Year New You dinner party. The Nolans and the Ridges retreated, and it wasn't until Penny finally revived the family text chain that they decided it was time to get the band back together. So, in late January, the Nolans and the Ridges were crammed into William's Subaru, headed north on Route 108 toward the base of Mount Mansfield. Penny didn't know who had decided that the cousins should go snowshoeing, but at 10:30 that morning, Chris had told her to suit up in her warmest winter gear and meet outside in five and to please convince Halsey to come. The snowshoeing was supposed to bring resolution about what to do, even though no one could come close to agreeing, and Halsey finally agreed to come after Penny promised her she would keep her and Laurie separated the entire time. Why Halsey had attacked Laurie's car was still a mystery, but Laurie had kept her mouth shut about the entire thing, which said plenty. Penny sat in the back, wedged between Chris and Halsey, her legs bent like twigs on the rise between the back seats.

Halsey was huffing into one window and Laurie was huffing into the passenger window up front. William and Laurie were arguing over what music to play.

"Why can't we just leave it on the Point?" William said, turning the tuning dial to the right.

"Because I'm not my mother, may she rest in peace," Laurie said, turning the tuning dial back to the hip-hop station.

"Your mother was lovely," Halsey said from the back. Penny inwardly groaned.

Laurie turned her head around to the back. "My mother *was* lovely. Not that you knew that, not really." Laurie punched each word she said into the air.

"I think we all knew our mother was lovely," Chris said, putting his hands in the air and moving his eyes frantically at Laurie. "And now we are here, in this car, forced together, in an effort to do something outdoors."

Laurie took the hint and turned back around with a huff.

"I knew your mother was lovely," Penny heard Halsey murmur out the window. Halsey had not been herself for weeks, longer if Penny counted the shadows of insight she'd caught amid her own spiraling. It had been three weeks since her brother and sister found her in Palm Springs and two weeks since she'd started talking to a therapist in earnest. It had been one week since she'd finally called Andrew back and one day since she had made a promise to herself to try and figure out how to save her family's land. Even if they could barely ride in a car together without a fight breaking out, these were her people, and it was time to start fighting for all of them.

~

The rest of the car ride was silent, save for the radio—which William turned back to the Point after taking advantage of an ad break on Cool

102.7—where music and static were wrestling for airtime. By the time William turned the Subaru into the Toll Road parking lot, finding a spot under a span of large pine trees all weighed down with snow, Penny had forgotten what they were even doing there.

~

They hit the trailhead just after noon, a little late for this point in the season. If the weather held up, they had three solid hours of daylight, with another hour and a half in the shadows before twilight really set in. Penny registered she was knee-deep in her second full Vermont winter. Did that make her a Vermonter yet?

The cloud cover was light enough that Penny didn't think it would start snowing. But it was cold, cold enough that saying it was cold didn't quite say the full picture, and Penny wished she'd worn her proper long underwear and not a pair of spandex pants. She made sure the flaps on her hat were down over her ears. Laurie was the only one properly dressed, in light snow pants and an athletically cut parka. She even had a wicking headband squeezed under her hat. When had Laurie figured out activewear for winter sports? Penny looked at her sister gliding as she shoed over the packed trail. She was at once perfectly put together and utterly untouchable, making it all seem more facade-like than anything else. Laurie was a house of cards without the veneer of pulling it off. It made Penny want to hug her and then watch her break from impact.

"Should we talk about stuff?" Chris asked a few minutes into the snowshoe. He walked awkwardly, like the snowshoes might have skis on the bottom and he didn't want to get out of control. It looked like a billy goat trying to wade through a river without getting too wet.

"Now?" Laurie asked.

"Would you rather wait until after the deadline?" Chris shot back.

"I just thought we could enjoy the scenery for a little while," Laurie said.

"In what world is this snowshoe enjoyable?" William said. He was even more uncomfortable than Chris trying to navigate the snow.

Laurie looked wounded. Halsey had still not said a single word since they left the car.

"We could talk about our options?" Penny said, surprised at her own voice.

"Yeah, yeah, that," Chris said, turning around and mouthing *thank you* when the others weren't looking. "We should weigh the pros and cons of each. Pros of keeping the land, pros of selling it."

"The only way we benefit is if we all make the decision together," William said. "As much as I'd love to leave you people in the dust, thanks to Grandpa, I can't do that."

"Basically, if we don't sell it, we have to pay to keep it," Chris said, weighing his words carefully. "Does it make sense? Who here actually has the cash to keep the Compound running?"

Penny knew the answer to this one. Chris and Laurie were the only ones with real jobs, with *careers*. The rest of them had never really launched.

Laurie spoke first. "I don't want to float your lifestyles. With all due respect, none of you ever got off the ground."

Halsey harrumphed behind them, causing Laurie to stop in her tracks and turn around.

"I'm sorry, Halsey, did I get that wrong? Did you find some success you forgot to mention over the past, I don't know, ten or fifteen years?"

Now all five cousins were frozen in place.

Halsey stared at Laurie, her face like a brick wall. "Tell me, Laurie," she said, "are we supposed to be impressed by you?" She let the question linger, and just when it looked like Laurie was about to answer, Halsey started talking again. "I haven't heard much about your fancy career lately." Halsey turned to face the others. "Have any of you? Does Laurie seem consumed by meetings or emails or briefs? Don't you think it's weird that books and television shows and movies and hell, even Trevor

Durkin, posit that being a lawyer is one of the most demanding pro-
fessions in the country, and yet here she is, casually taking a snowshoe
with her family in the middle of the day?" Halsey turned back to Laurie.
"Does that seem weird to you? Or am I just, I don't know, reading into
something that isn't there?"

Laurie's face had paled beyond a ghost. No one said a word.

"Just because you tried to keep it a secret doesn't mean it worked.
We all know about Paul. And I know why you've had such a quiet few
months. He realized he had more power selling you out than sticking
by you, and you got fired because he reported you. And now you're
here, desperate and alone and wondering what you'll ever be able to do
because you've been disgraced by anyone who knew you in New York.
You can't float this land anyway. But you don't want us to know, so you
pretend it's because you're above us. When really, your apartment is long
gone, and you're cobbling together enough to make sure you can pay
taxes in April. You have nothing, and yet you're acting like it's really the
rest of us who have nothing."

"How did you—how do you—" Laurie sputtered.

"How did I find out?" Halsey asked.

Laurie nodded, her lips a straight line, her jaw clenched. Penny
could see she was fighting back tears.

"Don't make threats you can't uphold," Halsey said. When Laurie
still didn't register, Halsey said, "You threatened me. I found out what
I needed to."

Laurie turned around and started walking, easily sidestepping
William and Chris and stepping boldly over the rocks ahead of the
group. Penny started to follow her, but Chris pulled at her elbow.

"Let her be," he said. "I wouldn't want to be followed after that."
He turned toward Halsey. "Why are you such a bitch?"

Halsey shrugged and crinkled her eyebrows. "Truth hurts, little
cousin."

"Come on, Hals," William said, his voice an octave lower than normal. "What is wrong with you?"

"Oh, get off it," Halsey said, miraculously unfazed by the wrath around her. "She needed to hear it. We've put up with her pretention for long enough, always dangling her career at us like a carrot of failure. Well, I had enough. Time for her to get off her high horse."

William was shaking his head, blinking rapidly, like he was willing the shock to subside. "I always knew you were hard. I didn't know you were awful."

Halsey stood with her hands on her hips and shrugged. "I'm not awful. I tell the truth."

Penny took a step toward Halsey. She looked her cousin up and down and felt her insides boil with rage. This person had ridiculed and bullied and pushed Penny around her entire life, and for what?

"Do you tell the truth?" Penny asked.

"What do you mean by that?" Halsey shot back.

Penny mouthed, *H-E-A-T-H-E-R.*

Halsey furrowed her brows and squinted.

"You weren't alone that day the snake bit you," Penny said calmly. "You're lying, just like Laurie."

"That's not the point," Halsey said.

"What is the point?" Chris asked, finally interjecting.

William stood, resting his body weight on his poles. Everyone stared at Halsey.

"The point is that Laurie lied, and she shouldn't have," Halsey said plainly.

"Aren't we all lying?" Penny said. "To ourselves, to each other. Who of us actually wants to let this place go? No one. I know that for a fact. And yet, we can't actually admit that we need each other in order to make it work. We keep saying we need to decide, when really, we need to make a plan. That's all this is. It's not about a shared account or who pays for what or who even calls for a vote."

Penny met her brother's eye and he smiled. She swelled with pride. She knew her mind was clear again, and she wanted to celebrate every nonspiraling, unanxious thought.

Halsey turned around and started snowshoeing farther down the trail.

"Halsey!" Penny cried.

She stopped in her tracks and turned around.

"Where are you going?"

"Your sister threatened me and then lied to all of us about her livelihood. About who she is and what she's doing. I am not interested in a decision or a *plan* until she comes clean to all of us. No more lies."

Halsey started stomping away.

"Then you stop lying!" Penny shouted. Chris let out a soft whistle at the outburst.

"I am not lying!" Halsey screamed back.

"Don't lie to yourself, Halsey Ridge! It's only going to catch up with you."

"Enough with your Glennon Doyle bullshit. We get it, Penny—you are crawling out of the depths of despair, but that does not make you a guru. Do not tell me how to live my life. My life is just fine, thank you very much."

~

Chris was the one who noticed the dark clouds overhead.

He gestured to Penny. "You go find Laurie. We'll catch up with Halsey." Penny nodded and turned to go, but William piped up.

"I'll go with Penny, just in case something happened to Laurie," he said.

Chris was gone down the trail before Penny had even fully turned around.

CHAPTER THIRTY-SEVEN

Five days had passed since the cousin snowshoe. It was as if each cousin had their route dug into the snow, none of the routes crossing or bumping up against each other. Penny would talk to Chris, but not to Laurie. Laurie tried to talk to Penny but avoided Chris. Chris would acknowledge William but turn his back on Halsey. Halsey spoke to no one. William didn't let this stop him from posting new content to his Instagram account. Chris communicated with Trevor, and somehow bought them more time, though Trevor was not shy with his disapproval. At this point, all five of you are contributing to the purgatory, he wrote in an email a few days after the missed January thirty-first deadline.

Penny found Chris on the terrace looking out over the frozen pond, like he was scanning for birds. His hands were stuffed in his coat pockets, and she watched his breath hit the cold air.

"What's happening out here?" she asked, leaning against the house next to the sliding door. Halsey and Miles were sledding across the hill.

"Who cares?" Chris said, continuing to look out. "It's cold. Animals are looking for food. Miles is screaming with glee we can't feel."

Penny scanned the mountains. It was amazing to look out and not see a single man-made structure. Not even a road.

"How can we give this place up?" she asked her brother.

Chris didn't say anything for a long time. Penny watched him look around, watched him watch a bird land on the birdhouse their mom had planted so many years earlier. The bird alternated between tweeting and looking inside the house, then flew off, down the hill toward the woods. The air was cold enough to believe that spring would never come. They were only a few weeks into the new year, and yet—Penny put her own hands in her pockets for warmth—nothing even hinted at being new. They were all stuck.

"We weren't prepared," Chris finally said.

"What do you mean?"

"Everyone died too early. To run a place like this. We're all just kids in adult bodies, you know? Did Dad ever sit you down and really go through the accounting of this place? Did Mom?" She realized he was really asking her.

"No. Neither of them did. I always assumed they were talking to you. I'm not sure either of them expected much of me," Penny said. It hurt to say that out loud.

Chris shook his head. "They weren't talking to me either. And I know they weren't preparing Laurie, even if she was supposed to be the big lawyer in the family. Obviously, no one talked to Halsey. And forget William. Uncle Harry could never take him seriously with the influencing stuff."

Penny laughed at the image of her old-school uncle and his content-creating, influencer yogi son.

"Couldn't we learn now?"

"I think it's too late," Chris said, resigned.

Penny opened her mouth to speak, but nothing came out. Chris's phone buzzed from his pocket. He checked it. Thumbed a reply.

"I gotta go, Pen, but I'll see you later, yeah?" He was gone before Penny could reply.

Was that it? They weren't properly prepared and so it was all over?

~

Penny walked through the house to the mudroom, looking for her boots. She couldn't bear to face Laurie, who she knew was still hiding in the basement. Laurie hadn't yet admitted being fired or why she was fired, and Penny was infuriated by the double standard. Laurie's wall was so high around her, and now by hiding, she was building a moat. Penny laced up her boots and grabbed a pair of snowshoes and poles and headed back outside. She would do a loop around the property. If they were really going to let this place go, she wanted to imprint every square inch of it in her mind.

There were snowmobile trails throughout the property, looping around both houses and down the hill into the woods, and Penny started at a trail steps from their deck. She would walk the long way and try to notice everything. The sun was high today, too far to offer any warmth, but enough light she was happy to be wearing sunglasses. The trees had enough snow on them from a storm a few days earlier that with every gust of wind, they shimmied snow onto the ground, leaving bullet-hole-size darts in the ground. She didn't walk with music, not since her thoughts got so loud that they drowned out the sound, forcing her to choose. But that was changing too: ever since Palm Springs, when her siblings had shown up and showed her that she was worth saving, her thoughts had gotten a little quieter.

When she finally walked into the woods, she heard enough rustling behind her to turn around. A tall figure was walking behind her, maybe a football field away.

"Hello?" she called, nervous it was an off-season hunter who had mistakenly walked onto their land. "This is private property!" She tried to sound brave.

"I know it's private property!" the figure called, and Penny suddenly realized it was Andrew walking toward her.

"What are you doing here?" she shouted, exhilarated to know it was him.

"Penny!" Andrew called out. He picked up his gait.

"What are you doing here?" she shouted again, the last word getting caught in her throat.

Andrew finished walking the distance between them. He wasn't wearing snowshoes, so his feet stepped deep into the snow, nearly up to his knee on each step. He stopped a foot away from where Penny stood.

"I have been looking for you for a long time," he said. He was trying to stay calm, but his eyes were frantic.

"I've been right here," she said.

"What are you talking about?" he said, getting heated. "We meet. I call you Penny Lane; we have what can only be described as the best three months of my entire life, where I cannot believe I've been lucky enough to find you. You are a little high-strung. Definitely private. It takes me a little while to realize you don't really have any friends, and you spend most of your time freaking out about the fact that you've inherited this property no one knows how to manage. You slowly bring me into the fold. I get to know your siblings and your cousins, and then we have a fight when I ask you what you want to do with your life—a totally reasonable question, by the way—and beyond a half-assed phone call that made little sense and definitely didn't make me feel better, I never hear from you again. Literally, never again. I didn't know what had happened. I finally got Laurie on the phone, and she told me that you'd just gotten back from Palm Springs. I was busy falling in love, and you disappeared. What happened, Penny?"

He exhaled loudly.

"Are you finished?" Penny asked, even though she had no idea how to respond to this.

"I think so," he said.

"Was it really the best three months of your life?" she asked.

Andrew nodded.

No one had ever told Penny she was the best part of anything before.

"Really, the best?"

"Really. The best," Andrew said. His eyes were watering a little.

Penny looked down and kicked the snow.

"And you were busy falling in love?"

Andrew bit his lip and nodded.

"I'm pretty messed up, you know," she said. "Sometimes I can't get out of bed. And I like to line up rations of food and drinks. I do that a lot. I do that almost every day."

Andrew nodded, like he wasn't surprised. "I know," he said.

"You know?"

"I saw you do it once when I slept over."

Penny bit her lip and closed her eyes for a second. She couldn't do this yet.

"I have to circle the car twice at the end of the day," Andrew said, his voice a mix of hope and confession. Penny cocked her head. She'd seen him circle the car before; when he slept over, he would sneak out on their way up to bed and do it, but she always assumed he'd forgotten something inside.

"Why? Every night?"

Andrew nodded. "Every night. When I was a kid, my mom took our family wagon down to town, to the grocery store, but on her way, one of the front tires burst. Don't worry. She was fine, and it was thirty years ago. But. My six-year-old brain didn't understand, and my six-year-old brain was petrified my mom would never come home from the hospital. And for whatever reason, my six-year-old brain decided that every night he would circle the car twice to make sure the tires all looked good for the next day. And it's been thirty years, and I know I'm not six anymore, and my mom is completely fine, but I can't not do it. I can't not circle the car." Andrew gave a little smile as he finished talking.

"That's weird," Penny said, not meaning to. Andrew started to laugh.

"Penny, do you know how this works? I share something personal, something honest, and then you share something personal back." Andrew smiled the whole time he said this, and somehow Penny decided she was not going to run in the other direction.

"A few years ago, I was at a bachelorette party. And I did too many drugs, and I took the wrong person back to the room everyone was sharing, and I passed out, but he robbed us. And I haven't been able to face any of those girls since."

There it was, Penny's secret. The reason why she didn't have any friends left.

"And here I thought you missed your parents," Andrew said, incredibly sweetly. "That must have been really hard. When guilt and shame mix together, it's like one plus one equals eleven."

"That's exactly what it feels like. And then my parents going only made it worse. Like I didn't know where to go, except for up here. And now we can't even keep up here, and I have no idea what to do with my life. I don't even know what I care about, I don't think." Penny hadn't ever been so honest before. It felt exhilarating.

Andrew took a step toward where Penny stood.

"I think you might like growing things?" he suggested.

"What do you mean?"

"Can I show you something through my eyes?" Andrew said. Penny nodded. "Follow me." He started walking the way they had come into the woods. Penny followed. When they reached the edge of the meadow, Andrew took out his phone and thumbed to his music app.

They started walking through the meadow toward the frozen-over pond.

"Is Dispatch really playing right now? Really?" Penny asked, smiling and rolling her eyes.

"'The General' is a classic song," Andrew said. "A classic."

"'The General' was played to boarding school kids in the early 2000s. East Coast boarding school."

"They actually toured extensively," Andrew said empathically, turning up the volume and holding his phone high above his head. Penny picked up her pace so she could walk alongside him. The pine trees at the edge of the woods opened up onto a field that stretched for thirty acres. It was breathtaking, even in the snow. She loved that she was walking through this field on snowshoes with a boy who ran a gear shop and still listened to jam bands. He made her feel safe and seen and like maybe she could make a real life for herself in Stowe.

Andrew stopped at the foot of the hill, where Penny had fenced in a garden last spring. The same garden she'd been showing her father when he collapsed. Now it was no more than dirt and snow mixed together, but Penny could see the raised beds poking through, and the wired walls were holding up nicely.

"So what I see," Andrew said, leading them both through the gate and into the middle of the garden, "is a plan."

"What do you mean?" Penny asked.

"You could do this," he said, motioning over to the garden.

"I could do what? Garden?" Penny asked.

"Exactly."

Penny let out a snort. "Are you serious? How on earth did you think of this?"

"I'm glad you asked, Penny Lane." Andrew took his phone and moved it to the photo app. Penny peered over his shoulder. He opened his arm so she was now leaning against his chest and looking at his phone.

"Look," he said, thumbing through photos Penny recognized from her Instagram account, all from before she and Andrew had even met. She had posted so much garden content without even noticing, and she watched as an album bore witness to a season of growth: tomatoes hanging on the vines, squash and zucchini and snow peas growing madly, eggplant tucked into the earth, even hot peppers shining red in the middle. She saw her attempt at butter lettuce, which hadn't worked, and kale, which had.

"Think about it. You have one hundred and fifty acres of land on quality and undeveloped soil. Think of what you could produce up here."

Penny considered it.

"How would we ever do that?" she asked, meaning it.

"I'll help. Chris can handle the business side. Put Halsey to work; she's great with logistics and working with her hands, even if she doesn't know it—think about how awesome Miles is. Clearly, she's doing something right. And Laurie, Laurie needs a change, whether she admits it or not. I don't mean to be so forward, but, Penny, I've watched your family in action. Trust me, none of you wants to lose this property, but every single one of you is petrified about actually keeping it."

Penny leaned over and brushed some snow off what she knew would be soil in a few months. She looked out at the land, the rolling fields that poured right into the woods. Even a twenty-acre farm could yield a tremendous amount of produce to start. They'd still have so much property left. They could develop a farming business gradually, just enough to keep the property going. The hills would soon start to thaw, the new year's growth poking through the ground. By April it would be an explosion of faraway greens, and by May the mud would start to recede. Inuit had fifty words for snow. Vermonters, Penny thought, had at least double the shades of green.

CHAPTER
THIRTY-EIGHT

Just before the January 31 deadline, the Nolans and Ridges had pooled enough money together to push their meeting with Trevor another eight weeks, buying them until the end of March to call it. Halsey had transferred the $5,000 and, for the first time in her life, had no idea when or how she would get another $5,000 to refill her account. It was petrifying to be in her midforties, with a child, and realize she wasn't equipped to do anything of value. The rest of February and into March passed with Halsey hiding at the house, fooling Miles into believing they were on a staycation whenever he wasn't at school, as she toggled between the reminder for their final meeting with Trevor and her now-dormant text chain with Heather. She wanted both to disappear yet could look at nothing else.

She knew the inevitable: that they would sell this place, and she needed to figure out a life that was actually hers. William said he would stay long enough for her and Miles to get settled somewhere else, hopefully in town, so Miles could keep the life he recognized. Even Chad was being nice, which meant Halsey really was in trouble. Or at least officially pathetic. She needed a job, and she needed to figure out how to make herself employable. If they sold this place, money would come in, of course, but the life Halsey wanted so desperately for her son—the magic of living on this hill and engaging with the land—disappeared. Even if she moved to town, her attachment to this place was not replicable. She felt like her parents when they used to tell her that this place was not about money. It was about the place itself.

Miles came bursting through the door that led from the kitchen to the terrace.

"Jeremy is here!" he shouted.

Halsey got up, dropping her phone in the process, at once startled by her son's volume and petrified that he was telling the truth. Jeremy meant Heather. She had not seen or spoken to Heather since Christmas, and she had not thought of anyone else since the early fall. She knew she would never think of anyone else ever again.

"Hey, buddy, what do you mean, Jeremy is here?" she asked. Miles was running circles around the jungle gym, his pants immediately wet from the snow.

"Check the driveway," Miles said, utterly nonchalant. *"Jeremy! I'm back by the slide!"* he shouted, loud enough to startle the birds perched in the big pines by the house.

Halsey straightened her shirt under an oversize cream sweater and smoothed over her black corduroys. She ran her hands through her hair. Coughed a little and stood up straighter. She peeked through the door and could see all the way through the front door to the driveway. There was Heather, standing outside her car. She was in snow pants and a parka. Jeremy was audibly running around the house to where Miles was still shouting.

"Hi," Halsey said, once she opened the front door.

Heather looked up but didn't smile. "Hey."

"What are you doing here?" she asked, not meaning for it to come out so accusatory.

"Jeremy has been begging to see Miles, and I finally relented. Chad mentioned you were probably at the house, so I figured I'd give you a break and take them skiing."

"You talked to Chad?"

"Only because he had Miles last weekend and the boys had a play-date. I didn't know if Miles was with him or you," Heather said.

"And it would have been simpler if Miles were with his dad today?" Halsey said.

"It would have been a little simpler, yes," Heather said. She smiled as she said it, and Halsey felt the familiar butterflies take flight in her stomach.

Halsey bit her lip and put her hands in her pants pockets. She finally noticed the skis in the rack on the roof of Heather's car. She imagined the poles and ski helmets and extra-warm layers were in the trunk. She felt like she was going to throw up, but instead of running inside, locking the door, and hiding behind the sofa, Halsey said, "I could go with you. I'm sure the boys will want to ski themselves, but it'll be easier with both of us there."

Heather raised her eyebrows at Halsey's suggestion. "Really?"

Was that a hopeful "really" or a skeptical "really"? Halsey couldn't tell, but she prayed it was a hopeful "really."

"Yes. I'll come with you if that's okay. I can make some sandwiches to eat at the lodge?" she said, starting to feel a little braver.

"Grab chips too," Heather said, but she looked down at her phone as she said it, making sure Halsey knew she was not flirting.

~

An hour later, they parked at the lodge at Spruce Peak. The boys were just big enough that they could carry their own skis to the lift, but Heather and Halsey walked close enough to pick up any dropped items. Miles waddled with his helmet on, and at one point almost whacked an unsuspecting woman with his skis. After much discussion, it was decided that the four of them would ride up the quad chair together, but the boys could ski down a trail on their own. The quartet would meet at the bottom and do the same thing again. Halsey breathed a sigh of relief that she and Heather would not be on a chairlift alone together.

At the top of the chair, the boys took off down Sunrise. Heather suggested they simply ski a little slower so they could stay behind the boys.

"We aren't really letting them ski alone, right?" Heather asked.

"Why are you being so nice to me?" Halsey asked just as Heather had started to ski down. Heather stopped and planted her skis against the mountain. She looked up at Halsey but didn't say anything. Halsey didn't know if she was contemplating an answer or torturing her or both.

"Your son is my son's favorite person after his parents. And my son is my favorite person. If that means I need to figure out how to be friendly with his favorite person's mother, then I will."

Halsey didn't know what she'd expected, or hoped, Heather would say. She didn't deserve much right now; she knew that deep in her core. And yet: being in love with someone when you can't admit it makes you hope for impossible things. In that moment, watching Heather leaning against her ski poles, the winter vista of early-spring skiing spread out behind her, Halsey hoped she was still worthy of love. Even if it scared her. Even if it meant doing something she never thought she'd have to do.

A breeze whistled through her helmet, knocking Halsey out of her own head.

"Thank you," she whispered.

Heather looked up. Met her eye. "You're welcome."

They skied down in tandem. Heather glided over the snow, at home on her skis after a lifetime with the sport. Halsey compared her own jagged movements, how she seemed to feel every bump, easily jostled by the slightest change in conditions. She briefly closed her eyes and tried to channel Heather's comfort, her confidence. Could such a state of being be contagious?

The rest of the afternoon was a blur of awkward chairlift rides in which both women worked too hard to remove tension from the air and runs where neither woman said anything and Halsey watched Heather fly down the hill. The world felt like it was closing in on her, the earth suddenly a room with walls and a door.

~

When Halsey and Miles got home, he immediately plopped down in front of the television. This winter had been a real wash for monitored screen time, and Halsey was just relieved that Miles was so easily amused by the likes of *Paw Patrol*. She sat with him for a few minutes, stroking his hair and wondering when this feeling that she was ruining the best thing that had ever happened to her would end. Could such a feeling end, if she were in fact ruining the best thing that had ever happened to her?

A reflection from down the hill caught her eye. She blinked, thinking it was just an odd ray of sunlight, until it happened again. Halsey got up and went to the living room window. Penny was down in the garden, the ground equal parts dirt and snow, with some sort of device that involved Penny lifting it over her head and slamming it into the ground. Halsey still hadn't spoken to any of her cousins since that snowshoe, and she couldn't believe it had been nearly two months. Even when they'd decided to push the meeting, Trevor had coordinated everything. Maybe she could start with Penny, confirm one by one the reality that they would sell the property.

Halsey entered the garden and said an awkward, "Hey, hello," just as Penny had lifted the instrument over her head. The greeting startled her, and when Penny turned her head to see who had entered, the tool went with her head and flying out of her hands toward Halsey, who thought Penny had done this deliberately and ducked as she shouted, "What the hell, Penny! I'm just saying hello!"

To which Penny screamed, ducked herself, and shouted back, "Why would you creep up on me like that! What is wrong with you!"

To which Halsey screamed, "I didn't creep up on you! We both live here! You shouldn't be so skittish!"

To which Penny screamed, "I have a lot going on right now, Halsey! You should have thought of that!"

Now the cousins were standing upright and shouting at each other, each trying to top the other.

"I have a lot going on too, you know!" Halsey shouted. She put her hands on her hips for effect.

"Oh, come on. You have a girlfriend you're embarrassed about. It's 2022. Everyone is gay now. Catch up," Penny said.

Halsey opened her mouth, but nothing came out.

"That's what it is, right?" Penny said. Her voice softened slightly. "Seriously, Hals, it really isn't that big of a deal to us. Especially if you like her."

"I do like her," Halsey said, almost without meaning to.

"Wasn't she just here?" Penny asked.

"How could you tell?"

"Her car was parked in the driveway when I was walking down to the garden," Penny said. The fight had left both of them.

"What are you doing?" Halsey asked.

"Right now?" Penny asked.

"Do you have an answer prepared for a larger kind of question?" Halsey asked, and Penny laughed.

"I'm trying to hoe a new row or fight with the still-frozen ground. I want to see how many rows we could actually fit in here," Penny said, leaning over to pick up the tool again but gesturing toward the fenced-in area as she did.

"Does it matter, though?" Halsey asked.

Penny cocked her head.

"Our meeting with Trevor is in a few days, at which point I imagine we'll all finally admit failure and start prepping this place to sell. The ground will still be frozen. Won't the garden be a problem for the next people?" Halsey said.

"Our meeting is in five days," Penny said. "But I had an idea. Or really, Andrew had an idea that I can't get out of my head."

"I'm listening," Halsey said.

Penny laughed before saying, "I'm not sure I've ever heard you utter those words."

"I'm *listening*," Halsey said, smirking. "Better talk before the moment passes."

"Okay, fine. So, as Andrew reminded me, we have one hundred and fifty acres of primo land here. Primo land means quality soil." Penny gestured around the garden. "I planted this last spring on a whim, without even knowing what I was doing. And I took all these photographs, not actually paying attention to them, but it was Andrew who noticed. Thank you, Instagram Stalking Your Girlfriend. But he saw something real, and it's sort of wild that we didn't even notice. But it grew, Hals. It grew."

Halsey followed Penny's eyes and hands and remembered that the garden had been exploding the summer her father died. It was mostly flashes of green, but she dug into her memory and remembered: of course, they'd thrown an entire dinner party with vegetables just from this garden.

"We could start small; Andrew said we could probably test it out on ten acres or so and then build gradually."

"Can we just do that?" Halsey asked.

"I have no idea," Penny said. "But I know you don't want to sell this place."

"I really don't want to sell this place," Halsey agreed.

"What do you think?"

"Do you want to sell this place?" Halsey asked.

"I don't. Truly. I think I would do anything not to sell this place," Penny said. Halsey didn't recognize this calm side of her.

"What did Laurie and Chris say?" Halsey knew William wouldn't know anything about this yet.

"I haven't said anything yet," Penny said. "I'm still figuring out if I think it's possible."

Halsey looked around, at the garden, at the hill, at the pond below. The field stretched out almost thirty acres; they could raze the land without even taking down trees to start. It was nearly April. The ground would thaw in a few weeks, and they could get started immediately.

"It's possible," Halsey said.

"Would you do it with me?" Penny asked.

"What would I do?" Halsey asked. She meant this. Most days she didn't believe she could really do anything. That's what a life of no jobs will do.

"Operations," Penny said quickly.

"What?"

"Think about it. What is raising a child if not extensive experience in logistics and operations?"

Halsey considered it.

"Plus, you're divorced. That's, like, extra logistics and operations under duress. You can do anything." Penny smiled while she said this, making Halsey feel like maybe this was possible.

"What else do you have up your sleeve?"

"Honestly, most of this was Andrew," Penny said.

"He's pretty great," Halsey said.

"So is Heather," Penny said.

"So is Heather," Halsey said.

"Will you tell the others with me?" Penny asked.

Halsey imagined the five of them sitting in the living room in Halsey's house, where the garden was perfectly in view, each one asking too many questions to count. But then she imagined them getting on board, one by one, and for the first time in their adult lives, actually and truly agreeing on something.

"I'd love to," she said.

"I want to wait, though, and figure out exactly how we'll do it. If we tell Chris too early, he will only see the risk," Penny said.

"What about at the meeting with Trevor?" Halsey asked.

"That could work," Penny said, nodding.

Halsey started walking out of the garden. Miles had either fallen asleep or lost his mind to *Paw Patrol*. "I gotta go," she said. Penny nodded and started surveying what to do next in the garden.

"Hey, Hals," Penny said, causing Halsey to turn around. "Andrew came to find me, and I'm so glad he did, but he almost didn't. Go find Heather. Tell her how you really feel."

"I don't know how to do that!" Halsey said, a little louder than necessary, as she walked up the hill.

"None of us does!" Penny shouted back, the hoe already over her head and piercing into the ground.

CHAPTER
THIRTY-NINE

"You're early," Trevor said, looking up from his desk. Laurie stood at the doorway after knocking softly on the wall.

Today she would ask him for a job.

"Isn't our meeting set for two?" Trevor asked, going so far as to look at his wristwatch.

"It is. I know I'm a little early," Laurie said. She was nervous all the way in her feet.

"Do you want to go get a sandwich?" Trevor asked. "I haven't had lunch yet, and we've got twenty minutes until the meeting."

"Um, sure," Laurie said. "I'll walk with you."

Trevor got up from his desk and grabbed a blazer. He was the only person in Stowe who walked around in a suit. Laurie noticed, maybe for the first time, that he was adorable. Every day he looked a little less like a boy dressed in his father's clothes.

They left the building, an old wooden house painted a dull white, and crossed the street to the Mercantile.

"I'm a sucker for their tuna salad," Trevor confessed, holding the door open for her.

"I'm a sucker for the samples downstairs," Laurie confessed back. *Ask him for a job* ticked through her mind like a mantra.

"Hey, how are you doing?" Trevor asked the young woman standing behind the counter. "I'd love a—"

"I need a job!" Laurie blurted out, immediately throwing her hand over her mouth. Here? She'd shouted that she needed a job here, at the Mercantile. What was wrong with her?

Trevor turned his body very slowly toward Laurie. "You need a job?"

"I need a job," she said, nodding. "I want to stay up here, even if we're selling. But I need to work. Because I need to and because I love it. I'm a good lawyer. I could help with whatever you need help with," she said. Her voice was getting softer with each word. Trevor looked at her for a long time.

"Did you want to order the tuna salad sandwich?" the young woman said from behind the counter, her eyes darting between Trevor and Laurie.

"Ye-yes, yes please, to the sandwich," Trevor said quickly. He turned back to Laurie. "I don't have anything right now; I'm really sorry."

"Of course, of course, I understand," Laurie said. She was mortified. Six months ago, she was a partner at a firm in New York City. Then she'd been fired because the guy she had actual feelings for realized he could get much further ahead by reporting their relationship. She didn't blame him. How could she? Laurie never, ever should have entertained that relationship, and she knew it. She was finished in the New York City law scene. But today she was being rejected by a small-town lawyer she had known since he was in diapers, which meant she was also finished in the small-town law scene. It served her right, she thought, looking behind the deli counter and wondering if maybe she needed to forget about the law and just get a job. Any job, in any place. It didn't matter, but this existence of hiding from the truth and avoiding anyone who knew the truth wasn't working.

Trevor paid for the sandwich, and Laurie noticed how the server sneaked in a little flirting. Laurie felt like her legs lost their bones at the same time her lungs stopped processing oxygen. She had to get out of here.

"I will see you in a few minutes at the meeting," Laurie said, leaving the restaurant before Trevor could say anything back.

She stumbled onto Main Street, walking as fast as she could down the block so she'd be out of Trevor's view. The tears came as she passed Black Cap Coffee, and her face was wet by the time she hit the hardware store. It was 1:50. She had ten minutes to gain her composure and come up with a life plan.

Laurie walked down behind the hardware store to where a parking lot led to the path that was just melted enough to welcome runners and bikers again. She watched a woman who could be her push a running stroller over a small bridge. Where did one find a life plan? If she was just over forty, and unemployed, and chronically single, and arguably no fun to be around, was such a plan really on offer? Laurie clenched her jaw in an attempt to curb the crying, which only made her jaw hurt. Where had everything gone so horribly wrong?

What surprised Laurie in this moment wasn't her emotions coming out full throttle or that she felt like at any second the earth would literally swallow her up. It didn't even surprise her that she felt like she had nowhere to turn and no one to turn to. What surprised Laurie was that she didn't want to run. She looked down at her feet planted firmly on the ground. She'd found a patch of grass just off the bike path, and she was standing like someone deciding where to march. But marching was different from running. Marching was what you did when you had somewhere to go. *We march toward things. We don't march away from them.*

Laurie looked up and saw the light bounce off the bell tower of the church. Her feet were still planted. Her hands were on her hips. The answer was here, in Stowe, somehow. In an instant, when every particle on earth briefly froze, Laurie saw that having nowhere to go meant she could stay put. Was that the plan? To stay put long enough to get to the next moment, whatever that moment was?

Her phone buzzed at the alarm she'd set for two p.m. She walked up toward Trevor's office, still crying a little and without a real plan, but somehow, she felt okay about both. If Penny could go from lining up mini liquor bottles to gardening, Laurie could figure out what to do next.

~

The Nolans and Ridges were already in the conference room when Laurie entered the office.

"Hey, guys," she said, sitting between Penny and William. She couldn't quite read the energy of the room; it was somewhere between resigned and determined.

Trevor gave her a small smile and then lightly tapped the table with his knuckles.

"So today is the day. What do we think?" he asked. The Nolans looked around at each other, silently deciding who should speak on their behalf.

Chris cleared his throat and leaned forward. "We are going to sell. The property is too much for any one of us to handle and way too much for all of us to handle. I know it hasn't been the full year, but we've made no progress on how to move forward, and it's better for everyone to walk away."

Trevor nodded as Chris spoke. He opened the folder in front of him and began sifting through papers.

"Actually," Penny said, breaking the silence, "we had a different idea."

"Who is we?" Chris asked. His eyebrows were furrowed into a deep crease.

"It was Andrew's idea to start. Then mine. Then Halsey's."

"This should be good," Chris said.

Penny rolled her eyes. "Brother, it's really time for you to lighten up a little. Okay?"

"What is that supposed to mean?" Chris said.

Halsey held up her hands. "Hear us out. Penny, tell them your idea."

Penny took a deep breath and put her palms facedown on the table, with her arms outstretched.

"You know the garden I built last spring?" she asked. Her cousins nodded. Laurie thought of how surprised she'd been to see just how much produce had grown over the summer. "We have one hundred and fifty acres of rich, untouched soil. We could start small, with fifteen or twenty acres, and gradually increase."

"What are you saying?" Laurie asked.

"If we farm the land, it lets the land work for us a bit. It helps take care of the property. Of managing it. We can give back to the land, to Stowe, but we also get to keep it," Penny said. Laurie didn't think she'd ever seen her sister so excited or resolved about something before. Her eyes were shining, her skin clear and bright.

"How would that work, though?" Chris asked. He was still skeptical.

"I would run the actual farming. Well, the growing at first. I have a lot to learn. Halsey would be operations. We need help with business development, and we need help with accounting, which maybe one of you might be interested in," Penny said, looking between her brother and sister.

"Can you just start a farm like that?" Chris asked Trevor.

Trevor considered it. "I don't see why not. You own the land outright; it's under your jurisdiction to decide how to use it."

"Chris, do you understand—this lets us stay?" Halsey asked him.

"I don't want to live in Vermont forever," Chris said a little softly.

"I do," Laurie said, the first thing she'd said since the meeting started. Everyone looked at her. "I could do what you're asking for. Figure out the business side of things."

"This would definitely help your tax bill," Trevor said. "But I'd want you to hire a proper accountant."

"Hey, Trevor," Laurie said, getting an idea. "What about our forest acreage? Can we put that to use?"

Trevor looked down at a map of the Nolans' land. "Absolutely. We could make a deal with the forest service," he said.

Laurie turned to her family. "I think we can really do this," she said to Penny and Halsey. "Both the farming and the forestry."

Even Trevor could sense the heightened energy in the room. Chris shrank into himself. Penny turned to her brother.

"What do you think? If we don't have to sell, are you okay with us giving this a shot?" she asked.

Chris was quiet. He looked at his hands clasped together. The whole room held their breath. Laurie realized this wasn't about forcing him to their side. She wanted him to be happy about it too. She looked around the room; Penny, Halsey, and William all looked at Chris, their expressions intent, compassionate. A wholly different look from a few months earlier, when everyone had marched in here with their own agendas. This seven-month span had felt like a languishing waste of time, and yet, it had delivered them here, to this moment. If Chris needed more time, they would give it to him. Laurie felt this in her bones.

"I'm really proud of you," Chris said after a while, his voice shaky. "I can't believe we might actually pull this off." His eyes were wet, which immediately made Laurie start to cry again, and soon Halsey and Penny followed suit.

"We might pull this off," Penny said, smiling through tears.

"At least we get to try," Halsey said.

"Just think of the Instagram opportunities," William said without a trace of irony. Even Trevor started laughing.

~

The Nolans and Ridges left Trevor's law office with an energy they hadn't felt in a very long time.

"Should we celebrate?" Penny asked, her eyes bright.

Laurie and William both nodded in agreement. "How about Idletyme?" Laurie suggested.

Chris stood with his hands in his pockets, looking toward the mountains.

"Chris?" Laurie said, jolting him out of his daydream.

"Yeah?"

Halsey sucked in a breath. If Chris was still on the fence, that meant this really wasn't the plan. They'd all agreed, once and for all, that they would be united in the decision. No one was walking away with $100.

"Do you want to go celebrate with beers and wings at Idletyme?" Laurie asked.

It was like Chris was still not listening. Halsey was about to burst out when Chris finally looked at them.

"It's so cool that we're going to build a farm," he said. "That's so much cooler than what I was expecting."

William made the cousins gather for a selfie before posting and tagging it.

"I'm going to call Andrew, but let's meet at the restaurant in, like, a half hour?" Penny said, walking to her car. The group agreed.

CHAPTER FORTY

Three months later

Penny's knees were dug into the ground, even with knee pads, and even with an extra foam roller. Her lower back ached and her shoulders were hunched, and when Penny took off her gardening gloves to check, her fingernails were so caked with dirt, it seemed unlikely they would ever look clean again. The sun was at its highest point overheard, the late-June days stretching on and on. Penny exhaled and wiped a bead of sweat off her forehead. This was *work*. She had no idea what she was doing, and she was exhilarated. Her manager at Harvest Market had been the first to place an order, for exactly one crate of artichokes. Penny had cocked her head to the side, confused.

"They're the earliest to grow. That way you have a confirmed order for May. Let's see how the artichokes do and we'll go from there," her manager said.

They had razed five acres below the pond into rows of produce-ready soil. They'd put up the fence themselves, Andrew shouting instructions as they all learned the art of a hammer and a nail. The fence wasn't exactly perfect, but it was theirs, and the wire mesh meant it was safe from critters.

"Hey, Chris," she called up the hill to her brother. "Can you tell me if we have any orders for radishes?"

She watched Chris thumb around on his laptop. "Yeah, looks like both the Stowe farmers market and the Morrisville farmers market think you should bring some around on Wednesday."

Penny nodded to herself, calculating what that meant in terms of radish heads. "How about broccoli?"

Chris thumbed some more. "Broccoli got Stowe, Morrisville, *and* Shelburne!"

"Shelburne is competitive!"

"They are all competitive!" Chris shouted back. Penny could see him smiling from the porch. "Hey, Pen?" he asked.

"Mm?"

"Why are we growing such boring vegetables? Why aren't we doing, like, tomatoes and squash and that stuff people Instagram about?"

"Because these boring vegetables are in season for seven months a year. Tomatoes are in season for two, maybe three. And strawberries, what any person with a taste bud is after, are in season in Vermont for exactly one month." Penny couldn't believe how much she'd learned in three months. It had taken three weeks of around-the-clock studying to formulate a plan she presented to her family. She had never felt so alive in all her life.

"I guess this is why you are leading the charge on Nolan Ridge Farm," Chris said with a hint of pride in his voice.

"Plus, don't quit before the miracle happens," Penny said. Chris cocked his head in confusion. "We're selling tomatoes. Obviously. Those orders won't come in for another month."

As soon as the group had decided to try their hand at farming, Penny had planted the broccoli seeds in small plastic containers and set them up in their kitchen. When the days started getting longer and the temperatures slowly rose, she had moved the seedlings outdoors with an audience of her siblings and cousins. When the first head of broccoli had sprouted up eight weeks later, there wasn't a dry eye on the hill. Even Trevor had come over to see this head of broccoli in all its glory.

A car door slammed out of view, and a few moments later, Andrew walked around the house to the top of the hill.

"Howdy," he called, waving. Penny swooned. Since that day he'd chased her down and said they could save this land, he'd been by Penny's side, offering everything from marketing support to advice on pricing to back rubs. He walked down the hill to the fenced-in garden and kissed Penny square on the lips.

"Hi," she said.

"Hi," he said back, smiling as he kept kissing her.

"What'd you learn?"

Andrew stood back and opened a folder he'd been holding under his arm. "I learned a lot. I learned that the produce commissioner for Stowe is a big fan of Nolan Ridge, and I'm pretty sure if we play our cards right, by next summer we will have a permanent booth at the market. And"—he flipped through a few pieces of paper for effect— "Daedalus has inquired whether we might be the right produce partner for their store."

Penny squealed with delight, which made Andrew laugh. Store placement was the dream, especially as Laurie and Halsey were spearheading expansion into products like goat cheese and milk and honey.

"This really might happen?"

"It might."

"Get a room, you two," Chris called from the porch.

"Stop spying on us!" Penny yelled back. "Or go inside! Or get a life!"

Chris raised his arms out in salutation. "This is my life! And as soon as you survive this selling season, I'm going back to my company full time!"

Penny rolled her eyes but smiled ear to ear.

$\sim$

Andrew knelt down to start picking the radishes and heads of broccoli. Penny could see that the cabbage was only a week or so away from also being ready. She walked a few paces back to the edge of the garden, the corner that inched its way closer to the woods, where they'd planted a variety of different potatoes.

"Are Laurie and Hals coming down soon to help pick?" Andrew asked. He pulled a bunch of radishes that almost glowed pink in the sun.

"Halsey should be down here soon, and Laurie is researching the rules and regulations of owning goats."

Penny bent over to pull up a potato. She knew it wouldn't be quite ripe, but she wanted to check how they were coming in so she could have Andrew start boasting about them to his contacts. She pulled up a baby new potato, but it was shriveled, a little like it had been suffocated by the earth. The leaves attached to the plant were yellowing and wilting in places.

"Hey, A," she said, "can you come look at this?"

Andrew dropped the radishes and the basket holding them and walked over.

"Yellowing leaves can't be good, right?" Penny asked. Her stomach fell at the idea of the potatoes being ruined. They couldn't afford to miss out on clutch produce like this. Suddenly Nolan Ridge was slipping through her hands. She felt her breath leave her body.

Andrew fingered the leaves and the dirt around the plants. He took out his phone and took a picture of the leaf and of the pinched baby potato.

"What is it?" Penny asked. By now, her thoughts were fully spiraling, and her body was playing along. That was the thing about anxiety: if the mind signals to the body that there is a crisis, the body only eggs the mind on, even if there's nothing to worry about. Penny's insides were boiling, which made her thoughts spiral faster, which made her insides boil more.

Andrew looked between the phone and the leaves. "I think it's verticillium wilt."

"What the hell is that?" Penny asked. Now she was sweating.

"It's a fungal disease, I think. It lives in the soil and then infects the plants." Andrew bit his lip. "Potatoes are especially susceptible to it."

In the time that Andrew had been surveying the potatoes, both Laurie and Halsey had made their way down the hill. Their smiles turned flat when they saw Andrew and Penny.

"What's happening down here?" Halsey asked. Her voice lacked the aggression Penny was so used to hearing.

"It seems our potatoes have got a wilting disease," Penny said, her voice shaking.

"What does that mean?" Laurie asked. Her voice was sharp, and Penny watched both Andrew and Halsey give her a look that said to soften her edge immediately. She course corrected: "Sorry. Whatever it is, we'll figure it out."

Penny wiped her eye. She didn't want to be crying.

"I think we probably need to start over with the potato patch," Andrew said. The group looked at the corner. The potatoes covered almost a third of the entire garden.

"We miss this year?" Halsey asked.

Penny nodded and tears streamed down her face.

"But we plant for next year, right?" Laurie said, forcing a smile. "We can do this."

"What about all those lost sales?" Penny asked. Laurie was in charge of keeping the books, and she had them all on exceptionally tight financial plans.

"It means we don't take that family trip to Disney World this fall. We can go next fall," Laurie said simply.

"That's it?" Halsey asked. Even Andrew cocked his head at Laurie's calm.

"Is it ideal? Of course not. But we are in year one of an experiment that might keep this family on this land, and we were bound to run into something. We ran into it. We keep going. Penny, I know you can figure out exactly what happened with the soil and then pivot. In the meantime, we have rows and rows of other plants that are giving us produce," Laurie said.

"So you're saying that potato plants with ver-whatever-it's-called wilt is better than sleeping with an associate and having him report you in order to get ahead in his career?" Halsey asked, smirking.

By now, Associate-Gate was an oft-mentioned rib on Laurie. She took it in stride.

"I am saying that verticillium wilt is far worse but that we will get through it and I thank you in advance for bringing that up again." Laurie smiled as she spoke.

"Is anyone else hungry?" Andrew asked.

Penny and Laurie both nodded. It was well past lunchtime. The group started walking up the hill to the driveway.

"Is going to get tater tots too on the nose?" Halsey asked.

CHAPTER
FORTY-ONE

A few weeks after the potato debacle, Laurie was surveying the garden against her balance sheet. By now, the vegetables that were growing had a place to be sold, which was good. But, as Laurie counted the cabbageheads coming in and looked at the ledger, there was a reason why produce farms needed to run at a certain size. All the cabbage in the world paid for only so many bills.

No matter, she decided, moving on to the tomato plants. These were still weeks away, but they were beauties—even Laurie, a true hater of tomatoes, could see it.

She'd gotten a text from Paul. Out of the blue and after all this time, all he said was, Hey, how r u?

In before times, she would have thrown the phone out the window and then expensed for a new one. Current times didn't allow for such frivolity, so instead, she shouted into a pillow and then blocked his number. She had stopped thinking she would hear from any of her old partners. The letter from HR had said it all, that women were disposable after proving they weren't perfect.

Still. She never should have entertained anything with Paul, and she knew that. Laurie didn't need to blame Paul for reporting her, and she didn't need to blame her company for responding. If this year was about anything, it was about letting the anger go and letting the truth in.

Laurie walked up the hill toward the house, planning to go sit at the makeshift desk she'd put in by the window in the living room. Chris had the proper office, and Penny had the long bar in the kitchen. It felt right that Nolan Ridge had started on a TV tray with an uncomfortable chair.

Halsey was standing on the porch when Laurie walked up.

"Well, hey there," Laurie said. The anger between her and Halsey had long since left the room. They were both too pathetic to be angry.

"What's up?" Halsey said without looking up from her phone. When Laurie stretched her eyes to see the screen, Halsey was just thumbing through Instagram, her eyes not really focused on anything.

"Just doing the books as we head into the next quarter," Laurie said.

Halsey didn't respond.

Laurie stopped right before going inside. "Hey, Hals?" she asked.

Halsey looked up. Her eyes were rimmed with red. Her shoulders were hunched over. Her hair was limp in a low ponytail.

"I'm just going to say this once, because it will probably be pretty weird coming from me. But. I love you. You are a really important part of this family, and no matter what, you deserve even unexpected happiness."

She was talking about Heather, of course. Halsey had never been so happy as when she and Heather had dated, and ever since that fateful snowshoe, she had been a shell of herself.

But they all deserved happiness. Didn't they?

~

264

Laurie walked inside before Halsey could say anything.

She checked her phone for the two hundredth time that day. There were no notifications, and it was just before noon. Miles had camp in the morning and then a "Welcome Back to School" kickoff party at the mountain. Why a first-grade class needed a party nearly a month before school started was beyond Halsey, but at least Miles loved parties.

What was she supposed to do with Laurie's comment?

Halsey walked up the hill, debating what to do with each step. Laurie was talking about Heather, obviously, and Halsey could think of nothing else. The women hadn't spoken in months, not since the snow was three feet deep and the sun was gone by midafternoon. What was Halsey supposed to do, just call Heather out of the blue? She'd probably moved on by now, Halsey thought, winding around the stone fence that dotted the property between the driveway and the hill.

Without totally understanding why, Halsey got in her car and dialed Chad. He'd had Miles the past few days, and he would have him tonight. But maybe he would be willing to play family for a few hours, so she could hold her son close.

"What's up?" Chad said when he answered.

"Hey, what are you two doing?" she asked, putting the car into gear. Chad, and she guessed his girlfriend, lived just a mile out past the Shaw's on 108.

"We're headed up to the mountain for that back-to-school party. Did you know the kids' school rented out the Alpine Slide to get them jazzed up for the year? That definitely did not happen to me growing up," Chad said.

Duh, she thought. She literally had just told herself that Miles had a back-to-school shindig. Her head was not in the game. The car rumbled to a stop at the end of Shaw Hill Road. She crested right to head down Moscow Road.

"How far are you?" she asked. She turned right onto Barrows Road and let her eyes scan the mountains as she drove up another hill. Everywhere she looked, it was green.

"Just a couple of minutes out. Do you want to meet us here? Ashley is coming too, just so you know."

"Yeah, I'll meet you there," Halsey said, looking between the clock and the long trail of cars ahead of her waiting to merge onto the mountain road. She was probably twenty minutes out.

She dialed Penny, who answered on the first ring. "What's up?"

"I need to do something quickly," she said.

"That's cryptic," Penny said. Halsey laughed. She was still getting used to having a shorthand with Penny.

"Sorry. Chad is driving Miles there now because the school rented the Alpine Slide. And I feel like I should go too. You know, celebrate the start of the school year," Halsey said, leaving out a big chunk of the truth.

"And where Miles goes, Jeremy follows," Penny said in a singsong voice.

Halsey didn't say anything.

"You ready to finally get her back?" Penny asked.

"We'll see," Halsey said.

"That's awesome," Penny said. Halsey could hear her smiling.

"Let's see about that. She's probably totally over it," Halsey said.

"Do you know how good it feels to finally say what you want?" Penny asked.

Halsey nodded without saying anything. Her throat was swallowing down emotion.

"I'm proud of you, cous," Penny said. "We all are. Go get her."

Halsey rolled into the parking lot at the mountain fifteen minutes later. She was already pooling sweat under her arms and she wasn't even positive she would see Heather. She did not have a plan, but she saw Chad's car parked closer to the lift that went up to the top of the Alpine Slide.

Are you here? Just arrived, at the bottom of the quad, she texted Chad.

We're at the top. Miles is about to go down. All by himself! Chad responded.

When she got to the top of the lift, she scanned the people milling around the start of the Alpine Slide. She found Miles and Chad were next up and rushed over to meet them before they left.

"Hey!" she said, causing Miles to turn around.

"Mommy! I am riding the slide by my*self*!" Miles shouted.

"I can see that, buddy," she said, smiling. "Hey," she said to Chad. Ashley was next to him.

"Hey." Both of them waved back.

"Are you ready for this adventure?" Halsey asked Miles.

"Yeah, Jeremy is about to go," Miles said. She could tell he was pretending not to be nervous.

"Is Jeremy going by himself?" she asked. This meant Heather was here. In an instant, every cell in her entire body started to go haywire. She half expected to levitate.

"Yeah, look," Miles said, pointing to the front. Sure enough, Jeremy was on the deck, with the attendant giving him the three-second countdown.

"Wahoooooooo!" Jeremy yelled as he started the slide.

Halsey saw Heather was on the next slide, cheering on her son. She looked perfect in a baseball hat with a ponytail through the hole and sunglasses. She wore a Patagonia windbreaker over spandex, and Halsey wished she were sitting right behind her on the slide, being the big spoon.

"Heather!" Halsey called, starting to push her way up the line.

Heather turned around and saw Halsey. Her face stiffened.

267

"Heather, wait!" Halsey called again. She was only two people away, but she could see Heather was moving up to the top of the slide. The attendant started to count down from three. "Heather!"

Heather put her hand up to the attendant and turned her neck to see Halsey, who was now standing right next to them. "Yes?"

"Hi." *"Hi"*? That was all Halsey could come up with? She wanted to die.

"Hello," Heather said, her voice steely.

"I need to—"

"I'm going to go down the slide now. Okay? I really wish you luck in everything. I do. I want the best for you. But I'm going down the slide to get Jeremy."

With that, she signaled to the slide attendant and started down. Without thinking through it, Halsey knocked the person sitting in the cart right behind Heather, assuring them she'd get them reimbursed and settling into the cart herself.

"I'm sorry; I'm sorry," she kept saying as everyone, including the attendant, shouted at her to stop what she was doing and get out of the car.

She closed her eyes and counted to three and sped down the slide, determined to catch up with Heather.

"Heather!" she called as the sleds got closer. The slide was an old track of concrete that threatened all sorts of skin burns should the sled topple over. Halsey had always hated this thing. She hated concrete, she hated fast speeds, and she definitely hated being out of control.

"Heather! Okay. It's me. It's Halsey. Here's the deal." She braked the sled so it wouldn't actually crash into Heather. "I'm a total wimp, okay? I never should have tried to keep you—to keep us—a secret. You are amazing. You're an amazing mom. You're an amazing friend." Halsey gulped in air. "You're an amazing girlfriend. I love you, okay? I love you!" Halsey took a few more breaths. Heather still hadn't turned around. She got ready to scream. *"I love you, Heather Johnson."*

The scream was so loud, it echoed off the trees and into the mountain. Halsey had no idea how many people heard it, but she yelled it again. *"I love you, Heather Johnson, and I will never keep you a secret."* And then softer: "I'm so sorry I was so scared, and so weak, and I can only promise you I will never be that scared or that weak ever again. And if you can't forgive me, just know you changed my life. And I'll always love you for that." Halsey stopped talking and rode the rest of the slide in silence. She let tears fall down her cheeks and tasted the salt on her lips. Even if it was over, really, truly over, she knew she deserved it, and she knew she would be okay.

Heather got out of the sled without turning around. Halsey landed at the bottom just a few seconds after. She steeled herself for Heather to continue walking away, and she'd accepted it, accepted that she'd tried but she was too late, and she couldn't have expected anything after how she'd treated her. But then Heather stopped walking and turned around. Halsey saw her face was wet too. Halsey took a few steps toward Heather, and Heather took a few steps toward Halsey.

"That was very sweet, you know," she said quietly.

"It was all true. Every word," Halsey said. They were standing right in front of each other.

"You love me?" Heather asked. She was looking down at the ground, her fingers clasped in front of her, like she didn't know what to do with her hands. Maybe she was nervous too. Halsey took one more step forward, close enough that they were touching, and gently took Heather's chin in her hand. She leaned forward and kissed Heather, softly, lightly on the lips, her other hand grazing Heather's shoulder.

"I love you," Halsey said, their noses touching.

"That's good," Heather said. They kissed again, deeper this time, their hands now clasped at their sides.

When they finally broke apart, a small circle with their sons and Chad and Ashley had collected. Miles and Jeremy looked confused without being upset about it, while Chad and Ashley were both smiling.

"It's about time," Chad said, looking between them.

Halsey let out a laugh and looked at her son. He opened his mouth to say something, and she prepared herself for a question she wasn't quite ready to answer but also knew she needed to. She glanced at Heather, who she could tell was thinking the same thing.

"Can we have a snack and watch *Paw Patrol*?" Miles asked.

The adults all started laughing, then howling, Miles and Jeremy clueless as to why. Halsey and Heather were still holding hands and crying a little.

"Yes, we can have a snack and watch *Paw Patrol*," Halsey said. She looked at Heather. "But only if Jeremy and his mom come too."

Miles rolled his eyes. "Of course *they're* coming. Where else would they go?"

Heather squeezed Halsey's hand and whispered, "Exactly. Where else would we go?"

EPILOGUE

One year later

Penny finished carrying a box of freshly shucked corn to the bed of the Nolan Ridge pickup truck as her phone started buzzing incessantly. She fished the phone out of her pocket, her fingers fumbling on the too-slippery case, only for it to buzz again. Andrew's friends had become Penny's friends, and little by little, she'd made new friends in town as well. Penny smiled as one conveyed frustration at her husband via an assortment of emojis. She had friends again.

Tell Tim that for every golf hole he plays, he owes you an hour of peekaboo with Harriet, Penny typed, adding a golf club, golf ball, and baby face emoji.

Halsey and Heather were sitting on the back porch overlooking the hill. Penny waved and walked over.

"Hey, you two," she said.

"What's up, little cous," Halsey said. Heather nodded her hello.

"Just loaded the rest of the corn onto the truck. Any interest in a ride into town with me? Commodities is expecting us," Penny said. Really, she needed help carrying all that corn their farm had produced, but Halsey, though happy now, had not changed, and asking her for help still demanded a gentle touch.

"We'd love to come," Heather said, patting Halsey's leg and standing up. Penny caught Halsey give Heather a look that said, *Why would you make us do such a thing?* Heather, seeing the look and seeing Penny see the look, said, "We would love to come for a ride to town because very obviously you will need help with the corn, and given that we are all benefiting from your exceptional farming skills, we are here however you need."

Halsey smiled, rolled her eyes, and stood up. "Fine. Yes. We'd love to come, but only if we can get maple creemees on the way home."

The trio made their way to the truck, an upgrade from their first summer of hauling produce out of Halsey's RAV4.

"You drive," Penny said, throwing Halsey the keys and jumping in the back seat.

They made their way down the driveway, the truck bed weighed down by the corn. Penny couldn't believe they still had four complete rows to pull. That was at least three more truck runs to town.

The hill had transformed in the past year. What had started as a few hundred feet of garden had spanned into an acre, then five, and now thirty acres of farmland. Penny and Andrew had tackled learning everything they could about farming, Laurie handled the books and business development, and Halsey had regained her marketing chops.

"Have you heard from your brother?" Penny asked. Halsey glided the truck off Shaw Hill onto River Road.

"He's loving Boston," Halsey said. "And still with his girlfriend."

"His girlfriend who is *not* Alison," Heather said.

"His girlfriend who is not his cousin's ex-fiancée, no, despite his current girlfriend having the same name and the same hair color," Halsey said.

Everyone in the truck laughed at the memory of putting two and two together, with a very confused William throwing up his hands and shouting, "I would never date your girl, bro!"

To which Chris had shouted back, "Thank you very much for clarifying!" And then suddenly the men had been hugging, and the women had shared expressions of deep, deep relief. Chris had never found out who Alison was dating, and after a little while, he'd realized he didn't care.

"I can't believe he left Hudson," Penny said, shaking her head.

"I can't believe he realized that being a yogi influencer was not an actual life plan," Halsey said. They all laughed. "I guess we might finally meet her if he brings her to the hill party."

The hill party was three weeks away, the Saturday after Labor Day weekend, to welcome in fall and celebrate a second summer with Nolan Ridge Farm. They were opening the hill to visitors, with tractor rides and hay bales and even bobbing for apples. Most surprisingly to Penny, this had been Laurie's idea.

~

The truck pulled into Commodities, where the store manager was already standing by the loading dock.

"Are we late?" Penny asked, hopping out even before Halsey had put the truck in park.

"No, no," the young man answered, putting his hands up. "I just figured you'd need help." He surveyed the truck's contents. "Is that all coming here?" he asked, his eyebrows raised.

Penny and Halsey looked at each other.

"Yes," Penny said, though cocking her head to the side in case she was ultimately wrong.

The guy turned around and grabbed a clipboard off the ledge. "It says here we're only expecting fifty pounds." He looked up expectantly.

Halsey had already pulled out her phone and dialed Laurie, and, like magic, Laurie was only three doors down at the butcher's.

Not two minutes later, Laurie pulled into the Stowe Naturals driveway, her blonde hair now long and wispy past her shoulders. Her typically translucent skin now tanned in a late-July glow.

"Ben, you know very well you ordered one hundred pounds from us, and just because you got cold feet about moving all that corn this week does not mean you are taking any less than one hundred pounds," she said, talking, parking, and getting out of her car all in one movement.

Ben opened his mouth—

"Don't even try it. We've been here before. You say one hundred, it's one hundred. It's not one hundred crossed out in pencil and fifty written over it," Laurie said. Penny and Halsey and Heather all stood up a little straighter. Laurie was their bookkeeper and their bulldog.

Ben put up his hands and whistled. "Fair enough. Let's unload this sucker," he said, grabbing a box of corn.

The truck was unloaded in minutes, with each woman laughing at Laurie swooping in to save the day.

"Teamwork makes the dream work," she said, getting back in her car. "Are we doing burgers at your house?" she asked Halsey.

"Burgers at *our* house," Halsey said, looking at Heather.

"Are you two finally making this official?" Penny asked. Heather and Jeremy had become fixtures at the other house. Miles now bragged to everyone he knew that his best friend lived at his house now because their moms were also best friends.

"It seems you all are not going to get rid of us anytime soon," Heather said, a smile peeking through. She looked at Halsey and kissed her shoulder.

"Welcome to the hill, officially," Laurie said. "You need to start contributing for covering costs and we need to talk about parking this winter once the snow comes. We can't have you pulled up on the snowbank again. There's no dignity in that."

Penny watched her sister walk to her car and couldn't believe who Laurie had become. The hard-shelled, brittle lawyer from New York City had morphed into an assured, cheerful woman in Vermont. She giggled. She cooked. She even dated sometimes. Penny smiled at her sister's happiness.

Her phone buzzed in her pocket.

Andrew.

"Hey, you," she said, holding the phone to her ear. "We're just headed back now."

"Good. I've got a bike ride to the waterfall with a cheese plate and half bottle of champagne with your name on it," he said.

"You know, Heather and Jeremy are officially moving onto the hill," she said.

"And?" he asked. She could hear the smile in his voice.

"You can't live in that condo in town forever," Penny said. Holding her breath as she spoke.

"And?" he asked again.

"I think it's time for both of us to move. You move out of that condo. I move out of the Birds Nest. We both move into the room down the hall. And"—Penny took a breath; she couldn't hold it any longer—"next year, if we're enjoying ourselves, I think you and I should build a little house down the hill by the pond. We are the farmers, after all. We need a farmhouse."

Andrew started laughing, a deep belly laugh that made Penny catch her heart in her throat.

"Is that a yes?" Penny asked.

"Penny Lane, I would be honored to build a farmhouse with you."

"See you at home?" Penny asked.

"See you at home," Andrew said.

∽

The women drove back to Nolan Ridge, the late-afternoon sun shining gold over the mountains. It had been nearly two years since that fateful day in the garden, when Penny had thought the world she knew would never be her world again. And she'd been right, she thought, watching Mount Mansfield fade in the distance. That world was gone, and in its place was a world Penny had never loved herself enough to dream of before. But it was hers. It was theirs.

ACKNOWLEDGMENTS

Writing might be a solitary activity, but publishing is not. A huge thanks to my editor Alicia Clancy, It was so fun to do this again—you are deft, nimble, and gracious in your work. Thank you for seeing the book club author within me. Thank you for Jen Bentham, Kellie Osborne, and Stacy Abrams for such a seamless production experience. Jen Richards, you are a PR dream! I'm so incredibly grateful we get to collaborate again. Alexandra Machinist, the first book may have been a lark, but the second cements us as the rare breed of agent-client-friend. Let's go back to that first lunch in September of 2009, when we were both overflowing with dreams. So much started that day, but most important was a friendship that's brought me so much joy and invaluable mentorship. Thank you.

Wendy Wolf, you are the shining star of mentors, and to have you in my corner as one of my first readers is an embarrassment of riches. *Thank you* doesn't cover it. Connie Tallman, my other first reader, it's been an utter joy to have you and Cliffster as part of my life.

Recently someone asked me if I would be getting a tattoo that said *Verve*. We're four years into Verve Publishing, and to everyone there, please know: I just might.

If *All Are Welcome* considered the family you are born into, then *The Family Compound* is about the family you inherit. To my inherited family, grandparents, aunts, uncles, and cousins: my memories with you are among the richest in my life, teeming with love and humor and warmth. When I started this story, the cousins were always going to find a way to stay together. Family is worth staying for.

Mom, Dad, Mike, Giegs: I'm a lucky girl to have you as my fam.

Sarah Tallman, look at the life we've built! You are my North Star. You are the reason why anything goes right, and you are the salve when anything goes wrong.

To my readers, thank you. I promise to keep writing you stories.

ABOUT THE AUTHOR

Photo © 2021 Leanna Creel

Liz Parker is a literary agent at Verve Talent & Literary and the author of *All Are Welcome*. She has written for the *New York Times*' Modern Love column and lives in Los Angeles with her wife, Sarah, and their three dogs. For more information visit www.lizparkerwritessometimes.com.